TRADING UP

TRADING UP

Nancy
Bazelon
Goldstone

E.P. DUTTON NEW YORK

AUTHOR'S NOTE

*The events in this book really happened, although a series
of events in some instances has been telescoped to a single
scene. The characters in this book are based on real people;
although again some individuals appearing in the book are composite
characters, and I have disguised the identity of the people upon which
the characters are based.*

*Published in the United States by E. P. Dutton,
a division of NAL Penguin Inc.,
2 Park Avenue, New York, N.Y. 10016.*

*Published simultaneously in Canada by Fitzhenry and Whiteside,
Limited, Toronto.*

*Library of Congress Cataloging-in-Publication Data
Goldstone, Nancy Bazelon.
Trading up.*
1. *Goldstone, Nancy Bazelon.* 2. *Floor traders
(Finance)—New York (N.Y.)—Biography.* 3. *Forward exchange.*
4. *Financial futures.* I. *Title*
HG3853.G65   1988   332.4'5'0924 [B]   87-19975
ISBN: 0-525-24621-5

Designed by REM Studios

3 5 7 9 10 8 6 4 2

to Larry, who gave me back my dreams

CONTENTS

vii

CONTENTS

TRADING UP

PROLOGUE

8:29 A.M.: The trading room of a large commercial bank on Wall Street. The room is filled with people. The United States government is about to release key information on the state of the economy. It is deadly quiet.

The head foreign-exchange trader stands nervously behind his desk. He knows this information will move the dollar. If the data are good, the dollar will go up. The head trader will order his traders to telephone their counterparts at other banks and buy. If the numbers are very good, he will buy at least $100 million. If the numbers are bad the dollar will fall; the head trader will sell. The decision to buy or sell must be made immediately because the price will begin to change the instant the information is released. The head trader

1

alone will make this critical decision. There is no time for consultation. If he is correct, he may earn a million dollars for his bank in minutes. If he is wrong, he could lose a million just as quickly.

8:30 A.M.: A junior trader stands at the Telerate machine. A bell rings. The news is moving across the wire.

"Up 3.4 percent!" the junior trader shouts. He runs back to his desk and grabs his telephone.

Great news!

"Buy!" the head trader orders.

Six traders scream into six telephones.

"Mine! Mine!" they shout, buying the dollar.

8:31 A.M.: Countless traders at other institutions across the globe are also trying to buy. The value of the dollar jumps. The head trader takes a quick look at the scrawl on his trading blotter. His traders have bought $150 million in the first minute. The head trader grins. The dollars he bought have risen in value. A profit of $1.25 million.

8:32 A.M.: The bell at the Telerate machine rings again. The junior trader drops his phone and races to read the new information on the wire.

"Revision!" he shouts. "Last month's numbers revised down by 4.5 percent!"

The head trader freezes. The economy is weaker than expected because it grew less in the previous month than the first flash indicated. The dollar will crash.

"Sell it!" he hollers.

Six heads bend once again to their task.

"Yours! Yours!"

But other traders at other institutions have also seen the revision. No one is willing to buy the dollar. The traders have no one to sell to. The dollar begins to

2

plummet. The head trader looks on helplessly. Finally, after what seems like an eternity, the price falls so low that traders at some of the other banks are ready to buy the dollar again. The head trader sells his dollars.

8:40 A.M.: From plus $1.25 million to a loss of two million dollars. Lunch is still three hours away.

On Wall Street, decision making is power. A head trader can make or lose millions in seconds. That's power.

    This is the story of how I, Nancy Bazelon Goldstone, at age twenty-seven, with no previous experience in currency trading, became the head trader for currency options at one of the largest financial institutions in the country. I did it in three months. Was it talent? No. Was it experience? No. I didn't know a deutsche mark from a benchmark. Suddenly I was making decisions on millions of dollars of the bank's capital every day. My friends were impressed. My peers were envious. My family was horrified.

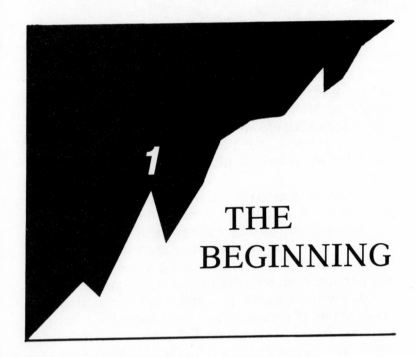

THE BEGINNING

I grew up in Highland Park, Illinois, an upper-middle-class suburb of Chicago. Highland Park is one of those places untouched by the current of human drama. Be there war, famine, pestilence, economic, political, or social upheaval in other cities or nations, Highland Park will remain aloof. Through the filter of a television set, sitting in a living room surrounded by prints of Expressionist art, with a scotch in one hand and a handful of Planters dry-roasted peanuts in the other, the residents of Highland Park monitor, judge, and finally dismiss the passion and turmoil of the outside world. These things happen, of course, they murmur. But not in Highland Park.

Upon reaching adolescence, I experienced an acute

5

sense of guilt over having to grow up in such a privileged environment. I considered it quite unfair. It was the early 1970s and we were at the tail end of the Vietnam War. Many people had suffered. The country was divided. New issues were coming to the fore.

At my house, the principal topic of conversation was whether to have lamb chops or broiled chicken for dinner.

Applying a fairly standard technique for relieving my conscience, I took everything out on my parents.

Striking out blindly against them, I rarely missed an opportunity to do the opposite of what they said. Their reasoning was dismissed out of hand. They were my parents, and, by definition, always wrong.

I saw my struggle as a noble act of rebellion and an assertion of independence. As it turned out, my parents made very convenient foils. After all, there's no safer way of asserting independence than when you know full well you aren't going to get it.

So how did I rebel? Did I drop out of society and go to work on a commune? Did I run away and join the French Foreign Legion? Did I start a home for unwed mothers in my bedroom?

Don't be ridiculous. I told you, this was Highland Park.

My rebellion took the tangible form of: (1) heroically resisting all of my mother's entreaties to straighten up my room; (2) boycotting the country club during the summer; (3) wearing torn Levi's instead of stonewashed Calvin Kleins; (4) turning down an invitation to the prom; (5) refusing to learn to play either golf or tennis; and (6) applying to colleges outside of the Chicago area.

Tough measures, but necessary.

But, like all teenagers, while fighting them, I desperately sought my parents' approval. One way to win their respect and affection was through education. They thought grades were important. As schoolwork always came easily to me, this seemed at first a painless way of earning their praise. But, after a while, it seemed they expected good grades. I brought home As, and, although they still praised me, they no longer went to the trouble of hiring a marching band or writing their congressman.

Interpreting this slight falloff in enthusiasm as disapproval, I raised my already high standards. You could say I was something of an overachiever.

To escape the pressure, I sought a refuge. Some kids do drugs. Some kids do sports.

I did books.

Long books. Short books. I read all the time—everything I could get my hands on, never bothering to discriminate. Thus I would finish Hemingway and begin on Irving Wallace.

(My mother, noting my attachment to the written word, suggested that perhaps I might wish to try my hand at writing. I immediately registered for an advanced mathematics course.)

I remember stumbling onto *War and Peace* during my senior year in high school. I loved *War and Peace*. I read it day and night to the exclusion of all other activities, intensely displeasing my high school sweetheart. Why would I want to stay home all night with a book, he asked plaintively, when I could spend the evening with him watching the Celtics play the Lakers on television?

Whenever I read, I give myself up to the world I'm reading about, unconscious of events happening right under my nose. In the case of *War and Peace*, this state of affairs lasted for over a month.

Consequently, I missed the announcement of an impending examination in European history.

I found out about the test thirty seconds before class,

7

in the hallway outside the room. All the other kids were standing around comparing notes. I froze. I'd read not one word of the assigned text and had not listened in class for nearly a month. What time period were we covering? What countries? I had no idea. Mechanically, I followed the rest of my classmates into the room and sat down at my desk. Everyone was quiet with the usual hush that precedes an examination.

The teacher handed out the test. It consisted of a single question: "Do great men make their circumstances, or do circumstances make great men?"

I stared down at the question. What luck! For over an hour, taking everything directly from *War and Peace,* I wrote happily about Napoleon invading Russia. Tolstoy and I received one of the highest grades in the class.

Though I didn't know it at the time, it was a sign of things to come. All I thought was, Thank God it wasn't math.

I went on to an Ivy League university, my first time away from home. Independent at last! Time to show my parents that I could manage perfectly well on my own, thank you very much.

My major changed three times in the first year and a half, running the gamut from playwriting to nuclear physics. (I had an idea that I would look terrific in a white coat— a notion I got from an old episode of "I Spy.") Finally, I came under the influence of a professor who taught power politics under the guise of American history. It was rumored that he'd be up for secretary of state if so-and-so were elected. So-and-so never made it, and neither did my professor. However, he did manage to pass on his ambition to most of his students.

Determined to follow in my professor's visionary though frustrated footsteps, I enrolled in graduate school at Columbia University in New York City to prepare for an entry-level position in the State Department. There I met Tom Smith, a graduate student in the School of Business. Tom was brilliant and determined. He knew exactly what he wanted. He had his whole life mapped out. He was going to enter an investment bank and become rich and powerful.

I was attracted to his intelligence and self-confidence. We started to date. I confided in him my scheme to enter the State Department, do great works, become famous, etc., etc.

He shuddered.

"What do you want to go there for?" he demanded. "That's just a bunch of bureaucrats."

He said it as though they were a new species of vermin.

"Well, where should I go?" I asked.

He never hesitated.

"Wall Street."

At first I thought he was crazy. Wall Street? I didn't know very much about Wall Street, but it seemed incompatible with my ideals. I was interested in doing good works. I wasn't particularly interested in making money.

But Tom was very determined. Unsure myself of what I wanted out of life, I began to listen to him. Suddenly, I noticed that most of the intelligent people I knew at school were following his example. Surely they knew what they were doing. Besides, power and money were attractive lures. I didn't want to spend my life as an ineffective naïf. It became something of a competition for me, trying to prove that I was every bit as determined and ambitious as my peers.

I didn't know it at the time, of course, but I was falling prey to one of the most insidious influences of my generation.

I was becoming a Yuppie.

Switching out of my World Hunger class, I enrolled in Basic Accounting and Finance. For the first time in my life, I read the business section of the newspaper and saw reports of billion-dollar deals and million-dollar salaries. Approaching graduation, I dreamed of power, money, action.

What I got was a job as a loan officer.

And a loan officer I remained for three years, achieving the position of assistant vice president at $40,000 a year.

It was my job to lend money to companies who traded in gold and silver. From my customers I was able to pick up a rudimentary knowledge of the precious-metals market and the basics of gold trading. Unfortunately, my term as a loan officer coincided with a slump in the demand for precious metals. The companies I was supposed to lend to didn't really need the bank's money. Faced with this reality, my days flew by at the breakneck speed of an English cricket match.

I came to dread my morning strategy sessions with my manager, Charles. Charles had dark hair and eyes, and a moustache of which he was very proud. He went out almost every night with customers of the bank so that he could eat at the most expensive restaurants and carouse at the liveliest nightclubs. In this way he affected a jet-set life-style without the necessity of a jet-set income.

Our conversations were nearly always the same.

"Good morning, Nancy," Charles said, examining his fingernails. Charles was always a bit superior, an attitude due, no doubt, to his keen regard for the high position he held within the bank. Charles was a "global manager." This meant he managed me and three others. I never did figure out why we were global.

"Good morning, Charles," I replied. "What can I do for you?"

10

"Nancy, how many customers do you have?"

"I have five customers, Charles."

"In that case, I expect you to lend out $10 million today to each customer. That's $50 million altogether."

"Wait. I called them all yesterday and they told me they don't need money this week."

"Call them back. Make them take the money." Charles glared at me.

"What do you mean, 'Make them take the money'? I can't force people to borrow, can I?"

"Call them."

With that Charles stalked off to his desk in a corner and stared at me until I picked up the phone. Then he folded his arms across his chest, put his feet up on the desk, and fell asleep.

I was driven to despair by Charles's rigidity and my customers' lack of enthusiasm for more money, despite my offer of a free toaster for every $10 million borrowed. So I approached Charles one day at 3:00 P.M. Months of experience had taught me that Charles was at his best immediately following his afternoon nap but previous to his cocktail hour. I caught him just as he was finishing up a telephone conversation. He had been trying to scrounge up a date for the evening's entertainment. This activity generally took up several hours of his day.

"Charles, may I speak with you for a moment?"

"Of course, Nancy." Charles was genial. He had apparently scored.

"I've been thinking, " I said. "Since I'm having so much trouble lending to our usual customers, why don't you let me go out and try to drum up some new business?"

Charles frowned slightly and lit a cigarette.

"Are you sure you have the time for it?" he asked suspiciously.

I assured him I had.

11

"Whom do you intend to visit?"

I told him about a relatively new product I'd heard of called *options*. I understood that there were companies that were devoting themselves entirely to trading options. I thought these companies might need to borrow to finance their purchases and sales.

"I don't think so," said Charles. "Sounds too risky for us."

But I knew how to get to Charles.

"Just think, Charles!" I exclaimed. "This is a new product. We could be the first people on Wall Street to finance options. People get their names in the newspaper for being the first to try something new."

"I suppose," said Charles, straightening up a bit, "there's no real harm in letting you investigate. Just make sure that I'm informed every step of the way. With something innovative like this, you'll need my signature on every memorandum."

"Of course, Charles."

Cheered by the thought of having something to do, I made an appointment with the treasurer of an options trading company. The treasurer told me that the company traded options on foreign currencies, U.S. government bonds, stocks, metals, and other commodities. He threw out technical terms, like *delta*, *gamma*, *theta*, and *volatility*. He was eager to borrow money and offered to post options as collateral.

I was quiet during this first interview. The terms the treasurer used were unfamiliar to me. However, I would have died rather than let him detect my ignorance. Smiling sweetly, I promised to get back to him.

I went to a bookstore and bought every book on options I could find. I spent the next two weeks studying. I learned that an option was like an insurance policy against an adverse price movement in the value of

12

a commodity. The purchaser of an option pays a premium up front for the right to buy or sell a commodity at a specific price for a finite period of time. This premium fluctuates with the price of the underlying commodity and the time left on the option. I became reasonably familiar with the term *delta*, which was a measure of how much the option's premium would increase or decrease in value given a change in the price of the underlying commodity. I never did figure out what *gamma*, *theta*, or *volatility* meant.

Charles was suspicious, but impressed by the flood of memorandums I produced for his signature. As copies of all memos were reviewed by the bank's senior management, it got around that Charles was becoming something of an options expert.

The more I learned, the more interested I became in trading. Although I couldn't pretend to understand everything I'd read, that didn't stop me from daydreaming about becoming an options trader. It seemed glamorous, fast-paced, and exciting. After three years of lending, I was in the mood for a little excitement.

This daydream haunted me so, that I actually did something about it. I went to apply for a job with the bank's trading department.

Most people don't know that banks speculate with their own capital. In fact, when I told my father, a respected lawyer in Chicago, that I intended to get a job trading options at the bank, he told me that I was crazy to think that a bank gambled with its depositors' money.

Of all the false images ever perpetrated on an unsuspecting public by advertising, surely the myth of the commercial bank as a financially conservative institution is the most blatant. Commercial banks are among the largest, and are certainly the most uncontrolled, gambling institutions in the world. This is a simple fact.

The trading departments of every major commercial bank in this country (and abroad, for that matter) are responsible for openly speculating with the bank's capital on the value of the dollar or the direction interest rates will take. More often than not, a bank trader will be allowed to bet a significant portion of the bank's actual capital base at any one time. The only difference between the trading room of a major commercial bank and a Las Vegas gambling casino is that in Las Vegas you can't lose more than you bet.

Therefore, I ignored the parental comment and approached the man in charge of the bank's Options Trading Unit, Paul Pepper.

He was large and genial, in his mid-thirties, possessed of masses of curly brown hair and an engaging grin. Though still young, he gave the impression of being middle-aged, which I attributed to the pressures of his job.

Paul had begun his career as an administrative assistant to a government bond trader. Later he became interested in options and succeeded in convincing senior management that the bank was falling behind the competition by not making this product available to its customers. He offered to study the situation and set up a currency options desk for the bank. His study took a year and a half, and at the end of that time he was appointed to head the bank's newly organized Options Trading Unit.

Trying to change jobs within a large organization such as a commercial bank is very tricky business. The whole matter has to be handled with delicacy, or you're liable to lose your old position without gaining the new one. The object is to get your prospective boss to think that hiring you was his own idea.

"Can I have a job trading options with you?" I asked Paul.

He looked at me, surprised.

14

"Do you know anything about options?" he asked me.

I handed him the pile of memorandums I'd written for Charles's signature. He looked them over.

"I wrote these," I said.

"Okay, leave them with me and give me a call tomorrow around four o'clock."

I walked away, holding my breath, dizzy with excitement. I'd done it! I'd made the first move! I rushed home to tell my fiancé, Larry, who gave me a thorough dose of reality.

I had known Larry for about a year. He had worked for a client of the bank, and one day he'd walked into my lending department. We gazed mutely at each other across the word processors.

Larry was unlike anyone I'd ever met before. Until now, all of my boyfriends had been a lot like Tom Smith: upright, industrious, boring.

Larry was anything but boring.

During his professional career, Larry had been (among other things) a political consultant, a banker, a gold trader, a model, an actor, and a member of a think tank. He'd helped organize a major gold-trading operation on Wall Street. He'd devised sophisticated risk-management programs as an outside consultant.

He was charming and extremely good-looking. He was also brilliant: it took him all of two years to get his Ph.D. in political science. His varied experiences had given him the kind of real-life outlook that is significantly underrepresented on Wall Street.

Larry had one motto in life: Go for it.

He was ten years older than I. I had a great deal of respect for his opinion.

"Do you have any idea," asked my fiancé, "how difficult it is to secure a junior trading position?"

I admitted I had no idea.

"Very difficult. Do you have any idea how many people want to get into trading who are far more qualified than you, and how few positions they compete for?"

I allowed ignorance as to the exact number of applicants in the field, or the size of the field, for that matter.

"Let me enlighten you, then," said my beloved. "The competition for a position in trading is fierce, because the potential rewards are enormous. It is the most sought-after career on Wall Street."

I pointed out, a bit defensively, that I wasn't without some skills. I had read books on the subject.

"I just don't want you to get your hopes up," said Larry, more gently. "The odds are a hundred to one against you. Go in there and give it your best shot. But know that it's an outside chance at best."

I didn't sleep all night.

I spent the next day at my lending desk, frantically poring over my books. The more I read, the more confused I became. By early afternoon I was absolutely convinced that I knew nothing whatsoever about options and could never learn. I would never get the job.

At 3:00 P.M., the phone rang.

"Nancy? This is Paul Pepper. Can you come up and see me in about half an hour?"

"Uh . . . well . . . sure," I stammered.

"Good," said Paul. "I'm going to have you sit down with Bob Green and myself. Bob is the other member of the team. Just come by the desk when you're ready." He hung up.

My hand trembled as I hung up the phone. I wanted the job so bad. But how to get through the interview? I prayed for divine intervention.

I made an excuse to Charles and escaped to the

trading room at the appointed time. Paul and Bob were there waiting for me. We shook hands, and they led me into an empty office away from the noisy, crowded room. We sat down facing one another. The moment of truth had arrived.

"Nancy," Paul began pleasantly, "you have excellent timing. As it turns out, Bob and I were looking for a third member of the options trading team."

So there was a job available! I prayed harder. I offered God my firstborn male child.

"There are a few questions we'd like to ask you first," the interview began.

Here it comes! I threw in the rest of my family.

"Could you start within two weeks?" Paul asked.

I said I thought it could be arranged.

"As a junior trader, you would have to come into work earlier than you do now, say seven-thirty instead of nine. Do you have a problem with that?"

I assured him that I was an early riser anyway. I am proud to say that this was the only real lie I told to get the job.

"Well," said Paul, settling back into his chair, "those are my questions. Bob, do you have any questions?"

"I don't think so," said Bob, looking bored.

"All right, then," said Paul, standing up, "I'll talk to John."

I looked from one to the other, bewildered.

"Did I get the job?" I asked Paul.

"Well," said Paul. "I've got no problem with you. Bob has no problem with you, right, Bob?"

"Right," said Bob, who was already on his way out of the office.

"Then it's only a matter of having you meet John."

"Who is John?"

"John Anderson," Paul explained, "is the head of the bank's trading operation. Our unit falls within his jurisdiction. If he agrees, the job is yours. Provided," he added quickly, "that you are willing to start within two weeks."

"Oh, absolutely," I said, just as quickly.

"Good," said Paul, shaking my hand. "I'll set you up with an appointment with John. Will you be available sometime tomorrow during the day? Okay. I'll call you tomorrow and let you know."

Larry made me repeat the conversation word for word that evening when I got home from work. He shook his head.

"There's something wrong here," he said when I had finished recounting the interview for the third time. "Are you sure that's all they asked you?"

I replied with dignity that I thought I could remember a five-minute conversation as well as the next person.

"Well," he said, "it must be that John Anderson makes all the decisions. That will be the tough interview. The one today must just have been part of the screening process. Still, it's odd that the two people that you will be working most closely with didn't bother to find out more about you."

Even I had to admit that the initial interview had been less than rigorous.

"Perhaps my memos were so good that they spoke for themselves," I suggested.

"Perhaps."

I kept the part about sacrificing the family to myself. But how else was I to explain the ease with which I had sailed through that first interview?

The next day I received a call from Mr. Anderson's secretary, Linda, who arranged for me to come and see him at 2:00 P.M. I spent the morning trying to find out everything I could about John Anderson.

It turned out that John was a rising star at the bank. He had come up through the ranks to achieve, at the age of forty-two, the coveted position of executive in charge of the Trading Sector. This meant that he was responsible for managing all of the bank's trading in its most sophisticated and complex financial instruments—everything from foreign-exchange options to interest-rate swaps.

The more I found out, the more impressed I became. I was to be interviewed by a man who was only two positions removed from the chairman of the board. No wonder the first interview had been so simple. A man of John's caliber would certainly detect my rudimentary knowledge of foreign-exchange and options trading immediately. I was keenly aware of my shortcomings.

Nonetheless I arrived at his office at the appointed time for the interview. I was ushered into the neat, uncluttered room and found myself face-to-face with one of the bank's most senior managers.

My first impression was of a well-groomed executive. Everything about him proclaimed his professionalism. He was perfectly dressed, from his immaculately clean white shirt to the gleam of the polish on his wing-tip shoes. He even had a freshly laundered handkerchief peeking out of the breast pocket of his conservative dark suit. Gold cuff links, a Rolex watch, and a wedding band were his only accessories. He was slim, energetic, and youthful in appearance, with an almost boyish charm. His posture was excellent. Although it was the dead of winter, he sported a beautiful suntan. He looked as if he hadn't a care in the world. He shook my hand briskly and asked me to sit down.

"Let's see," he began in a no-nonsense way. "Nancy. Yes. You're interviewing for a spot on the options team, is that it? You'll have to excuse me for not being entirely focused at the moment. You see, I've just come from a major meeting on asset-liability management."

I assured him that I understood.

"And in twenty minutes I must attend a senior-level risk-management meeting."

I thanked him for taking time out of so obviously busy a schedule to talk to me. He seemed to like that.

"Fascinating subject, risk management. Do you know much about risk management, Nancy?" He looked at me searchingly.

So Larry was right. This was going to be a difficult interview. I opened my lips to answer, but, to my surprise, he cut me off.

"I think that risk management is one of the most important issues facing those of us responsible for overseeing trading operations today. How, for example, do you manage the risk of an option position—?"

Worse and worse! Once again I started to answer, but he continued.

"—or of a forward rate agreement, or of a swap? What about forward foreign-exchange positions, Treasury positions?"

Damn! How was I to answer so many difficult questions during the course of a single twenty-minute interview? At least I did have some opinions on foreign-exchange options positions. I opened my mouth to speak but he interrupted again.

"These are the questions someone in my position has to deal with. Do you know my background, Nancy? No? Well, let me begin by telling you that I was an officer in the Marines during the Vietnam War. I joined the bank in 1973. . . ."

He spent the next eighteen minutes reviewing his

career. From combat he moved to junior bank clerk. From junior bank clerk to senior bank clerk. Then came a promotion to managing bank clerk. Then junior operations assistant, senior operations assistant—on and on, up and up, until his present position. Although I tried to listen attentively, I barely heard him. I thought he was just filling the time until the interview was over. I had obviously failed somewhere.

He had just finished speaking when there came a knock on the door. Linda poked her head into the office and reminded John that it was time to attend the next meeting.

He thanked her and rose to his feet. I stood up as well, not knowing what else to do, quite sure that I hadn't gotten the job. Now I was going to be dismissed.

He held out his hand to me. I took it limply.

He shook hands energetically, grinned, and exclaimed:

"Glad to have you on board!"

Larry didn't believe me when I told him I had gotten the job.

"Just like that?" he asked.

"Just like that," I replied.

"I don't understand it," he said. "All you know about trading is from what you've read in books." Suddenly he jerked his head up. "Unless . . ."

"Unless what?"

"You're certainly as smart and as capable as the next person. But you're also a lot better-looking than the next person, who would most assuredly be male. I'm sure that didn't hurt."

"That's not true!" I said, stung.

"Well, how many women did you see when you visited the trading room?"

"There were a few."

"Mostly secretaries or salespeople, I bet. How many of them were in their twenties? How many were pretty? How many had great legs?"

"I don't have great legs."

"You do have great legs. That's why I'm marrying you."

"I didn't get this job because of my legs."

"Are you sure?"

"I'm positive. It wasn't like that. There were no sexual vibes. I'm not sure they even noticed that I was a woman."

"Nancy," said Larry, "they always notice."

"I don't care. I've got the job now, and I'm going to keep it."

It was arranged that I would begin working on the options desk as soon as possible. I had to give Charles two weeks' notice, of course, and he would probably put up a bit of a fight about it, but since I had a firm offer from the trading side of the bank, there wasn't much he could do.

I spent those last two weeks as a loan officer in a happy daze. My associates were choked with envy. The trading side of the bank paid much better than the lending side. Although I wasn't getting a raise to begin with, my potential earning power was far greater as a trader. And I was going off to do something new and exciting. Already I could taste the fruits of success.

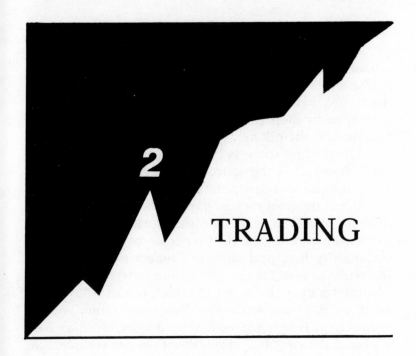

2

TRADING

Reality smacked me full in the face that first morning when the alarm went off at 5:30 A.M.

It was a bitterly cold day in early February 1985. The sun wouldn't be up for another hour and a half. Larry rolled over as I struggled out of bed.

"Good luck, babe," he murmured sleepily.

I was only half awake myself when I pushed open the swinging glass doors that marked the entrance to the trading room. I woke up with a start.

There were desks and computer screens everywhere. Wires hung down from the ceiling or lay piled in ropes on the floor. The fluorescent lighting intensified the glare from the machinery. The room was pulsing with heat and energy. It was only 7:15 A.M., but already the trading room was full of people sipping coffee and smoking their first cigarettes of the day. I made my way over to the options desk. Paul Pepper was already there, turning on computer screens and talking into the phone.

The trading room is the symbol of the life-force of Wall Street. It is the source of energy. Its fuel powers the impressive boardrooms where negotiations are conducted by quiet men in dark suits—negotiations that allocate and then reallocate the world's resources. Its influence pervades the deepest recesses of the financial community here and abroad. Traders sit in judgment on every action taken, every policy determined. The trading room is the arena in which modern-day gladiators meet to do battle for their institutions and for themselves. Telephones and computer screens may have replaced the swords and shields of days of yore, but the principle remains the same.

The telephones and computer screens relay information. Traders suck in information the way other people breathe. Trading rooms virtually hum with an incessant undertone of news. Improvements in communications systems over the last decade have made it possible for news reports to be almost instantaneous. Many traders keep Reuters screens at home so they can check on the overseas markets long after their office has shut down for the day. The whole world is on real time. What this means for the trader is that, from the moment of awakening in the morning until bedding down for a few hours of much-needed sleep at night, he or she is constantly bombarded with information.

All different kinds of news affect the market; it's not limited to "business" data per se. Factors such as political news: What candidate is running for which office and in which country? What bill is being passed in Congress and what effect will that have on other nations as well as our own? Then there is international news: riots have broken out here; terrorist activities are taking place there. And economic information: At what rate did the economy grow last month? What's predicted for next month? Who says so? Then there's general gossip: The Arabs are buying! No, they're selling! No, it's the Japanese!

Every new detail, fact or rumor, must be absorbed. To be unaware of even the most innocuous news item can mean the difference between winning and losing millions of dollars in a single day, even in a single hour, in what many consider to be the only game in town: the market.

The market is the sum total of all the traders in the world. It has a dynamic all its own, the result of a continual assessment of the value of a given commodity. For every buyer there is a seller. Price is determined literally by the total, on a macroeconomic scale, of what one trader is willing to pay versus what another will take to sell. As new information becomes available, opinions change, and so do the prices.

Successful traders are among the most respected individuals in the financial community. To do the job properly, a good trader must have, in addition to intellect, of course: stamina, to withstand the constant pressure and round-the-clock hours; boldness, to hold a position or risk large sums in the face of uncertain information; discipline, to acknowledge an error and take a loss today to save a larger loss tomorrow; speed, to grasp all of the implications of a piece of information instantaneously as one hears it; and creativity, to stay ahead of a community that places a high premium upon innovation. No other position demands all of these particular qualities to the extreme that trading does, and well the trader knows it. This usually adds arrogance to the list.

Trading rooms are large, open areas, filled with many people, mostly men. (Trading is one of the most purely male-dominated fields. It is almost taken for granted that one's masculinity, as much as one's capital, is on the line when one trades.) Some are standing, others sitting, but all are peering intently into tiny computer screens that transmit even tinier fluorescent numbers, while speaking into telephones—sometimes two at once. A trader is very conscious of time and never wastes words. The price could change during the exchange of even the most limited pleasantries and an opportunity to buy or sell would be gone. The atmosphere crackles. The air is hot and dry, fired by the heat given off by both the computer equipment and the sheer number of people crammed in per square foot.

Traders buy and sell and hope to make a profit by the effort. Gold traders buy and sell gold. Stock traders buy and sell stock. Currency option traders buy and sell currency options.

A gold trader's responsibility is to make money by betting that the price of gold will rise or fall. If, for example, the gold trader thinks that the price of gold will rise in the future, he will go into the marketplace and buy gold. He will buy the gold from traders at other banks (who are betting the price of gold will fall) or from one of the public exchanges that were established for this purpose. (Just as there is a stock exchange where it is possible for an individual to buy and sell stock, so there is a commodities exchange where it is possible to buy and sell gold.)

Currency options, of course, are harder to visualize than gold. Unlike gold, a tangible asset (something we can see and touch), a currency option is an intangible asset, a right. A currency option is the right to buy or sell foreign currency at a specific price for a specific period of time. Although not something you can touch or see, rights are real nonetheless. Since it is difficult to imagine a "right," think of a currency option as a piece of paper on which is written "The Right to Buy" or "The Right to Sell."

Like the gold trader, the currency option trader's responsibility is to make money by betting that the price of currency options will rise or fall. Currency options can be bought from traders at other banks, or from a public exchange, just like gold. Currency option prices rise or fall in correlation with the rise or fall of the dollar.

Traders are hired by banks for one reason and one reason alone: to make money.

Paul and Bob traded currency options from a desk in the center of a large room. To their right were the spot foreign-currency traders; to their left the interest-rate desk. The spot currency traders were responsible for speculating on whether the dollar would increase or decrease in value. The interest-rate traders were supposed to do the same thing for long-term and short-term interest rates. Both of these desks were run by men with ten or more years of experience in the marketplace.

But this was not the case at the options desk. Paul had only been trading options for a little over a year, and Bob for eight months. The options market was not so developed as the interest-rate or spot foreign-currency markets. Options were a new and complex financial instrument that not that many people understood, certainly not senior management at the bank. Paul and Bob could trade pretty much as they pleased.

By the time I arrived on the scene, Paul and Bob had managed to amass quite a sizable options portfolio—close to $1 billion in face value. Every option has a *face value*. For example, Paul and Bob could buy an option to purchase $5 million at a specific price for a specific date. The face value of that option would be $5 million. The aggregate of all the options they had purchased and sold was the face value of the portfolio. They were very proud of the size of the portfolio and of their reputation as being "aggressive" traders. They were willing to buy or sell at prices under the market in order to increase their volume of business. They said this was the best way to promote the bank's name throughout the industry.

The first few days at any new job are difficult. The first few days on a trading desk were bewildering.

Paul and Bob sat at a small table on which were stacked six computer screens, four push-button phones, and a telephone console. The phones rang constantly so it was often necessary to speak into two receivers at once. The computer screens blinked little green numbers that changed from second to second. Occasionally a bell would ring and one of the screens would flash an important news item.

Paul went out of his way to be helpful. In between phone calls and trading he would explain how one screen was linked to an exchange in Chicago, and another to Philadelphia; a third reported spot currency prices in New York; a fourth, options prices out of Switzerland. Whenever he bought or sold an option he would stop to show me exactly what he'd done and how he had priced the trade.

Nothing I had done as a loan officer prepared me for the grueling work and absolute concentration of those first few days in the trading room. There is no aspect of lending that can be remotely characterized as fast-paced, unless you count the speed at which everyone runs for the elevators at lunchtime.

But by 11:00 A.M. of that first day I was exhausted. I wanted to go home. The level of attention demanded was staggering.

And nothing I had read in any of the books I'd

studied so religiously prepared me for the reality of trading. Forget learning about the options market. I had to learn about the spot foreign-exchange market before I could attempt to understand the options market.

Paul called my attention to a screen that listed the current prices of each of the major currencies: deutsche marks, Swiss francs, Japanese yen, British pounds, Canadian dollars. I stared at that screen. Concentrate. Concentrate. Every time one of the numbers on that screen changed I would ask myself a series of questions. The deutsche mark number changed. Was the dollar going up or down against the deutsche mark? Up—no, down. No—up. Okay. If the dollar was going up, did that mean other traders were buying it or selling it? Selling it—no, buying it. Wait! The British pound number just changed. Did that mean the dollar was going up or down against the British pound . . . ?

I could hear the spot foreign-exchange traders, at their desks across the room, trading. Mine! They shouted. Did *mine* mean they were buying or selling the dollar? I asked Paul. Buying. Okay, if they were buying did that mean the dollar was going up or down? And against which currencies?

Wait! A bell is ringing! That means there's news. Oh my God! *All* the numbers are changing! The mark, the pound, the franc, the yen! Are they going up or down? What does that mean . . . ?

All day long. Constant. Unremitting.

"How'd it go?" asked Larry when I got home that first evening.

I collapsed on the sofa.

"That bad, huh?" he murmured sympathetically, sitting down beside me and putting his arm around me.

"Oh, Larry," I sighed, stifling a sob, "I can't do it. It's too hard."

"Don't you think you should give yourself more than one day at it before you chuck it?"

"I guess so," I sighed again. I was very depressed.

"Why don't you let me help you a little?" Larry asked.

"Oh!" I said, eagerly. "Do you think you can?"

"Sure. I know how the market works. C'mon, keep your chin up." He winked at me.

I'd written down every one of the trades that Paul had done that day. He'd tried to explain them to me at the time, but I hadn't understood. I figured if I wrote them all down, there was a chance of making some sense of them later. I showed the sheets to Larry.

"Terrific!" he said. "Now we've got something to work with. Let's look at this very first trade. What does it say?"

I looked at the trade steadily for about five minutes.

"Beats me," I said.

"Well, let's go through it slowly," said Larry, laughing. "It looks to me like you bought $5 million worth of a put on the deutsche mark expiring in June."

I looked at the trade again. Now that he mentioned it, it did look like Paul had bought $5 million of a put on the deutsche mark expiring in June.

"Now, what does that mean?" Larry encouraged.

I closed my eyes and tried to concentrate. I remembered something I'd read in one of my books.

"Well," I said slowly, "when you buy a put on the deutsche mark, you are buying the right to sell deutsche marks at a specific price for a specific period of time."

"That's right," said Larry, nodding. "Who says you don't know your stuff? Now what does that mean, the 'right to sell deutsche marks'?"

I closed my eyes to concentrate again. Then I opened them.

"Beats me," I said.

"Well," said Larry, "when you sell deutsche marks, doesn't that mean you are going short the deutsche mark? And when you go short the deutsche mark, doesn't that mean that you are actually going long the dollar? Isn't that the same thing as buying dollars?"

"You really think so?" I asked.

"Think about it," he said.

I hadn't thought about it that way before. It seemed right. At least, I could see nothing wrong with the reasoning.

"Did the dollar go up or down against the deutsche mark today?" Larry asked.

I'd remembered to write down the price of all the currencies when I came in in the morning and just before I left. I dived for the paper. After some intense calculating (I had to start over once from the beginning when I lost track in the middle), I was able to answer the question.

"The dollar went up against the deutsche mark today," I said finally.

"There you go!" said Larry. "So if you bought a put—buying a put is the same thing as buying dollars—and the dollar went up, did you make or lose money on this put?"

"I guess if we bought dollars and the dollar went up we made money on the put," I said.

"Exactly."

"Gee! We made money on that put?" I asked, looking at the sheets with renewed interest.

"Looks like," said Larry, dryly.

"Think of that," I said, just as pleased as if I'd thought to buy the put myself.

"Don't get cocky," said Larry. "Let's look at the

next one. It looks to me like you bought a put on the Japanese yen. . . "

Larry never lost patience. I don't know what I would have done without him. Day after day of those first two weeks I would struggle out of bed in the morning and steel myself for another day of frustration and concentration. Night after night I would bring home handwritten notes of the trades that Paul and Bob had executed that day, and Larry and I would go over them, painstakingly, one at a time. It took hours.

But bit by bit I started to learn. I didn't learn enough to trade. But I learned enough to start asking questions.

There is no one standard method for trading options. In many ways, it's like going to the racetrack. A bettor can make educated guesses by studying the racing form and knowing something about the horses, but it's best to have luck on your side. The most successful options traders try to structure trades that make money in three out of four scenarios—and then hope that the fourth doesn't happen.

Paul tried to explain the rationale behind some of his trades.

"Now this trade," he said, pointing an ink-stained finger to one of many numbers scrawled on a handwritten sheet, "this trade makes money if the dollar increases in value anytime during the next two months. It has a maximum profit potential of $100,000."

I looked at the trade.

"What if the dollar doesn't increase in value?" I asked.

"Well," Paul answered, "if the dollar stays pretty much where it is today for the next two months, this trade will make about $20,000."

"And if the dollar declines in value?"

"If the dollar declines slightly in value, the trade will lose about $30,000. You always have to take some risk," he added.

"What if the dollar declines significantly in value?"

"If the dollar declines significantly in value?" Paul repeated. "Nancy, I've been trading options for over a year and a half now. In all that time I have never seen the dollar decrease significantly in value. In fact, the dollar has been steadily increasing in value during the entire time I've been trading. It is extremely unlikely that the dollar will decrease significantly in value during the next two months, which is the time period of this particular trade."

"But what if it does?" I persisted.

"Well, if the dollar started to fall dramatically, the loss on this particular trade would be unlimited. But I tell you, it's not going to happen."

"I see," I said.

Almost all of my instruction came from Paul. Bob just ignored me.

Bob came from Connecticut. His father was a corporate lawyer, his mother a psychiatrist. Bob's scholastic credits read like a sample from a how-to book on résumé writing: prep school, Ivy League university, Harvard Business School. (Hobbies: golf and tennis.) He had wavy blond hair and blue eyes. The freckles on his nose belied his real age, which was close to thirty.

The first thing that struck me about Bob were his clothes. His expensive suits were cut in the European style and were tailored to perfection. Cary Grant would have envied the crease in his trousers. He scorned the traditional red or yellow neckties popular on Wall Street in favor of muted colors and patterns. A pink silk handkerchief adorned his breast pocket. When I was introduced to him, we shook hands, and I noticed to my chagrin that his fingernails were better manicured than mine.

Bob had begun his career marketing foreign exchange to the bank's customers. His sense of self-assurance combined with an understated humor held a universal appeal. He charmed both men and women (particularly the latter) and was considered to be one of the bank's most successful young salesmen. Bob could, and often did, convince people who had no need whatsoever for foreign currency to buy large quantities of it, and at overstated prices.

Bob loved to trade. Here was an opportunity to sell anything to anybody. He was particularly interested in selling options that no other trader was willing to sell.

"Why did you sell that option?" I would ask Bob of a particularly complex trade. Bob never volunteered information; he would only respond to a direct question. Whenever I spoke to him, he would look at me so blankly that I was never sure he remembered who I was.

"Because it puts customer business on the books."

"Isn't it risky, though?" I would ask.

"What do you mean, risky?"

"Can't you lose a lot of money on it?"

"Nancy," Bob would say, with a finality that signaled his patience was at an end, "these are options. You can't lose a lot of money trading options."

I believed everything they told me. It seemed that they traded with ease and confidence. I wanted to know how much money they made for the bank, but something in their attitude suggested that it was inappropriate to ask.

It turned out I didn't have to.

Once a month, the options position was assessed for profit and loss. One day, soon after I'd started, Paul,

Bob, and I sat down to value all the options in the portfolio. That is, we had to decide what every option was worth on that day. This is called *finding the market value of an option*. The difference between that market value and the amount of money that had been paid for the option if the option had been purchased, or the amount of money received for that option if it had been sold, was then tallied by hand by the accounting representative, Kashir Rameshwar. Whatever the resulting number came out to be was assumed to be the profit or loss for the month.

Paul handed me a sheet of paper on which were listed the options that I was supposed to value. There were over one hundred options on my list.

Some of the options had been purchased from or sold to one of the public exchanges that offer currency options. The exchanges list the market value of all their options on a daily basis, so for exchange-traded options I just put down whatever the exchange said was the market value of that particular option.

But exchange-traded options were only a very small percentage of the options in our portfolio. For over 80 percent of the portfolio there were no listed market values.

"How should I calculate the market price for the options that are not listed on the exchange?" I asked Paul.

"Eyeball it," he advised me.

Eyeball it?

Paul's method for determining the price of an option that was not listed on the exchange was to pretend it was listed on the exchange, and extrapolate a price. He showed me how to do that, and I copied his method and went to work. It took about three hours for all of us, working steadily, to value the portfolio this way.

I was aware almost immediately that there were two dangers with this system. The first was that because Paul and Bob and I were assigning the market values (using the rigorous "eyeball" method), we could more or less assign any value we wished. There didn't appear to be any second checks. Almost no one at the bank knew what an option was, so there was no one to monitor our work. This meant that, if we'd wanted to, we could have shown whatever profit we wished.

The second danger was that Kashir seemed to have absolutely no idea of what he was doing. Not only could he not provide the necessary second check on our calculations, he didn't seem to know what to do with the data we provided.

However, as no one but I seemed to have any problem with this arrangement, we handed in our market values to Kashir and awaited the result.

A week after we assigned the month-end market values, Kashir, whose office was located just off the main trading room, came by holding a slip of paper behind his back. Kashir was of medium build. He wore his jet-black hair slicked back off his face, and had a fondness for bow ties. He spoke with a heavy accent.

Kashir had been with the bank seemingly since its inception, and over time had performed a wide variety of tasks all having to do with the operations side of the bank. That's where the bank performs its internal accounting, makes and receives payments, and monitors the traders' positions. The operations department of any commercial bank or trading house is absolutely crucial to the financial health of the institution. Operations are ultimately responsible for guarding the bank against fraud and theft. Unfortunately, operations work is also boring, which results in a high turnover rate for personnel. Kashir had achieved his position principally by outlasting the competition. As the most senior person in his department, he was responsible for verifying the profit and loss of the entire trading floor. When Paul and Bob started up the options desk, senior management deemed it unnecessary to go to all the trouble and expense of hiring an individual experienced in accounting for currency options, and assigned the additional task to Kashir.

Kashir made his way over to the desk and addressed himself to Paul.

"Ahem!" he began, clearing his throat and rolling his eyes nervously. "I haf here de profit-and-loss numbers," he announced, sneaking a glance at Paul to determine his reaction to this piece of information.

"Yes?" Paul replied pleasantly.

"I haf here de profit-and-loss numbers," Kashir repeated for emphasis.

"Yes?" Paul replied again, a shade less pleasantly. "What is the number?"

Here Kashir lost his nerve. "Ahh . . . " he drew in his breath, held it, and then finally let it out. "Ahh . . . " Suddenly, his face brightened with a new thought. "What number do you think eet should be?"

"It doesn't matter what number I think it is," Paul replied. "You're the accounting person. It's your responsibility to determine the profit or loss on the position for the month. It's you who are representing to senior management how well or how poorly this area is performing on a monthly basis." Here Paul paused for effect. "If you misrepresent the number, it's your head, not mine."

"Yes, I know." Kashir cleared his throat again. "But what number do you think eet should be?" he persisted, finally raising his eyes to meet Paul's pleadingly.

"I told you, it doesn't matter what I think!" Paul was exasperated now. "What is the number?"

Kashir couldn't bring himself to say the number, so instead he handed Paul the slip of paper he had been twisting around and around in his hands. "Here eet is," he said glumly.

"A loss? A $250,000 loss?" Paul's voice reflected astonishment and anger. "It's wrong."

"Eet's wrong?" Kashir repeated hopefully, his eyes still on the ground. After all, he had finally ascertained one figure the profit and loss was not. "You think maybe dees loss is too beeg? You think maybe de loss should be smaller?"

"I think it should not be a loss," Paul said emphatically.

Kashir lifted his head, his eyes searching Paul's face as if to find the answer there. "You think eet should not be a loss," he repeated thoughtfully.

"Of course," Paul's tone was more casual now, "if you wish to represent this number to senior management . . . " He left the sentence unfinished.

"No, no," Kashir interrupted hurriedly. "Dees ees only an interim number," he explained. "I haf to go back and recheck eet."

"Okay," Paul said, turning his back to end the conversation.

Two days later Kashir reappeared and sidled up to the desk, clutching a new piece of paper. He stood behind Paul's chair, a little off to the side, waiting to get his attention. Paul made him wait about five minutes before turning toward him.

"Yes, Kashir," he said. "What can I do for you?"

"I haf now de profit-and-loss number," Kashir announced, head slightly bent, staring at Paul's kneecaps. "You were right. Eet ees not a loss." He paused.

"Oh?" Paul queried. "What is it?"

"Eet ees a gain."

"Yes?" Paul stared directly into Kashir's bowed head, where a heavy film of hair tonic combined with the overhead lighting to produce a rainbow effect. "How much of a gain?"

Pause.

"Eet ees a gain of $5,000," Kashir whispered, staring at the paper in his hand.

Now Paul paused.

"Five thousand dollars?" he said incredulously. "Five thousand dollars? Do you think I worked that hard last month for a lousy $5,000? Five thousand dollars is not a gain! You can make more than $5,000 a month if you invested the money in a Treasury bill!" Paul sputtered. "Jesus! You could make at least $250,000 a month just investing the money in a crummy Treasury bill!"

Kashir caught the magic number. Raising his eyes to Paul's belt buckle, he repeated, "Two hundred and fifty thousand dollars a month?"

"Of course!" Paul was contemptuous. "Over $250,000 a month," he added.

"I see," Kashir nodded slowly.

"Of course, if you want to represent this figure to senior management—"

"No, no!" Kashir cut in. "Dees ees only an interim number."

About a week later Kashir returned, beaming. We were by this time two weeks into the next month, not yet having a profit-and-loss number to show management for the preceding month. Kashir walked proudly up to Paul's desk and waved a piece of paper under his nose.

"I haf here de profit-and-loss number for last month," he announced.

"What is it?"

"Eet ees a gain of $300,000!"

"Really?" Paul broke into a smile. "Hey, that's terrific! Hey, John!" Paul called over to the boss. "Come over here! Kashir has the profit-and-loss number for last month!"

"Finally!" John came racing over to the desk. "What is it?"

Before Kashir could say anything, Paul cut in.

"It's a gain of $300,000! Isn't that so, Kashir?" Paul turned and stared at Kashir.

"Ahh . . . well . . . ahh . . . "

"Wonderful!" John bellowed. "Let me congratulate you!" he shook Paul's hand. Then he turned back to Kashir. "Now, are you sure that number is correct?" he asked.

Both pairs of eyes bored into Kashir's bowed head. "Ahh . . . yes, eet's right," he mumbled.

"Wonderful!" John took the paper to his office.

Kashir slunk back to his desk.

The first time I saw this happen, I approached Paul, puzzled.

"If you knew the profit for the last month was $300,000, why didn't you just tell Kashir what you thought in the first place? Couldn't you have gone over his numbers with him to find the error, so it wouldn't happen again next time?"

Paul looked at me. "I didn't know that the profit for last month was $300,000," he said.

"You didn't?" I asked, surprised. "What should it have been then?"

"How should I know?" Paul shrugged. "It might have been a loss for all I know."

"But . . . ," it was my turn to stammer. "Kashir . . . "

"Hey." Paul was stern. "It's Kashir's job to figure out the profit-and-loss number, not mine. It's not my fault if he misrepresents the situation to senior management."

Thus were the profit-and-loss numbers determined monthly for the options section of a large commercial bank.

I was coming home from work one night. It was about six-thirty on a Thursday evening. I had been working at my new trading job for almost two weeks.

I got off the subway and climbed the steps to the open air, bracing myself for the chill of the February night. I moved slowly. I was still unaccustomed to my new hours. Having to wake up every morning at five-thirty was throwing off my internal clock. It was like having perpetual jet lag.

I fought the wind, clutching my copy of the day's work to me. After two weeks, I had a grasp of the absolute basics. In order to avoid confusion, I turned over my newfound knowledge constantly in my mind, memorizing it until it took on the unreal singsong quality of a nursery rhyme.

If I buy a call, I'm long the currency, short the dollar.

If I sell a call, I'm short the currency, long the dollar.

If I buy a put, I'm short the currency, long the dollar.

If I sell a put, I'm long the currency, short the dollar.

A vast improvement in understanding from a mere two weeks ago. Still, something less than what was needed actually to trade.

But tonight I did not repeat my lessons under my breath. Tonight I had other things on my mind.

For the first time I had discovered that the dollar was actively traded abroad while I was at home asleep. According to Paul, the Far Eastern market, which included Singapore and Tokyo, began trading at around eight o'clock in the evening New York time, and stayed open until the traders in Europe and London came in. Although I knew that the dollar traded while I was sleeping (the morning price was almost always different from that of the previous afternoon), I had not understood that the foreign markets were every bit as active as the one I traded in. In fact, the London market was actually larger than the New York market.

I had been surprised to learn that Paul regularly monitored the market in the Far East from his home at night. I myself was exhausted when I got home from work. It was all I could do just to force myself to work through the day's trades. How did Paul manage? My respect for him increased.

Then the blow fell.

Paul was bemoaning his inability to trade the London and European markets when they first opened in the morning, sometime around 3:30 A.M. New York time. He couldn't very well trade Singapore until 11:30 P.M., get up again at 3:00 A.M., and expect to put in a full day's work at the office.

Suddenly he looked at me.

"Hey! I've got a great idea," he said. "Why don't you come in every morning at three-thirty and trade London for us?"

I looked around to see whom he was talking to. There was nobody else in the immediate vicinity.

"Me?" I choked.

"Sure. Why not? It's not like you'd have to stay all day. I wouldn't be so unreasonable as to expect you to work until six every night. You'd be the early morning shift. You come in at three-thirty and stay until, say two-thirty in the afternoon. Bob and I would come in at our regular time." He thought about it. "We could even come in a little later. I mean, you'd be here to cover."

I started to laugh.

"It's a joke, right?" I giggled. "You're putting me on?"

"What's wrong with it?" Paul demanded.

I stopped laughing.

"Why . . . uh . . . ." I searched frantically for an irrefutable objection. "Why, I can't even trade yet! I haven't put on a single trade by myself. I just sit here and watch you. I don't even know what to do yet when somebody calls and wants to trade. I can't be here all by myself!"

"Well, I'm not saying we have to start tomorrow," said Paul. "Maybe in a couple of months. You can always call me at home if there's a problem."

"But, Paul!" I was desperate. "I can't. I mean, I wouldn't feel comfortable alone here . . . at that hour . . . "

"Nancy," said Paul. "Sit down."

I sat.

"Nancy," said Paul. "I look at you, and Bob, and myself, as a professional team playing an intensively competitive sport, like football. We have to give up everything to win. It's a question of giving it our all. Of self-sacrifice and determination." He saw the blank expression on my face. "Maybe you don't watch football," he continued. "But do you know what I'm talking about? It's like a team sport. Everybody plays team sports in school. Nancy, what sport did you play in high school?"

"Water ballet."

Now, walking home from the subway, I reviewed this conversation. This is going to be some short career, I thought. If I say no, I will not come into the office at 3:30 A.M., Paul will probably fire me. If I say yes, I will come into the office at 3:30 A.M., I'll be killed taking the subway alone at that hour. That's not quite correct. I'll be killed walking out of my apartment building at that hour of the morning. I'll never make it to the subway.

On this cheerful note, I put my key in the lock and opened the door of my apartment.

For a second I thought I was in the wrong place.

The apartment had been cleaned, and there were

43

three big bunches of roses in vases around the room. The table had been laid for a candlelight dinner for two. There was a bottle of champagne cooling in an ice bucket. From the kitchen came the pleasant aroma of food cooking. The room was warm and cozy, and shadows flickered on the wall from all the candles. The scene was romantic and inviting.

Larry, dressed in black tie, was standing at the table lighting candles.

"What's all this?" I asked.

"Happy Valentine's Day," said Larry, putting his arms around me.

Valentine's Day! I'd forgotten all about it.

"Dinner for two coming up," he said. "May I pour you a glass of champagne?"

I just stood there.

"You can put your papers down now," said Larry. "We're not doing any options tonight." He went to open the champagne.

"It's beautiful," I said finally. "It's wonderful."

We ate the dinner and drank the champagne. All thoughts of the bank, the market, and Paul's latest suggestion were forgotten.

Later that evening, lying in bed, I told Larry of Paul's suggestion.

"That's absurd," he laughed. "You can't ask a young, attractive woman to be traipsing around Manhattan in the dead of night. Besides, you don't have a clue to what you're doing. If they really want to trade London, they should hire an experienced trader to work out of the bank's London office."

"You mean you think I can tell him that I won't do it?" I asked.

"Absolutely. Stick up for yourself."

By the end of February I had advanced to the point that I could handle several tasks: confirming the daily trades with the proper counterpart, writing out instructions for wire transfers, computing premiums. However, I was no closer to knowing what Paul and Bob's trading strategies were than I was when I was a loan officer. I told Paul that I really couldn't see myself coming in alone for the opening of London every day. At first he protested, but then he dropped the subject altogether. I could tell that he didn't like my refusing him like that.

To make matters worse, I became aware that Paul and Bob were paying more and more attention to each other and less attention to me. They were always whispering together, or speaking in half-sentences that I knew they didn't mean for me to understand. This made me feel left out, and I wondered if they were disappointed with my progress. When I first took over the administrative duties, I had made some mechanical errors, like sending a payment to the wrong bank. But these mistakes were corrected quickly, and I never made the same mistake twice. Still, I couldn't shake the suspicion that something was very wrong.

I was ready for the worst when Paul approached me on the last day of the month.

"I'm calling a staff meeting this evening at five. Just you and me and Bob. We'll meet in my office."

We had never had a staff meeting before. What was on Paul's mind? He'd said it pleasantly enough, but by now I knew that Paul was always pleasant.

Paul and Bob were already in the office when I arrived. They clearly had been discussing something, but stopped when I entered. I pulled a chair over to where they were sitting.

"So what's up?" I asked, to break the silence.

Paul and Bob exchanged glances. In their look I read my doom.

"Bob and I have some news for you," Paul began

cheerfully. "There's good news and there's bad news. Which do you prefer to hear first?"

I'm of the school of thought that believes in getting the worst over quickly.

"The bad news," I said.

"The bad news is that Bob and I are both resigning from the bank. I am going to run the options desk at another bank. Bob is going to work for a brokerage operation."

"How soon?"

"By Friday."

Three days!

"Does John know yet?"

"He'll know tomorrow."

I was speechless. No one at the bank except Paul and Bob knew anything whatsoever about options.

"Don't you want to hear the good news?" Paul asked.

"Of course."

"I'm recommending that you take over the desk."

"Well!" said Larry that evening after I had relayed these latest developments to him. "That explains a great many things."

"What do you mean?" I asked. I was still grappling with the enormity of the situation.

"Well, the kind of deals that Paul and Bob made take months to come to fruition."

"So?"

"So they knew they were going to leave when they hired you."

"What exactly are you saying?"

"I'm saying that they needed to hire someone so that they could both leave the bank at the same time without appearing overly irresponsible. They probably would have hired a chimpanzee if they thought they could get away with it."

Early the next morning, I saw Paul disappear into John's office. Bob flashed me a conspiratorial smile.

Already I had noticed a change in Bob's manner. Normally he would have been too absorbed in his own affairs to take much notice of me. This morning, however, he made an effort to be friendly.

"When this is all over," he whispered, "you and I will go out for a drink and we'll have a nice talk."

I said I thought that would be fine.

"And before I go," Bob continued, "I want to give you my new phone number. You know, I'm going to be brokering currency options. I don't see any reason why you and I shouldn't do some profitable business together. After all, I feel kind of responsible toward you. You know I've always tried to help you whenever I could."

Paul came out of John's office and wandered over to where Bob and I were standing.

"Your turn," he said to Bob.

"Right!" said Bob. "This is going to be fun!"

I asked Paul how John had taken the news.

"Not badly," he said. "But then again, he doesn't know about Bob yet."

"I see."

John came tearing out of his office.

"Both of you?" he asked Paul.

Paul nodded.

"Back into my office!" John ordered.

Paul, Bob, and John were closeted for the whole day. I waited to see if John intended to talk to me, but they were still at it at six-thirty in the evening. I decided to give up and go home. I was relieved. I needed time to appraise the situation.

"What do you think I should do?" I asked Larry.

"Well, that depends," he replied. "Do you want to run the desk?"

I weighed the advantages and disadvantages of the situation. On the negative side I listed the following: I didn't know how to trade; I didn't understand Paul's and Bob's trades that were already on the books; the bank had no accounting system to help me keep track of the position or the profit and loss; there was no one at the bank who could help me to learn the business; and Paul and Bob were leaving approximately $1 billion worth of trades to manage, too much for one person to handle alone. The amount of work involved would be staggering, as I would have to watch the New York, London, and Singapore markets by myself. That alone was a twenty-four-hour job.

On the positive side there was only one factor: I would never have this chance again.

"I want to do it," I said.

Paul had been induced to stay on an extra week. I spent as much time with him as I could, working frantically to understand the trades that would be left to my management.

John asked to see me.

"We have to talk," he said.

"Certainly," I replied.

"Why don't you come into my office right now so we can chat for a minute?"

I decided to set the rules immediately.

"I think that what we have to say to each other will take longer than a few minutes. Besides, I have to trade now."

He was taken aback.

"Oh! Of course." He thought for a moment. "Well, how about dinner tonight after work? That should give us enough time."

"That will be fine."

That evening, John relaxed comfortably against the soft leather of the booth.

"I hope you like steak," he said. "This place has the best T-bones in town."

We ordered drinks. John raised his glass.

"Cheers," he said, taking a long pull of scotch and soda.

"Cheers," I seconded, sipping my wine.

Silence. I waited for him to begin.

"Nancy," John said, breaking the silence, "have I ever outlined for you my global plan for the trading sector of the bank?"

I said I didn't think so. I didn't bother to mention that, as this was only the second time we'd ever spoken, it seemed unlikely that I'd know of his global scheme.

"Well then!" He sat up a little straighter. "Let me give you some background. I was an officer in the Marine Corps during the Vietnam War. When I joined the bank back in 1973 . . ."

Drinks came and went. Appetizers were served.

"After I was promoted to vice president I was assigned to London . . ."

The steaks came. Mine was quite good.

"I told the chairman of the board that I wanted to run a global operation . . ."

The waiter cleared the plates and brushed the tablecloth for crumbs. Dessert menus were passed around. I ordered chocolate cake.

"I'm planning on expanding into Hong Kong . . ."

Finally, coffee was served.

"Well, that's about all I have to say." John paused to take a sip of coffee. "By the way, do you have any questions?"

"Just one," I replied.

"What is it?"

"Have you considered that I am the only person at the bank with any experience whatsoever in trading options, the only person who has any idea of the extent of the bank's exposure in currency options? That if I walk out of this restaurant and get hit by a truck the bank is at risk for millions and millions of dollars?"

He choked on his coffee.

"Something wrong, sir?" the waiter asked.

"Huh?" John asked, and then recovered. "No, everything's fine here, thank you."

Silence.

"So what do you want?" John asked, finally.

"I only want what's fair," I replied. "If I'm to take on all of this work and all of this responsibility, I deserve the benefits of the position as well."

"What do you intend to ask for?"

I took the plunge.

"I want an immediate 100 percent raise in salary. I want a bonus plan at the end of the year tied to my performance. And I want an immediate promotion to vice president and manager of the Options Trading Unit."

"That's rather a tall order," John replied uneasily.

"Look, John," I said. "We both know it will cost you twice as much to go out and hire an experienced trader and you still take the risk that whoever you get won't be able to handle the trades the bank has been left with. I at least have some familiarity with Paul's and Bob's trading styles and with our current exposure."

Silence.

"This is what I can do for you," John sighed. "A 50 percent increase in salary immediately. The other 50 percent increase in three months."

"What about the promotion and the bonus?"

"Promotions are harder to come by than raises. However, I believe that I can swing a promotion to vice president at the end of the three months."

"Vice president and manager," I corrected.

"Of course, vice president and manager," he echoed.

"And the bonus?"

"The bonus plan has to be approved by the board of directors," he said.

I waited.

"I'll do my best," he said.

I waited.

"All right," he said. "I'll recommend a bonus plan that is tied to performance. That's all I can do," he added quickly.

I thought about it.

"Okay," I said. "I'll do it. But there's something else."

"What is it?" John asked anxiously.

"I want all of this in writing."

"What's the matter?" John asked. "Don't you trust me?"

The next morning I walked into the trading room and over to the options desk. Both Paul's and Bob's chairs sat empty. Everyone in the room knew that I was going to try and fill the position of two seasoned options traders with only a little over a month's experience behind me. I could feel myself being sized up by both the spot foreign-exchange traders on my right and the interest-rate traders on my left.

I turned on all the computer screens as I had been taught to do. I took out the handwritten sheets that comprised the options position. I sipped black coffee as I examined the papers.

I was now the head currency options trader at the bank with a $1 billion options portfolio to manage.

What to do now?

3

THE LEARNING PROCESS

What I didn't know, couldn't have known, was that my solitary apprenticeship would mark by coincidence the advent of one of the most violent periods in the history of the currency markets: the beginning of the decline in the value of the dollar. In March 1985, when I assumed my new duties, the dollar was so high that it was difficult for producers of U.S. goods to sell their products abroad. American manufacturers were having trouble selling their products at home as well. Foreign goods were so much cheaper. The U.S. automobile industry, for example, was extremely threatened by a strong dollar. It seemed as if everybody was buying a Japanese car. The seriousness of the problem was reflected in the magnitude of the U.S. trade deficit.

The leaders of the industrialized world, led (some say coerced) by those in the United States, embraced the downward trend in the dollar as a panacea for the worsening economic climate. Not two weeks after the departure of Paul and Bob from my bank, the market began what was to become a two-year, all-out, free-for-all, come-and-get-'em, going-out-of-business, children-eat-free, fire sale on the dollar. This fire sale was punctuated every few weeks by panicked buying on the part of incredulous traders who, after watching the dollar appreciate for months and months, couldn't rid themselves of a strong-dollar bias and continued to buy the dollar periodically, almost from force of habit, as if against their wills. On the other hand, more astute traders profited by understanding that a major shift in opinion was taking place, and only waited for the chance to sell more. These competing impulses—the overwhelming rush to sell followed by short bursts of intense buying—resulted in wild swings in the value of the dollar, swings of such speed and violence that many veteran traders who understood the magnitude of the risks involved became frightened by the upheaval and chose to abstain from trading for short periods of time. I was not one of them.

I entered the world of trading with two advantages. As I had spent the last year and a half as a lending officer, I was oblivious to the dollar's recent appreciation in value and so had no bias in favor of a strong dollar. Furthermore, I was so inexperienced that I didn't know enough to be frightened. This resulted in my being able to take risks that would have made a seasoned trader shudder. Not that I knew I was taking risks. I thought I was just trading.

During those first three months of trading, through one of the most traumatic periods in market history, John left me completely alone. I was never asked to report on my position. I was never given any guidelines by which to trade. I was never told to limit the size of my positions. I'm not sure he knew that I was taking positions. (I'm not sure *I* knew that I was taking positions.) We communicated on the average of once a month, at which time Kashir would present the profit-and-loss numbers.

I found out later—much later—that the bank's board of directors approved limits under which each of its traders was to operate. But as nobody ever bothered to tell me what my limits were in the beginning, and as the bank had no system in place that enabled management to monitor my positions, I confess I don't see what purpose the limits served. In retrospect I realize that I must have been substantially over my limits often in those first few months. But who could tell?

To give an idea of the complete power that I was exercising, let me explain that if an officer of the bank wanted to commit $1 million of the bank's resources in the form of a loan to a customer, that officer would have had to have the decision approved by a bank credit committee. The decision to lend $1 million would have taken weeks, perhaps months. But for me to commit $20 million, $50 million, $100 million of the bank's resources to the purchase or sale of foreign-currency options, I had only to pick up the phone and make the trade. No one asked me what I was doing. No one seemed to care.

In the absence of any semblance of control or direction, I simply assumed that I had an unlimited source of funds behind me and operated accordingly.

The trading world reacted to the news of my taking over after Paul's and Bob's departures in the same way sharks react to the sight of a wounded man set adrift at sea.

My telephone console was blinking furiously with

unanswered calls by the time I got into the office at 7:20 A.M. The conversations were short and to the point.

"Options desk," I said, answering a call at random.

"Halloo?" said the voice on the other end of the phone through the static that indicated an international call. "This is Franz calling from Geneva, Switzerland. May I please speak with someone on the options desk?"

"Hello, Franz. This is Nancy on the options desk. How may I help you?"

"Can you make me a price?" Franz asked.

Making a price is trader jargon. It means: I-wish-to- trade- an- option- but- I- don't- want- you- to- know-whether- I'm- a- buyer- or- a- seller- so- that- I- can- take-advantage-of-you-if-possible. It is far easier to react to someone else's price than it is to have to make one up yourself. But that was a lesson that I learned later on.

"Certainly," I replied.

Franz wanted a price on a call option. The price of an option is determined by a number of factors: the current spot price of the dollar relative to the foreign currency in question; the date the option is to expire; the forward price of the dollar against the currency; the current U.S. interest rate; the interest rate in the country of the foreign currency; and the volatility of the currency in the market. I fed my computer this information as Paul had taught me to do. The computer responded with the price I should be willing to pay if I were buying, and the price I should be willing to take if I were selling. I quoted these two prices to Franz.

"Okay," said Franz immediately. "I sell $10 million to you."

I knew by the quickness of his response that I had made a mistake and that my price was too high. I'd seen Paul trade and knew that when there was no hesitation in the other trader's voice, there was something wrong. However, in trading your word is your handshake. I had just bought $10 million worth of an option from Franz.

"Done," I said, writing down the trade on a sheet of paper.

"Have you more to do there?" Franz asked casually.

Damn! The price must have really been high. Franz wanted to sell me more than $10 million.

"Not at that level," I hedged.

"Can you make me another price then?" Franz asked.

The man had no shame.

What could I do? I made him a new price but this time I lowered my bid substantially.

"Okay," said Franz. "I sell another $10 million to you."

Would this never end? What was I going to do with $20 million worth of a call option that gave me the right to sell the dollar at a much lower price than it was currently trading at, anyway? Buy a call, long the currency, short the dollar. That meant that the dollar would have to fall for me to make any money. Everybody knew that the dollar was going to rise in value, not fall. Here I was paying Franz all this money for an option that would most likely end up being worthless. Franz's gain; my loss.

"Done," I said again.

At this point I was thoroughly sick of talking to Franz. Before he had a chance to breathe, let alone ask me for another price, I cut in.

"I'm so sorry Franz, but the other phones are all ringing. I have to go now."

I hung up quickly without saying good-bye. I considered myself lucky to have escaped without having bought $50 million. The nerve of some people! Taking advantage of me like that!

Still, I took it in stride. After all, I consoled myself, they couldn't all be like Franz.

With renewed spirit I answered the next phone call. The voice on the other end of the phone was English this time.

"Can you make me a price?" it asked.

On the other hand, maybe they could.

Despite the merciless attack by colleagues here and abroad, I was able to turn my first few weeks of trading to good advantage. This didn't exactly happen by design. It was just that when the dollar started to fall, I panicked. I knew that I had inherited a large number of trades from Paul and Bob that were predicated on a strong dollar. If the dollar went down, these trades would lose money. So I sold a whole lot of dollars on the theory that if the dollar continued to fall I would make more on the dollars I'd sold than I would lose on the inherited trades. If the trend toward a lower dollar had reversed itself, I would have lost far more on the dollars I'd sold than I would have made on the inherited trades. It was a risky thing to do.

As it turned out, selling dollars was exactly the right thing to do.

In addition to that, the call options I had purchased as a result of my overly high price making turned out to be quite valuable once the dollar started to fall.

Looking back over the situation I see now that I was the beneficiary of a phenomenon not unknown to the trading community: beginner's luck.

I was just starting to breathe a little easier when events took a turn for the worse.

I was hard at work at my desk one afternoon when I heard a sound behind me. I turned around to find Kashir standing there holding a slip of paper in his hand.

I realized that the March profit-and-loss numbers were due.

This first profit-and-loss number was very important to me. I regarded it as justification for the long hours I had spent struggling through an extremely difficult period.

Although a lack of detailed information on the positions that I had inherited from Paul and Bob made it impossible for me to calculate the exact profit-and-loss number, I knew that I had been trading profitably. My most conservative estimate for the month's profit and loss was a gain of $250,000. I felt that I was actually doing better than this, but I didn't know how much would be recognized immediately, and how much would be deferred until the next month. In any event, I looked forward to hearing Kashir's report.

"Ahem!" Kashir cleared his throat.

"Yes?"

"I haf here de profit-and-loss number," he began.

There was something very different about Kashir today. He seemed to have had a change in attitude. He wasn't staring at the floor or twisting the paper nervously in his hands. His posture was erect; his manner threatening, even defiant.

"Yes?" I repeated.

"Eet ees a loss!" he announced, staring directly into my eyes.

A loss! "How much?" I asked.

"Eet ees a loss of $300,000!" he trumpeted.

A $300,000 loss! It wasn't possible! "Are you quite sure?" I asked, shocked.

"Absolutely!" He was actually grinning.

"Show me the numbers," I ordered.

Kashir handed me a disorganized pile of papers that represented his work sheets. On the sheets were scrawled figures in varying degrees of legibility.

"Leave these with me," I said. "I don't have the time to look at them right now."

"You don't haf to look at them," said Kashir. "I tell you de number ees correct."

It was my turn to stare Kashir in the eye.

"We'll see," I said.

He turned and walked away.

I studied the work sheets after Kashir had left. They were indecipherable. I called Kashir on the telephone, asking for explanations on some of his calculations. His answers were confused. The profit-and-loss numbers were produced by comparing this month's market values to last month's market values, so all of Kashir's calculations were based in part on numbers generated while Paul managed the desk. Last month's numbers had already been accepted by senior management and could not be changed. Nor, I realized helplessly, could they be disproved.

I knew that I had traded profitably in March. The only possible explanation for the loss Kashir was showing was that the profits that had been reported in prior months had been overstated. The overstatement (now reflected as a loss) was being reported in this, my first month of trading. And there was nothing I could do to prevent it. I was too inexperienced, too new at my job, for my version of events to carry any weight. Kashir had been with the bank forever. I had been there for fewer than four years. Kashir was a man in his late forties. I was a woman in my mid-twenties. I knew that if I attempted to argue with Kashir's results I would be branded as a troublemaker and, worse, as a woman who tried to blame her own mistakes on others. This, I knew, was an unacceptable sin in the eyes of the trading community. There was nothing to be done at the moment. I conceded the first round to Kashir.

But that didn't mean I wasn't going to get even.

▲ ▲ ▲

I was understaffed and needed some help. I pressed John, and in April I was assigned the services of an administrative assistant by the name of Phillip Lee. Phillip had been with the bank for over a year. He had spent most of this time on the spot foreign-exchange desk, where his most demanding duty was fetching the senior traders their coffee and doughnuts. Even after he was officially assigned to me, the spot desk refused to part with him for an additional two weeks. After that, they were forced to get their own coffee.

Of Asian descent, Phillip had come to New York to pursue a career in banking. He had received his graduate degree from Stanford, where he had graduated near the top of his class. His passion was computers.

In January, Paul and Bob had persuaded John to buy an options software package designed for personal computers. This software had arrived just before they left. The problem was that nobody (including me) knew how to use it. I asked Phillip if he thought he could adapt the software to accommodate our needs. We needed reports that were organized along the lines of our general trading style, rather than simply listing a long series of trades in no particular order. It was done within the week. I asked Phillip to generate a series of reports that would measure our overall exposure in the event of large currency moves. If the dollar rose or fell substantially overnight, what would be the effect on our portfolio? Should we be buying or selling the dollar? The reports were on my desk the next morning. I asked Phillip if it would be possible to produce daily profit-and-loss statements, rather than monthly. The reports were produced every afternoon and were on my desk by the time I went home in the evening.

I kept the existence of the profit-and-loss statements to myself for a while. As no one ever bothered to ask me how I was doing or what positions I was taking, this was not hard to do.

I continued to trade, and tried to keep my risk to a minimum by buying as many options as I sold. However, the daily P and L reported that while this conservative trading strategy made money consistently, the profits accrued slowly. I wanted a strategy that would make a whole lot of money quickly. After all, I had a $300,000 loss to make up, didn't I?

I decided to take a large position by either buying or selling dollars. It was, I knew, the only way for me to make back all of March's loss in April.

I analyzed the situation carefully. I was beginning to discuss the market on a much more detailed and informed basis with some of my colleagues on the spot foreign-exchange desk, and with traders at other institutions. I reviewed past data on the U.S. economy, and investigated what experts were predicting for the future. I analyzed technical data and surveyed charts. By degrees I arrived at a well-informed conclusion. I decided to buy the dollar.

Wrong.

I can still close my eyes and remember the horror of that first loss. The dollar started to fall precipitously in value almost from the moment I put on my position.

Not having yet learned the importance of exercising discipline in such cases, I stubbornly refused to cut my losses. It seemed impossible to me that the market wouldn't come back at least to where I'd bought in the first place. I held on to that thought and the dollars for three days, at the end of which time I had lost $500,000. That was in addition to the $300,000 loss that Kashir had already reported for March.

At this point I felt it was in my best interest to inform John of the situation.

I approached John's secretary first thing in the morning.

"I'd like to see John today," I said.

She looked over her glasses at me.

"Is it important?" she asked.

Was a half-million-dollar loss in three days important?

"Reasonably," I said.

She glanced down at her calendar.

"He's busy all day," she said. "But I think he can spare fifteen minutes between lunch and the weekly senior management meeting."

"I'll take it," I said.

I spent the next couple of hours contemplating my future. I felt terrible about losing the money. I understood now that I'd taken a risk with the bank's capital. I was playing with other people's savings deposits. Even though I had made the decision to buy dollars after an intelligent appraisal of the situation, I understood that it was the urge to make a quick and easy profit that had undermined me. I had become greedy, and the bank had paid. I had been rash, and the bank had paid. Although I recognized that everything I'd done had been motivated by the best of intentions, I was apprehensive about telling John. I wasn't sure but that I could be fired for making a mistake of this kind.

I was at John's office at the appointed time, but his luncheon ran late, and five minutes of my precious fifteen were wasted waiting for him to show up. Not that I minded the wait. It wasn't as if I were looking forward to this conversation.

"Have a seat," John said, breezing in. He flung himself into the chair behind his desk. "Sorry I'm late. I just couldn't get away."

"I understand," I said.

"So what's this all about?" John asked.

I took a deep breath.

"I've lost some money," I said. "Quite a lot of money, actually."

"I know," John said cheerily. "I saw Kashir's March figures."

"No," I said. "This is in addition to the March loss. This is the April loss." Before he could speak I rushed on. "I took a position. It was the wrong position to take. I lost $500,000. I'm sorry. It won't happen again."

"So you are now down almost $1 million, is that what you are saying?"

I nodded my head in misery. I couldn't even look him in the eye.

"Well, I suppose it can't be helped," said John. "Happens to everyone."

This was unexpected. He was taking it so well.

"You think you can make it back quickly?" John asked.

"Oh, absolutely," I lied.

"Well, then," said John smiling at me. "That's fine. I have to go to the senior management meeting now. But, hey! Thanks for letting me know."

"Don't mention it," I said.

I walked out of that meeting confused, but relieved. John must know, I reasoned, that the only way for me to "make it all back quickly" was to take yet another, larger position. In fact, I got the definite impression that it was my job to do so.

This time, though, I vowed to learn from my mistakes. If the position began to be a losing one, I would take an immediate loss rather than wait and thereby risk substantially more. If I was right, I would take some of my profit immediately, or hedge my exposure by using some of my profit to purchase options, which would increase in value if the market turned around and went against me. And, most important, I would take a large position only when I was thoroughly convinced that the market would go my way—not just because I had taken a loss the week before. I would take a large position only when I felt that technical and economic factors were signaling a move, and then only after I'd discussed the market with some of my colleagues at other institutions. These rules, in combination with a whole lot of luck, just might see me through this difficult period.

I continued to transact the conservative day-to-day trading that accumulated slow but steady profits, while waiting for the chance to take a large position. I did not contest Kashir's April figures, even though he reported a larger loss than was indicated by my own daily P and L.

Throughout this entire period, Phillip stood by me and became my friend and compatriot. I was lucky to have him.

Phillip is without doubt the most compassionate individual I have ever met. He always considers the other person's feelings and goes out of his way to be helpful or simply a good friend. I have never heard him say anything negative about another person. He is quiet and never volunteers advice. If you ask him for his opinion, he will choose his words carefully and they are always worth listening to.

Phillip is very intelligent. English is not his native language, so his speech is textbook-perfect. His manners are unparalleled; he could have taught Emily Post a thing or two.

Phillip's strengths complemented my own. I relied on him for computer prowess and technical analysis, two areas in which I was dangerously deficient.

On the whole I adored Phillip. There was only one small problem. Hardly worth mentioning.

He lived in another world.

▲ ▲ ▲

While Phillip was excellent at the large, terribly important computer-related aspects of the job, small human details utterly defeated him. My first tip-off of his problem came at lunchtime. The bank let us order free lunches from the cafeteria every day and had them delivered at noon in boxes so we could eat at our desks. That way we wouldn't miss a single second of trading. I ordered one of these free lunches once and decided not to repeat the experience.

Phillip, however, did not seem to mind the food, and took advantage of the bank's largess. He ordered the same thing every day: overcooked roast beef on Wonder Bread with raw onions, mashed potatoes accompanied by an unidentified green and brown gravy, and watered-down orange juice.

Unlike the other traders in the room, Phillip didn't wolf down his food as though it were his last meal. On the contrary, he would carefully unpack his lunch and then forget all about it.

The first time I saw this happen, I tried to be helpful.

"Phillip," I said, pointing to the sandwich, "why don't you eat your food now? It's one o'clock already. Aren't you hungry?"

"Huh?" he said, startled.

"Your lunch," I reminded him. "Eat your lunch."

"Oh!" He picked up the sandwich and opened his mouth to take a bite. Then he remembered his manners.

"May I offer you some?" he asked, extending the sandwich toward me.

"No, thank you anyway," I said, recoiling from the smell of raw onion.

"Oh! Okay!" he said, putting the sandwich down.

Another hour passed.

"Phillip, you still haven't eaten."

"Huh?"

"Your food. Eat your food."

He reached for the mashed potatoes. The gravy had hardened, coating the surface with a shiny cover of congealed fat.

"May I offer you some?"

"No, really, I'm not hungry."

Another hour passed.

"Phillip."

"Huh?"

"Please eat your food."

He ate.

"Oh! It's cold!" he said, surprised.

Lunch was only the beginning. This dreamlike state extended into other, more pressing areas.

"Phillip?"

"Huh?"

"Did you write the tickets yet so that the operations department can enter today's trades into the computer?"

"Oh! No! So sorry."

"It's one o'clock already. Let's try and get them done early today, okay? Otherwise the operations people have to stay late."

"Oh! Okay."

"Phillip?" I said later.

"Huh?"

"I don't see those tickets."

"Oh! So sorry! I forgot."

"Phillip, it's three o'clock," I reminded him after a while.

"Okay. I'll do them right now."

"Phillip?"

"Huh . . . ?"

This happened every day.

The simpler the task, the more difficult it was for Phillip to perform it. If it didn't relate to what he was plugging into a terminal, for Phillip it simply didn't exist.

"Phillip?"

"Huh?"

"The phone is ringing. Could you please answer it? I'm already on the other line."

"Oh! Sure! So sorry." He reached for the phone. "Good day? Good day?"

"No, I'm on that line," I said patiently. "Get the other line, please."

"Oh! Sure! So sorry," he said, starting to hang up.

"No! Wait!" I said. "You're about to—"

He hung up.

"—disconnect me."

"Oh! So sorry!"

"That's all right. Just get the other phone, okay?"

"Huh?"

I think I could have lived with all of this, except for one last thing. Phillip didn't like to trade options. It's not that he couldn't, it's just that he didn't want to. This can be a significant handicap for an options trader.

"Phillip?"

"Huh?"

"Could you please price this option for me?"

"Oh! Sure!"

"Phillip?"

"Huh?"

"Did you make that price I asked you for earlier?"

"Oh! So sorry!"

"Phillip, you can't leave people waiting like that. It's unprofessional."

"Yes, of course. So sorry!"

"Phillip?"

"Huh?"

"Did you make that price yet?"

He started to open his mouth.

"Never mind. I'll do it."

I decided I needed a third member of the team.

I gave the subject some thought and decided on an associate of mine from the lending side of the bank, Peter Poska. Peter was my friend.

He was two years younger than I, with a broad, open face that always had a well-scrubbed look to it. He kept his brown hair short and neatly parted on the side.

I had known Peter for two years. He'd been assigned to my unit while I was still in the lending department. He was just out of the bank's training program then and had graduated at the top of his class.

Peter's background was unusual. He came from a tiny town in the Midwest where his father raised cattle. It was an atmosphere as far removed from that of the city as it is possible to get without venturing into outer space, and even then I'm not sure that a small town set in the deep cold of the farm belt isn't one of the ends of the universe. There were no theaters, no restaurants, no social life for a teenager. The nearest farm was a half hour's drive, and the nearest movie (there was only one, of course) was even farther away.

In Highland Park, I spent my time going out with my friends or scooping ice cream at the local Baskin Robbins (a terrific after-school job; not only did I get to eat all the free ice cream I wanted, but as I regularly gave it away to members of the football and basketball teams I was enormously popular whenever one of them was hungry). By contrast, Peter was getting up at four o'clock in the morning to milk the cows or bale the hay or do whatever it is that is done on a cattle farm at four in the morning.

Peter is a quiet man. I put this down to his having spent most of his waking hours in the company of cows. Until you get to know him (and even then) it is difficult to get more than a "Yes" or "No" out of him, and then only in response to a direct question. Yet he had a dry wit and a commonsense way of looking at things that I found particularly refreshing.

What made Peter decide on commercial banking as a career is a mystery. No farmer has much respect for bankers, probably because farmers are actually forced to work with the financial community on a more or less regular basis.

Peter helped to handle his family's financial affairs at an early age.

"What was it like?" I asked.

Peter shrugged.

"Every couple of years or so the bank would give us a new loan officer," he said. "The new guy would drive out to the farm, and Dad would have to spend hours with him explaining the business." Peter shook his head. "Always the same questions. Always the same answers."

"What kind of questions did they ask?"

" 'Just how many head of cattle do you have, Mr. Poska?' " Peter imitated the fictitious banker in a high, squeaky voice. " 'We have ten thousand head of cattle, Mr. Banker,' " reverting to his usual delivery. " 'My! That seems like quite a lot, Mr. Poska.' " " 'Yes, sir, especially around milking time.' "

"I take it the cattle were put up as collateral," I said.

"Yup. They were always wanting to check out the collateral." Peter switched back to his banker voice. " 'Mr. Poska, I'm afraid that it's part of my job to count the cattle.' 'Count the cattle, Mr. Banker?' 'Yes, please, Mr. Poska.' 'All of 'em, Mr. Banker?' 'All of them, Mr. Poska.' "

"Well," Peter continued, "it was my job to drive those bankers around so they could count the cattle. I thought I'd make my job a little easier. First I'd drive around in circles to get them good and confused."

"Yes?" I prompted.

"And then I'd drive to the closest pasture and show them the one thousand head of cattle there. Then I'd drive around a little more and go back to the same pasture and show them the same one thousand head. I'd do it over and over until they'd counted their ten thousand head, and then they'd go home until the next time."

Peter went through a period of culture shock when he first moved to the big city. He had made a conscious decision to leave his past behind him and to mold himself in a new direction. But because he was trying so desperately to fit into an environment so different from that of his early years, he was unsure of himself. He hid his roots, but he was never quite satisfied that he wasn't giving himself away unconsciously.

Peter's lack of self-assurance touched me. I have a younger brother just Peter's age, living in Chicago. How would I feel if my brother moved to a strange city to begin a new career? Wouldn't I want someone to look after him, to protect him in his new endeavor?

Accordingly, I adopted Peter.

While we were still in the lending area, I encouraged him in every way possible. I gave him the benefit of my experience. I tried to protect him from superiors. If we stayed late at the office, I always made sure that he had enough money to get home and told him to call me when he got in so I would know he was all right.

"Don't worry, Mom," he would say.

I guess I overdid it a little, but my heart was in the right place.

When I got to be a trader, it was natural for me to want Peter on the desk. It was clearly better for his career. There was more money in it. It was more stimulating intellectually. I could continue to watch over him.

I secretly discussed the matter with Peter and found him enthusiastic. The next step was to take it up with his boss, Ralph Johnston.

Ralph had been with the bank for over ten years and was technically my senior. He was jealous of my advancement and would certainly object to my hiring Peter.

I put a phone call through to Ralph. "Hello, Ralph," I said when he answered. "This is Nancy on the options desk. How are you today?"

"What do you want?" he asked.

"Well, actually, Ralph," I said, "I'm calling about Peter."

"What about Peter?"

"I think you know, Ralph, that the options desk is somewhat understaffed due to the recent loss of some of our more senior people."

"So?"

"The fact is, the need for extra personnel is becoming increasingly urgent. Peter is the only person in the bank with any real knowledge of options—"

"Not a chance," Ralph cut me off. "No way."

"Just let me explain a little . . ."

"There's nothing to explain. Peter is to remain here. You are not to mention this to him, do you hear?" He hung up.

Six weeks, even a month, earlier, Ralph's attitude would have intimidated me. By nature a shy and reserved person, I would have abandoned any idea that led me into direct conflict with a superior. But regularly trading and managing large sums of money was beginning to have its effect. It was time to flex my muscles.

It was possible to advertise job openings throughout the bank by circulating a memorandum outlining the responsibilities associated with the work and listing the minimum qualifications. No one could be forbidden to apply.

I had such a memorandum circulated. I made the qualifications specific. So specific, in fact, that as far as I knew they fit only Peter.

I told Peter about the memo, and he was the first person to apply. In all, I had seven applicants. Three were grossly unqualified for the position. Two were discouraged by the amount of work involved. Peter had only one serious rival, and that person's knowledge of options was cursory.

"Phillip?"

"Huh?"

"Who do you think we should hire, Peter or the other applicant?"

Silence while Phillip considered the question. "Let me see," he said finally. "They are both very good."

"But Phillip, we can't hire both. Who would you prefer working with?"

"It's very hard to make a choice."

"I know. But I would really appreciate your opinion."

Silence while Phillip struggled to avoid saying anything negative, even by implication. "I think Peter is a little bit better."

Peter it was.

I had won my first round.

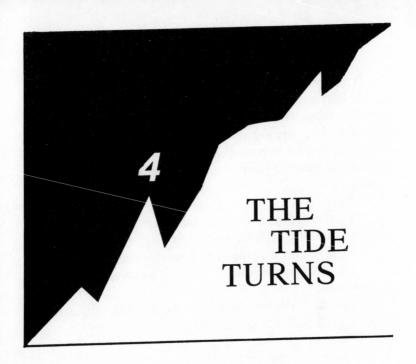

4

THE
TIDE
TURNS

Peter caught on to trading quickly and was soon able
to take over some of the day-to-day responsibilities. This
left me free to concentrate on the market.

By May I was convinced that the turmoil of March
and April was coming to a close. One look at the spot
foreign-exchange desk told me that the traders there
could not keep up their frenzied pace for much longer.
I concluded that the market would cool down during
the summer and the dollar would once again begin a
slow, measured descent. My conviction was so strong
that I took by far the largest position that I had yet
dared to take. If I were right, I knew that I would make
back all of the losses in one fell swoop. If I were
wrong . . .

It was the first week of July. I was once again hard at work at my desk when I heard a noise.

I recognized the sound immediately and turned to find Kashir standing upright behind me.

"Yes?" I encouraged him.

"I haf here de profit-and-loss number for June," said Kashir.

"Yes?"

Apparently my manner was not properly submissive because he repeated himself with more authority.

"I haf here de profit-and-loss number for June!"

"I heard you the first time," I answered. "What is the number?"

"Eet ees a loss!" Kashir had by this time developed a real flair for the dramatic.

"Really?" I asked. "How much of a loss?"

"Eet ees a loss of $300,000!"

I decided to give Kashir his one and only chance.

"Are you quite sure, Kashir?" I asked.

"Absolutely!" he insisted, throwing the papers on my desk and turning to go. "They will be distributed to senior management this afternoon."

"I wouldn't do that if I were you," I said.

Something in my tone made him turn around in midstride.

"Huh?" said Kashir.

"I wouldn't do that if I were you," I repeated.

"Why not?"

"Because it's not correct."

"How do you know?" he challenged.

I opened my desk drawer and took out a stack of my daily computerized profit-and-loss statements.

There is nothing so impressive as the sight of a stack of computerized reports. They are especially useful against the weak-minded.

74

Kashir took one look at the reports and turned pale. "What are those?" he whispered.

"These," I said, patting the papers lovingly, "are a set of daily profit-and-loss statements recording our progress over the last two months. Phillip and I have checked them over to ensure that there are no errors. The entire position has been input into the computer as a matter of record, and the computer automatically values the position. I can assure you that all of these figures are correct and can be accounted for."

I waited a moment to let the full impact sink in.

"I can also assure you that the computer reports are not showing a $300,000 loss for June."

Kashir was beginning to hunch over.

"What . . . what number are you showing?" he asked.

"Why do you care?" I countered. "You told me that you were absolutely sure that your number was correct."

"I . . . I never said that," he mumbled.

"Oh? I must have misunderstood you then. What was it that you said?"

"I said . . . I said . . . eet ees only an interim number."

"Oh?" I said. "You mean that you want to go back upstairs to recheck your work?"

"Yes."

"All right," I said.

Kashir didn't move.

"Yes?" I said.

"Perhaps I should take a copy of one of those reports with me," pleaded Kashir.

"Kashir," I said, "I will give you the reports so that you can check your work." He made a movement toward the papers. I held up my hand to stop him. "Please be advised that this information has been saved in the computer's memory, so that if any report is stolen or damaged I can always print a new one. If you have any questions, you can talk to Phillip about it. But I want you to work quickly. I intend to distribute my reports tomorrow afternoon to senior management whether or not you agree with them."

Not surprisingly, Kashir found that he had made a number of errors in his original calculation of the June profit-and-loss. After correcting these mistakes, he found that he agreed with the profit-and-loss figure demonstrated by the computer reports.

Senior management was pleasantly surprised to find that the options desk was recognizing a gain of $500,000 in June.

I was on my way.

My first three months as head trader were up.

In retrospect I understood that I had undertaken a task of almost Herculean proportions. I thought I'd done pretty well for the bank. Instead of a one-woman fiasco they had a three-person, fully functioning trading unit that was well on its way to profitability. Instead of a manual, error-filled accounting system they had a computerized program that monitored profit and loss and risk management on a daily basis. Instead of anonymity, they had a name that was recognized in the marketplace as a growing force.

Even though my three months had been up and I was owed a promotion and raise, I had not pressed the issue. I hadn't had the courage. Now that the desk was becoming profitable, my nerve returned. It was time for John to come through with his side of the bargain.

I went up to Linda's desk.

"I want to see John," I said. "Today."

Linda opened her appointment book.

"He hasn't got a second all day," she said. "He's booked all the way up until 6:30 P.M.."

"Fine," I said. "Tell him I'll see him at 6:30."

John was already in his office when I arrived promptly at 6:30. I walked in and shut the door behind me.

"Hello, Nancy," said John. "Have a seat."

I sat down in the chair across from his desk.

"Everything all right in the trading room?" he asked.

I assured him that everything was fine.

"That's good," he said.

Silence.

"So what can I do for you?" he asked finally.

"It's been three months," I said. "We had a deal."

"Is it three months already?" John asked vaguely.

"It's actually more than three months," I said.

"Oh," he said. "You know I've been so busy . . ."

I indicated that I appreciated the demands on his time.

"Well," said John. "I'm glad you reminded me. Let me get out your file and we'll discuss it."

Discuss it?

John called Linda into his office.

"Will you find Nancy's personnel file for me, please?" he asked her.

Linda went over to a file cabinet, picked out the appropriate folder, handed it to John, and left, closing the door behind her.

"She's just a wonder," said John. "Don't know what I'd do without her."

Silence.

John opened the file and flipped through a few pages.

"Let's see," he said. "What was it we had talked about?"

77

"We didn't just talk about it, we had an agreement," I reminded him. "After three months I was to be raised by another 50 percent, and promoted to vice president and manager. There was also to be a recommendation to the board of directors concerning my bonus."

"Nancy," said John, "let's examine each of these issues one at a time."

"Yes?"

"Let's begin with the additional 50 percent raise in salary," he said.

"Yes?"

"Although your performance has been adequate to date . . ."

Adequate?

"I don't see where you've earned an additional raise in salary," he said.

Silence.

"After all, you are still operating at a loss for the first three months, aren't you?" he asked.

More silence.

"I understand your difficulties and appreciate your efforts," said John. "I think you've made a fine start. Perhaps in another three months . . ."

Another three months? We'll see about that.

"I inherited those losses. I put in all new systems. We get daily profit-and-loss statements. Accurate profit-and-loss statements. By the end of this month the unit will be operating at a profit for the year. I've two people working for me that I've spent a significant amount of time training, and who show enormous potential. The bank's name is known in the market. The Options Unit is stronger today than it was the day that Paul and Bob resigned."

"I repeat that I commend your efforts," said John, "but I just don't see that an additional raise is justified."

Silence.

"I'm afraid I'm firm on this," he added.

"I'm sorry you feel that way," I said. "I'm afraid I don't agree with you." I stood up and started to leave the room.

"Where are you going?"

"Well," I said, "clearly there's nothing more to talk about. I'll have to reexamine the situation now. Perhaps I'll take a few days off to think about it. Of course, the market's pretty active now and someone else will have to try to run my position—"

Even John knew that there was no one else to run the position.

"Just a second," John cut in. "Let's not be too hasty."

I sat down again.

"Perhaps I was wrong after all," said John. "You have been working pretty hard and have had a number of obstacles to overcome."

I waited.

"All right," said John. "You'll get your raise."

"Thank you," I said.

"But about the promotion," he continued. "You know, Nancy, I feel very strongly about the title, vice president and manager. It's not a title one gives away lightly."

I waited.

"It usually takes at least seven years to receive such a title. As I understand it, this is only your third year with the bank; is that correct?"

I nodded.

"Don't you see that if I promote you you will be the youngest vice president and manager at the bank?"

Silence.

"I don't think you are ready to be a vice president and manager just yet," said John. "In another three months, perhaps . . ."

I stood up again.

"All right, all right," he sighed. "Vice president and manager it is."

I sat down.

"Thank you," I said.

"I don't suppose that you'd be willing to discuss the bonus recommendation . . . no, of course not. . . . I'll submit the recommendation to the board of directors at the end of this month."

"Thank you."

This time we both rose to our feet and shook hands. John smiled at me.

"Keep up the good work!" he said.

John kept his promise and I received both my raise and my promotion immediately. He was also successful in persuading the board of directors to approve a bonus arrangement that linked compensation directly to the earnings contributed by each trading unit. This made me one of the highest-paid individuals in the entire bank.

As it turned out, John didn't do too badly either. For the next six months I made one successful trading decision after another. He was more than justified in his decision to raise and promote me.

My power grew daily. I was alternately respected, feared, and hated throughout the bank. In three short months I had gone from a lowly loan officer to a position of recognized authority in a highly visible area of the bank.

My star was on the ascendancy.

It seemed that nothing could go wrong.

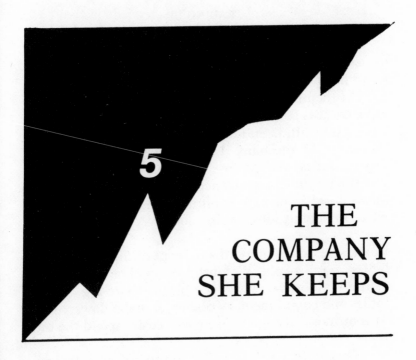

5

THE COMPANY SHE KEEPS

I fingered the cream-colored engraved invitation that had just arrived in the mail. A cocktail party was being given at the Waldorf-Astoria Hotel by one of the principal exchanges dealing in currency options. My presence at this function was requested.

I sighed as I turned the card over in my hand. Until now I had pretty much ignored the outside world, preferring to concentrate on matters closer to home. I had a hundred excellent excuses for putting off meeting my counterparts at other banks and financial institutions face-to-face. I told myself that I had my hands full at the bank; I had to organize my department, install computer systems, master my trade. Valid reasons, one and all.

But the truth was, I was scared. I wasn't sure I'd measure up to industry standards. It was safer and easier to hang back.

On the other hand, meeting the rest of the trading industry was something of a challenge. I couldn't get it out of my mind. Suddenly, it wasn't enough to have succeeded at the bank. I wouldn't be satisfied until I was respected as a professional by a jury of my peers.

Under the circumstances, there didn't seem to be much point in putting it off any longer. I was going to make my debut into trading society.

I took several deep breaths in front of the mirror in the ladies' room of the Waldorf-Astoria. The ladies' room at the Waldorf is a very nice place. There are dressing tables and complimentary cosmetics and a flowered sofa. At that moment I felt as if I could easily spend the night there.

This is it, I thought. I'm about to meet the most powerful and experienced traders in the options market. The crème de la crème. The elite. The chosen.

They know what they're doing. I don't. They're tough. I'm not. They'll be out there looking for weakness. My inexperience alone makes me an easy mark.

I'm in big trouble.

How can I even the odds? How earn the respect of people whose only definition of success is a personal net worth in excess of $20 million? These guys are killers! Sharks!

Sharks. That's it. That's the key.

I'm walking into a high-stakes poker game, aren't I? I thought suddenly. That's exactly what trading is all about. It's poker.

What wins in poker? Well, the cards, of course. But that's not enough. Good cards don't make a good poker player. Experience helps, too. I mean, you have to know the rules to win. But experience alone won't do it.

What really wins in poker is attitude. Attitude is the one quality that is absolutely necessary to win the game. There's only one thing to do, I decided.

Bluff 'em.

I walked into the crowded room.

The party was already in full swing. A rose-colored banquet room had been reserved for the occasion. The pinkish glow of the walls was set off nicely by the steel-gray cloud of cigarette smoke that forever shadows the trading industry.

I had been in New York for six years. This was the first time that I'd seen this many men all in the same place at the same time. There were men huddled in small groups. There were men clustered around the bar. There were men sitting and men standing up. There were men everywhere.

I had often heard my unmarried girlfriends wonder aloud at where all the men were in New York. Now I knew.

I'd never had any problem dealing with men in the past. It's just that I wasn't used to being in one room with quite so many all at once.

Oh, God, I thought. What'll I do if nobody talks to me?

At that moment a man stepped up to me.

Oh, God, I thought. Somebody's about to talk to me. What am I going to say?

The man in question was of less-than-average height with a mop of unruly dark hair that he made even messier by running his fingers through it every few minutes. He wore smudged horn-rimmed glasses and his shirt was wrinkled under his unbuttoned double-breasted blue pin-striped jacket. I judged him to be in his mid-twenties, perhaps a year or two younger than I. He was wearing a ridiculous bright orange name tag that read: "Hi! My Name Is Brian Henry!"

I recognized the name as belonging to a junior trader who worked at a competing bank.

He held out his hand to me. I took it.

"I'm Brian," he said.

"I'm Nancy," I said.

So far, so good.

"Pretty good turnout tonight," he commented, surveying the room.

"Oh, yes," I agreed, cautiously.

With this he fell silent, apparently having used up his entire store of snappy cocktail-party patter. Accordingly, I struggled to come up with something to talk about.

"How was your day today?" I asked.

Brian brightened immediately.

"Exhausting but profitable," he confided, grinning. "I captured 35 percent volatility in my Swiss book today and 28 percent in my yen book. And our theta curve is averaging $150,000 a day."

I stared at him. Was he speaking English? Perhaps this was some kind of a joke. I smiled uncertainly.

"Ah!" he said, puffing out his chest, which served to emphasize the food stains on his tie, "I see that you don't believe me. I don't blame you. Those are pretty impressive numbers."

What was the correct response? I searched frantically for some kind of answer.

"I believe you," I said.

"Listen," he said. "I can tell there's something else going on here. Maybe you think those numbers aren't so hot."

"I didn't say that—" I began.

"So what's the story?" he interrupted me. "You trying to tell me you're doing better than that? What's your time-decay number?"

I suppose if he could have told me what *time decay*

was, I might have been able to give him a number. As things stood, however, I could think of nothing better than to smile again.

"Not going to tell me, huh? What's the big secret? I told you mine."

I judged it best just to keep smiling.

"Two hundred thousand dollars a day?" he asked. "More? Two hundred fifty thousand dollars a day? Jesus! You telling me you're doing those kind of numbers?"

"I didn't say that," I objected again.

"You don't have to. I can see it on your face. I'm a pretty good judge of character, you know," he continued modestly.

"I think I need a drink," I said, edging away from him.

"Oh! Sure. But listen, let's sit down sometime and discuss the market, just you and me, okay? I have a feeling I could learn something from you."

"Uh . . . sure . . . sometime . . ." I said, backing off.

I went back into the ladies' room and wrote down every word he'd said. Perhaps there was a book somewhere that would explain it.

I returned to the party and moved in the direction of the bar, keeping as far away from Brian as possible. It was very crowded, and thus difficult to navigate.

I was stopped by a large group of traders who were arguing heatedly with one another. I was trying to find the best way of getting around them without simply pushing through. One of them noticed my efforts and pointed out my dilemma to the person next to him. They moved over to include me.

"Having trouble?" The trader laughed. He was about my age, but he had already lost a lot of his light brown hair and so looked older. His distinguishing characteristic was his height: he stood barely five feet four inches. As I stand five feet eight inches in my stocking feet and was at the time wearing three-inch heels, I'm sure we made an interesting couple.

"I'm afraid I am," I said, smiling down at him. I was trying to read his orange name tag to find out who he was, but I don't see long distances very well without my glasses.

"I'm John Wilson. You're Nancy, aren't you?" he said, taking me off the hook.

" Yes. Hi, John. I thought I recognized your voice." John worked for another major commercial bank and I spoke with him often.

"Nancy, this is Chuck Brown. Chuck, this is Nancy," he said, introducing the man next to him.

Another bank trader whose name sounded vaguely familiar.

"Pleased to meet you, Nancy," said Chuck. "I think we might have done some business last month."

"That's right," I said. "I remember."

"How's the market treating you?" John asked.

"Pretty well, I guess," I said cautiously. I certainly did not want a repetition of the last conversation. To throw him off, I changed the subject. "John, didn't I hear somewhere that you accepted a job at another bank?"

"That's right," he said. "This is my last week."

"What happened?" I asked. "Were you unhappy?"

"Not particularly," he said.

"Were you being held back?"

"On the contrary, I was given a free hand."

"What was it, then?"

Before John could answer, Chuck stepped in.

"It was the three months' supply-and-demand cycle," he said.

"The what?"

"The three months' cycle," Chuck repeated. "You know, every three months or so a new bank decides to get into the options business. So they steal an options trader from another bank. There is only a limited supply of us, so every time it happens the value of options traders in general rises."

"Then, of course," John continued for Chuck, "three months later another bank gets into the picture and steals the options trader from the first bank for a premium."

"You're kidding," I said. "I mean, I knew there was a high turnover rate . . ."

"I'm not kidding at all," said John seriously. "There's a good living in trading your salary. For instance, in the past two years I've worked for three different banks. I started out making $60,000 a year with a $10,000 bonus. Now I make $150,000 a year, and have an opportunity to make another $150,000 in bonus. Of course," he added quickly, "to make that kind of money I'd have to stay with the same bank for a whole year. I'm not sure I'd want to do that. It might be more profitable simply to move again, especially if prices keep moving up the way they've been."

"And if you keep trading the way you've been," Chuck cut in. "You don't earn much of a bonus for showing a loss at the end of the year."

"Who said I left a loss?" countered John.

"Oh, come on," said Chuck. "It's all over the Street."

"Who said I left a loss? I never left a loss! Who said I left a loss?"

"I must have been mistaken," snickered Chuck.

"You mean a new bank will hire you even if you've lost money at the old one?" I asked.

"Of course," said Chuck. "They don't care about

performance. They just want someone with experience."

"I see," I said, even though I didn't.

"Who said I left a loss?" John repeated hotly. "I never left a loss!"

"Oh, calm down, John," said Chuck. "How's the new house?"

"Great," said John sullenly.

"And the new car? What'd you get this time, a Porsche?"

"No," said John warming up slightly. "A Maserati."

"What color?"

"Fire-engine red."

I couldn't help smiling at the picture of this little balding guy zooming around in a red Maserati. How did he see over the dashboard?

"Well, I guess it's about time I went and got my drink," I said. "It was a pleasure meeting you both in person, finally. Be sure and call me if you want to do business."

As I walked away I heard John repeating:

"Who said I left a loss? I never left a loss!"

I got close enough to the bar this time to stand in line for a drink. The man in front of me smiled and held out his hand.

"Hi, I'm Sam."

"I'm Nancy."

"Nice to meet you. What can I get you?"

"Oh, just a glass of white wine, thanks."

He got the drinks and we moved out of the way of the bar.

"Cheers," he said, raising his glass.

"Cheers," I echoed, sipping my wine.

"The dollar's going down, you know," he said.

"What?"

"The dollar's going down."

"Is it?"

"Sure," he said. "Have a look."

He took a small metal object out of his pocket that looked rather like a hand-held calculator.

"What's that?" I asked.

"Why, it's my portable Reuters screen," he said, surprised. "Don't you have one?"

"Not only don't I have one, I've never seen one," I said. "What does it do?"

"It tells me the current prices for everything on a twenty-four-hour basis. See? I've got the Australian market right now. Pretty soon the Tokyo market will start trading. This way I always know exactly where everything is."

As I was staring at the tiny screen, I noticed that his hand was shaking. He quickly put the machine away and lit a cigarette.

"You must work awfully hard," I said.

"Twenty-four hours," he said proudly.

"Aren't you tired?" I asked with real curiosity.

"Sure I get tired. But I trade better when I'm tired."

"You do?"

"I love pressure. It sharpens my concentration."

"Don't you ever take any time off?"

"Not really."

"What does your wife think about that?"

"My wife?"

"I couldn't help noticing that you were married," I said, nodding toward his wedding ring.

"I haven't seen my wife in four days," he said.

"You haven't?"

"Nope. Either I'm working late or she is. She's a lawyer. She's asleep when I get up. She can't stand my trading at night. Says the phone calls wake her up."

"I can't understand why," I said under my breath.
"What?"

"I said, she doesn't seem to be very understanding," I recovered.

"Those are the breaks," he said. "It's the business. You've got to be tough to take it. Especially if you want what I want."

"What do you want?" I asked.

"I want to be the best. I've got it all planned out."

"You have?"

"Uh-huh. First I have to move to an investment bank."

"Where are you working now?"

"A commercial bank."

"What's so special about an investment bank?"

"The money."

"Is it really that much better?" I asked doubtfully. It seemed to me the pay was pretty good at commercial banks.

"See that guy over there?" asked Sam. "The one with the light-blue tie?"

I looked and saw an attractive man in his early thirties with blond hair cut very short. He was standing with an air of self-assurance, talking quietly to another man.

"Yes," I said. "I see him. What about him?"

"I hear he takes home almost $1 million a year."

I took a closer look. Damn! I wished I had my glasses.

"And there are others who make even more," said Sam.

"I see."

"It's not just the pay. It's the connections. The perks. The power."

"Are you close to making a deal?" I asked.

"Soon," he said. "But it's a secret. Don't tell any-one."

"I won't," I promised.

"I mean, I'm only telling my closest friends."

I made my way back to the bar and got myself another glass of wine. I stood back for a moment and surveyed the room.

"Allow me to introduce myself," said a voice be-hind me.

I turned around quickly, narrowly missing spilling my wine down the front of my blouse. It was the trader in the light-blue tie.

"Whoa!" said my new acquaintance. "Be careful. I don't usually have this strong an effect on women until the second or third date."

"Very funny."

"No, really." He stuck out his hand. "I'm Adam Tyler."

"Where's your orange name tag, Adam?"

"It doesn't go with my eyes."

"Well, it's nice to meet you, Adam. I'm Nancy."

"The pleasure is all mine, believe me."

I ignored his tone. He stared at me critically.

"I was wondering what you looked like," he said.

"I hope I haven't disappointed you."

"Not at all." He winked at me.

I laughed. He was so direct it was almost refresh-ing. I began to loosen up a little. Of course, the wine wasn't hurting any.

"That's better," he said, leaning over confiden-tially. "Listen. There's nobody here worth meeting other than me. Honest. Cross my heart. Why don't you and I blow off this group and go for a nice, quiet, intimate dinner somewhere? I know a lovely place not too far from here . . ."

"That sounds terrific, Adam," said another male voice at my elbow. "May I come along, too?"

A man of average height, also in his early thirties, had come up unobserved while we were talking. His dark hair curled over his collar, and his eyes seemed to take in the whole room at a glance. He was very intense. He exuded such a strong sense of confidence that he somehow diminished Adam's assurance.

"Thomas!" said Adam. "How wonderful to see you again. Why don't you get lost now?"

"Just when the conversation was getting so interesting? Not a chance," said Thomas, laughing. "I'm Thomas Richards," he said, shaking my hand.

I recognized Thomas as being an options dealer at another investment bank, one of Adam's principal competitors.

"Tell me," he said, nodding toward Adam, "has this man been bothering you?"

"Thomas," said Adam, "don't you have to go check the market in Australia or something?"

"That's funny coming from you. You're the one with the risky position."

"That's because you don't have the balls to go long the dollar."

"No, it's because I'm not stupid enough to go long the dollar."

They seemed to have forgotten about me completely.

"By the way," said Adam. "I haven't seen your name in the market for a while. Have you decided to take the summer off?"

"I was just about to ask you the same question," Thomas replied coolly. "We've been handling some pretty large deals. Too bad you couldn't get a piece of the action. I just figured you weren't up to it."

"You know I'm always ready to do size," Adam retorted. "Just name it."

"Fine. Make me a price."

"Here?"

"Sure. What's the matter?"

"This is a party, for God's sake."

"So? You have a problem with that? Are you telling me you don't know where the market is? Come now, Adam, I know you better than that." Thomas winked at me. "Unless, of course, you've started to slip in your old age . . ."

"Not at all. My market's 10 bid at 30." This meant that Adam was willing to buy at 10 or sell at 30.

"I don't call that being very aggressive," said Thomas. "I have to say that I'm disappointed in you, Adam. I thought you could do better than that. My market's 15 bid at 25."

"For how much?"

"Your size."

"Fine. Twenty dollars sold at 15." Adam had just sold Thomas $20 million worth of an option.

"Done," said Thomas. "Twenty bid for another 100."

Thomas was ready to buy another $100 million worth of options from Adam for five points higher than he had just paid.

I held my breath. I'd never seen anyone raise his own bid. It was a sign of real confidence. And for such a large sum, too! And not even being in the office!

Adam hesitated. In this business, he who hesitates is lost.

"I'll pass," he said, finally.

"Fine," said Thomas. "Well, it's been fun, but I've got to go make a phone call now. It's always a pleasure doing business with you, Adam." He turned to go.

"Oh, by the way, Adam," said Thomas, turning back for just a second. "You should have hit me. The real market's 10 bid at 15. Nancy, it was a pleasure meeting you. Do yourself a favor and don't listen to anything this guy says while I'm gone." He walked away laughing.

"Son of a bitch," said Adam to Thomas's back.

The cocktail party continued on for several hours. I had a wonderful time. Everybody wanted to talk to me. I learned more about the market in one evening than I had in four months on the trading desk.

I had walked in hoping that no one would notice that I was a woman, that I would be treated like one of the guys. What a mistake! Being a woman in this environment was a powerful advantage.

Sure, there were a few other women in the room. One or two of them were even traders. But I'd gotten most of the attention. Men who earned fabulous salaries, and who threw around hundreds of millions of dollars in the market as if it were so much chicken feed, had fallen over themselves competing for my attention. Nobody had tested my knowledge or experience. If anything, they'd gone out of their way to prove to me how intelligent, tough, and powerful they were.

Suddenly, I realized that it was very late. Larry had been expecting me at home hours ago. I'd been reveling in all the attention so much that I'd lost all track of time.

I started rummaging in my purse for cabfare home. In the process of the struggle I came across my notes. My elation was marred only slightly by the reminder.

What the hell was a theta curve?

I ran out into the warm summer night to hail a cab.

Larry was waiting up for me when I got home.

"Do you have any idea what time it is?" he asked.

"I'm sorry," I began. "I didn't realize—"

"Didn't realize that it was nearly one o'clock? That

you'd gone to a cocktail party that was supposed to be over by nine? Did it occur to you that I might be worried about you? That I had visions of you lying in the street somewhere alone and hurt?"

"Why would you be worried about me?"

"Why? You're four hours late without even bothering to call me, and you ask me why? Are you telling me you didn't once notice the time?"

"I'm sorry. The time just got away from me."

Boy. This was the last thing I needed.

I told myself that it was my success that was causing the argument. That he didn't like the fact that it was I who was holding her own among the big boys. Well, I wasn't going to split the credit with anybody, not even Larry, who'd helped me get started in the first place. I turned and went into the bedroom.

About half an hour later Larry followed me in and went to sleep.

I tried to sleep as well. But when I closed my eyes all I could see was Thomas's face offering to buy another $100 million at 20.

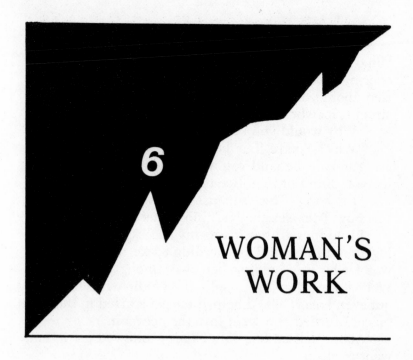

6

WOMAN'S WORK

There's one little piece of information I've neglected to mention. Larry and I were newlyweds. We'd been married one month after I got the trading job.

We didn't plan it that way; it just happened. We were engaged in September after having known each other for nine months. My mother had been firm in her insistence that it takes at least six months to organize a proper wedding (please note that this is approximately twice the time it takes to become a head options trader at a major commercial bank), so we'd set the date for April, never dreaming I'd have any trouble getting away. After all, who cares when a loan officer takes her vacation?

Much to John Anderson's displeasure, when the time

came, I actually insisted on attending my own wedding and—inexcusable irresponsibility—my own honeymoon. I must confess that I was surprised by his reaction. He showed so little interest in what I was doing that I naturally assumed his indifference would extend to my vacation plans. In this I was wrong; while he didn't particularly seem to care what I did on the desk, he did seem to care that I be there to oversee personally whatever it was that I did that he didn't care about. I think he believed he could talk me out of leaving right up until the time I got on the plane.

Mom did a great job, the wedding was beautiful, the honeymoon was even lovelier, and the whole event was marred only slightly by the fact that Phillip lost an additional $250,000 in my absence. Oh, well, you can't have everything.

I completely adore Larry. His good looks and intelligence are a hard combination to beat, and there's an energy about him that I find very attractive. You can't meet Larry, even briefly, without his leaving a definite impression on you, good or bad. How did I wind up with this spectacular guy? Timing. He's divorced. Twice.

Until this point, Larry and I had been living a fairytale existence. We had a terrific apartment, for one thing. Now, I know that in most cities, procuring an adequate living space is not a cause for wild rejoicings, but this is Manhattan. I, for example, had lived the first four years in New York without benefit of direct sunlight, unless you count the fact that if I stuck my head out of the window at exactly 5:33 P.M. between October 13 and December 10 I could see the reflection of the sun as it struck the windows of the thirty-fifth floor of the building directly opposite mine.

By contrast, Larry had an apartment on the fifteenth floor of a building on Central Park West. Not only was his spacious one-bedroom apartment flooded with direct sunlight whenever there was direct sunlight to be had, but to the apartment was attached a terrace, and to the terrace was attached—Oh, wonder! Oh, marvel! Oh, joy!—an unimpaired view of Central Park and the city surrounding it. On cold winter nights you could see all the way down to the Empire State Building. All this, and the man himself, for the unbelievably low price of $400 a month ($440 if you wanted to rent a parking space as well).

Naturally, I took the deal.

"How in the world did you ever get this wonderful apartment so cheap?" I asked Larry when he told me what he paid in rent.

"I've been here for ten years," Larry replied. "It was only $250 when I first moved in, but the neighborhood's changed a lot in ten years. It wasn't quite this nice when I first got here."

"How bad could it have been?" I asked.

"Let me put it this way," said Larry. "When I first moved in, on Sunday nights I would hear the sound of drums beating and weird chanting coming from the park. It was scary, let me tell you. Then, on Monday mornings, the park would be littered with dead chickens. I mean it, chickens with their heads cut off."

"Ugh!" I said.

"Yep," he said, nodding his head. "Dead chickens. The occasional dead goat. But mostly chickens."

"Why didn't you go to the police?" I asked. The Twenty-fourth Precinct was right down the block.

"I did," said Larry. "Talked to a sergeant. He told me he knew all about it. Told me it was the Haitians practicing their voodoo and such."

"Well, why didn't they go in there and break it up?"

"I asked the cop that very same question."

"What did he say?"

"He said: 'Didn't you hear what I said, man? It's the Haitians! That's voodoo going on in there!'"

"I see his point," I said.

Anyway, what the NYPD was unable to do, the Yuppies did. By the time I arrived on the scene the war had already been fought, and all that was left was to iron out a few of the finer terms of surrender: exactly which corner would be left available for drug distribution and during what hours; the exact period of time before the Army-Navy store would be converted into a Tex-Mex charcuterie; just the usual last-minute details. All I had to do was to relax and enjoy it.

When I first met Larry, he had chucked his business career in favor of the theater. It had always been his dream to be an actor, and he felt that this was his only chance to give it a try. We'd agreed that he'd give himself a full year to get a start in the theater. If he hadn't made it by that time, we would reevaluate.

Greater naïveté, I am convinced, does not exist on this planet. It would be easier to break into Fort Knox in a year's time than into the New York theater community.

We were therefore in the process of reevaluating. When I got the trading job, and Larry and I spent so much time going over the basics of options, he'd gotten the idea of trading himself from home. He was just getting started that summer.

But in the meantime, because it cost us so little to live, there was always enough money around for a good time, even before I got the trading job. Larry and I would get all dressed up and go dancing late at night during the week (while I was still a loan officer and it wasn't necessary to be awake to do the job). We went to the movies. We went to the theater. We went to the ballet. I love the ballet. We went to the Mets games. Larry loves the Mets.

We made love all the time. I couldn't have been happier.

Then I got the trading job.

The morning after the cocktail party, the sound of the alarm wrenched me from a deep sleep at 5:30. I longed to throw the clock across the room, turn over, and fall immediately back into a deep, satisfying sleep lasting a mere twelve hours or so. Then I remembered the fight.

We'd had fights before, of course, but this was our first major argument since we'd been married. In the quiet of the dark bedroom I suddenly felt terribly lonely.

I looked over at Larry, lying peacefully on his stomach, still fast asleep. His dark hair was curling around his face and his long lashes rested against cheeks flushed with the warmth of sleep. I felt a great rush of love for him.

He'd been right. It had been thoughtless of me not to call. He'd had every right to be upset. And why had I stayed at the party so long anyway? All the attention had gone to my head.

I nestled up closer to him and put my arms around him.

"Ummm," he mumbled sleepily.

"Honey, I'm sorry," I whispered tenderly, kissing his ear. "You were right. It was horrible of me not to call. I love you. I don't know what came over me. I acted like a big jerk last night."

He turned his head toward me and cocked open one eye.

"I know," he said.

The result of the cocktail party was that I found myself at the center of a network of information and shifting alliances.

Traders are the biggest gossips in the world. Bigger than professional gossip columnists like Rona Barrett. Bigger than male sports commentators. Bigger even than my aunt Agnes.

Until I'd had the chance to meet my fellow traders, I never realized the extent of this underground advisory service. Now I picked up bits and pieces of information almost daily. Suddenly, a large portion of the industry was calling just to talk.

What was the cause of my sudden popularity?

They liked talking to a woman.

A woman who knows how to trade is a great anomaly. Male traders feel more comfortable with a woman trader than they do with their wives or girlfriends. They can talk about the market with a woman who really understands what they are saying. A spouse who has never traded may appreciate the amount of time and effort her husband puts into his career and certainly respects the money he brings in as a result, but she could not identify with the feeling of doubling up on a losing position, nor could she properly admire the brilliance of a decision to buy when prevailing thought says sell.

But I could.

"Options desk."

"Hi, Nancy. This is Chuck."

"Hi, Chuck. How are you?"

"I'm hanging in there. What about yourself?"

"I'm just fine. What can I do for you? Do you want me to make you a price?"

"No, I shut down for the day. I was up late last night."

"Really?" I asked. "What happened?"

"Oh, I was the wrong way when the Japanese prime minister decided to open his big mouth."

Translation: Chuck had bought yen, expecting the yen to strengthen overnight. The Japanese prime minister had unexpectedly issued a statement that the market had interpreted in favor of a weaker yen. The yen had fallen. Chuck had lost money.

"Oh, I'm sorry," I said, sympathetically. "Don't worry. I know you'll do better next time."

I was getting used to my role as surrogate girlfriend, cheerleader, and den mother.

"I know it, too," he said. "I'm not worried. I just found out that a very large player in Switzerland will be in there buying Swiss francs at ———." He named a price.

"They will?" I asked. "How do you know?"

"I have a very good contact in Europe. Trust me."

If that was true, the Swiss franc could be expected to appreciate in value as soon as it reached that price.

"Oh!" I said. "Thanks for the information."

"Anytime," he said, ringing off.

I watched and waited until the price of Swiss francs got to the level that Chuck had indicated, and then I bought a very small amount just to see. Sure enough, someone came into the market and started buying large amounts of Swiss just as Chuck had predicted. The price of Swiss started to rise. Although I hadn't taken very much of a position, I still made some money.

Well! I thought. This is turning out better than I'd expected.

"Options desk."

"Nancy," said a deep male voice, "how nice to hear from you again."

"But, Adam," I replied, recognizing the voice instantly, "you called me."

"Did I? In that case, why haven't you called me?"

"I didn't have anything to say."

"That makes no difference," said Adam. "You'd be surprised the number of people who call me with nothing to say."

"I'll keep it in mind," I promised. "Now, what can I do for you?"

"I was hoping you'd ask that. Let's start with drinks and then dinner and then—"

"Let me rephrase the question," I said, cutting him off. "Do you want me to make you a price?"

"You cut me to the quick. Of course I don't want you to make me a price. I can get a price from anybody. But I can't go for a walk with just anybody. And it's a beautiful day for a walk. Don't you want to go with me?"

"I'd love to but I have to work."

"Work! That's a lame excuse."

"Lame but true," I said.

"What do you have to do?"

I sighed.

"For one thing, I have to figure out which way the dollar is going," I said. "I don't suppose you know the answer to that question?"

"Nobody knows the answer to that question, my sweet," said Adam. "But if it will allow you to unchain yourself from the desk for an hour or so and accept my gallant invitation to stroll along the streets of downtown New York, I can tell you that all the signs indicate that a rebound is in the works."

"You think the dollar's going up, then?" I asked, zeroing in.

"Well," said Adam. "From a completely technical point of view, a correction in the downward trend is long overdue. Just take a look at your charts."

The *charts* Adam referred to are graphs that record the price of the dollar over the recent past. Some charts are extremely sophisticated, utilizing all kinds of market information in addition to price histories. However, anyone can draw a simple chart by taking the price of the dollar relative to another currency (say, deutsche marks) and plotting it over time on a piece of ordinary graph paper.

People who follow these charts are, appropriately enough, called *chartists*. Chartists believe that there are patterns to market behavior. Properly interpreted, the charts reveal these patterns and help predict future prices.

Chartists, like the charts they employ, come in a variety of types. The most effective spend a great deal of time at their craft and have elevated charting to a science.

Unfortunately, because anyone can pick up a pencil and draw a crude graph without much effort, the vast majority of those who call themselves chartists are individuals who believe that any chart (particularly theirs) can predict the future. In their unrelenting search for quick and easy profit, these chartists have reduced the science to art.

This is how it works. The standard method for drawing charts is based somewhat loosely on the children's game Connect-the-Dots. You remember Connect-the-Dots. Children play it in school, behind the teacher's back. The essence of chart interpretation, then, is to draw lines through the dots on the graphs and to hunt for pictures resulting from this effort.

For example, a chartist will suddenly lift his head from his work to chortle: "Aha! A perfect head-and-shoulders formation!" He will offer to show you his work. You look, and, sure enough (after he has lovingly traced the outline for you with his finger) you will see a clumsy picture of what could be interpreted as a person's head and shoulders, particularly if that person were a hunchback. "What does it mean?" you ask the chartist. "It means the dollar is going down!" he shouts happily. "Sell the dollar!"

The first time I was introduced to a chartist's methods I made the mistake of wondering aloud whether he wasn't working too hard, and didn't perhaps need a vacation. But then I noticed something important. When all the chartists in the world (and their number is growing every day) decide to sell the dollar, there are so many of them selling that the dollar, by virtue of being sold so much, actually does go down. Chartists make fortunes during these periods.

Accordingly, I have learned to pay attention to the charts.

"In addition to that," Adam continued, "most of the economists on the Street are predicting a slight improvement in economic growth over the near term. Not very much, but enough. But none of that is really important. The really important thing is . . ."

"Yes?" I asked, all attention.

". . . I feel like the dollar is going up," he finished.

"You feel like it," I repeated.

"Yep," he said.

Well, there's no arguing with research. "Thanks for the insight," I said.

"Now, what about that walk?"

"Some other time," I said. "I promise." I hung up the phone.

"Phillip?" I said.

"Huh?"

"What do the charts say?"

"Huh?"

"The charts. Your charts," I repeated patiently. "Do they seem to indicate a rebound in the dollar?"

"Ah! My charts! Let's look at my charts!" Phillip loved his charts. He spent hours on them, keeping them up to date, drawing lines through points, erasing these lines and then redrawing them. Now he tenderly unfolded a large chart depicting the value of the dollar relative to the deutsche mark over the past three years.

"Let's see," he said, scrutinizing his own work. "Why, yes! I don't know why I didn't see it before! Look here. It's oversold. The dollar should be going up! Let's buy some!"

"Not so fast," I said. I wanted to make sure that Adam's information was real. "Do we have any numbers coming out this week?"

"Yes. Housing starts and the consumer price index," said Phillip, referring to a calendar that indicated the dates on which economic data were released monthly by the Commerce Department.

"What's expected?" I asked. "A slight improvement?"

"Yes," said Phillip. "A slight improvement is expected."

"Okay," I said. "Let's buy some."

We bought some.

Adam was right. The dollar was oversold. The correction began in Tokyo that very night and continued for a few days. The dollars that Phillip and I bought increased in value. We sold them for a nice profit.

And this industry has a reputation for being cutthroat! I thought. Why, everyone is being just as helpful as they can be!

"Options desk."

"Hello, Nancy. This is Roger calling from London."

"Hello, Roger. What can I do for you?"

"Nothing much. Just calling up to chat."

I was surprised and pleased. I hadn't met Roger face-to-face yet. I guessed that my name was getting around the market as a good person to talk to.

"How's it going for you, anyway?" Roger asked. "You getting along okay?"

"Pretty well," I said. "How about yourself?"

"Great month. Couldn't be better. What do you think of the dollar?"

I was thrilled. Imagine Roger asking me for my opinion! I had finally arrived.

"I think the dollar's going down," I said firmly.

"Really?" Did I imagine it or was there a hint of disapproval in his voice?

"I mean . . ." I faltered, "all the signs are there for a weaker dollar. . ."

"You think so?" This time there was no mistaking his tone.

"Of course, I could be wrong," I admitted, suddenly very unsure of my position.

"Did you hear about the retail sales number?" Roger asked.

Retail sales is a statistic released every month by the U.S. government. It's an indication of how well the retailing sector of the economy did in the previous month.

"What about the retail sales number?"

"Rumor says it's going to be up 6.5 percent."

Up 6.5 percent! For the past few months, retail sales had been averaging under 3 percent.

"But . . . the dollar will fly," I said, aghast. I was at the moment running a short dollar position. That meant that I had sold dollars I didn't own, intending to buy them back when the dollar was cheaper. A 6.5 percent retail sales number could kill me.

"Exactly."

I made some quick calculations. Today was Thursday. Retail sales didn't come out until tomorrow. I still had time to turn my position around and go long dollars.

As if he could read my thoughts, Roger continued: "Just look at the bonds."

I looked at the bonds. Bond prices were falling. This could be interpreted in favor of higher interest rates.

Such an interpretation was in line with a stronger dollar.

"Gee," I said. "Thanks for the information."

"Don't mention it," said Roger, hanging up.

I bought back all the dollars I had sold, and more. I also bought some very expensive options that would increase in value when the dollar went up.

I wasn't the only one buying. By the time I went home Thursday night the dollar was stronger. It was even higher in Tokyo when I checked the market at eleven-thirty before going to sleep.

Another example of male chivalry. I hardly knew Roger and I felt rather guilty for not having been friendlier toward him in the past. I wished I had had some information to pass along back to him. Maybe I could send him some flowers or something instead.

Friday morning at eight o'clock found me pacing back and forth behind my chair. The dollar had started to fall in London at three o'clock in the morning my time. It was already lower than where I'd bought it yesterday, so I was running a small loss at the moment.

I wasn't really worried, though. I knew how far up a 6.5 percent retail sales number would push the dollar. My only question was whether to buy more dollars at the cheaper price before the number came out at 8:30, or stay with the position I had. I decided to stay put.

8:30: One of the junior spot traders was at the Telerate machine. The bell went off. Silence. Then: "Up 1.5 percent!" shouted the junior trader.

Phillip and Peter and I exchanged looks of horror. It was a terrible number. Much weaker than expected. The dollar started to fall.

"Wait for the revision," I ordered.

Sometimes the government revises the previous month's retail sales number on the basis of more accurate information. I could only assume that Roger's information referred to last month's number.

We waited breathlessly to see if there would be a revision. The dollar continued to fall.

Suddenly the bell went off again. Ding ding ding ding ding!

"Revision!" shouted the junior trader.

Thank God, I mouthed silently.

"Last month's number revised down by 1.2 percent!"

I didn't even have to say anything.

"Yours!" shouted Phillip.

"Yours!" shouted Peter.

"Yours! Yours! Yours!" I shouted, selling dollars at a loss.

"London speaking."

"May I please speak to Roger?"

"Roger speaking."

"Hello, Roger. This is Nancy."

"Nancy, old girl! How are you?"

"I've been better."

"Really? Sorry to hear that. What's the matter?"

"Your information wasn't exactly accurate."

"What information?"

"The retail sales number," I said coldly. "Remember? Up 6.5 percent?"

"But—you don't mean—didn't you hear the later rumor?"

"What later rumor?"

"The rumor that said it was going to be up only 1.5 percent."

"I must have missed that one."

"What a pity. I hope you didn't get burned too badly?"

So much for male chivalry.

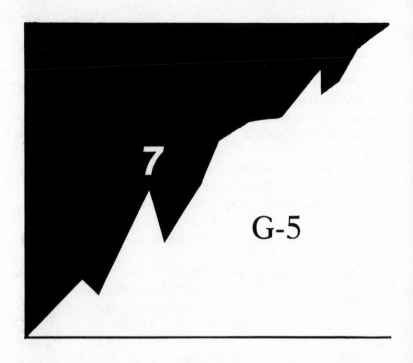

7

G-5

Something was happening to me. It crept up on me so slowly that I didn't even notice it. But it was there nonetheless. And it was growing stronger every day.

I was developing trader head.

Trader head is a syndrome in which one's ego grows at an accelerated rate at the expense of all other personality traits. Manifestations of the disease include a tendency on the part of the victim to look down his or her nose at other human beings, particularly those people who don't trade large sums of money for a living.

My exposure to other traders aggravated the pace of the illness. As I spent more and more time socializing with colleagues, I picked up not only their mania for all things market-related, but their arrogance as well.

I came home later and later in the evening and my talk was increasingly about who had sold what and to whom. I felt very important, being accepted as part of such an elite group. Home and husband lost by comparison.

My working environment contributed to the condition. On the trading desk, my word was law. No one questioned my decisions, or my right to throw ever-increasing sums of money at the market. If I told Peter or Phillip to do something, they did it. Fast.

This approach, however, did not seem to work as well at home.

It was the third Sunday in September. Larry and I were having a fight.

"What's your problem?" I asked coldly.

"You're my problem," he responded.

"That's not very helpful. Perhaps you could elaborate."

"Let me make myself clear."

"Please do."

"We don't spend any time together anymore."

"I have to work."

"Not all the time. Trading has become your whole life. When was the last time you took the initiative in this relationship? You're too tired to go dancing. You're too tired to see a film. You're too tired to go out with friends. The only thing you're not too tired to do is trade. That's a big drag."

"Anything else?"

"You are completely self-absorbed. The only thing that's growing in this relationship is your ego."

"It's my business," I retorted.

"It's not your business to turn into a walking, talking Reuters screen."

"You're just jealous. You're jealous of my success."

"That's untrue and unfair and you know it. I've helped and encouraged you from the beginning. That's

111

why I'm disappointed to see you turning out this way."

"Just leave me alone."

"Have it your way."

Larry went to read the Sunday paper outside on the terrace. I stayed in the apartment, fuming. What right had he to criticize me that way? Nobody else would dare do such a thing. Why was it that everyone else could see how important I had become but my own husband still treated me as though I were a mere mortal?

A half hour later Larry came back inside.

"Much as I hate to encourage you at this point in your chosen profession, I feel obliged to inform you that there's an article in the paper today which it behooves you to read."

I ignored him. Nothing he could say would interest me.

"Front page," he said, reading over my pointed silence. " 'Members of the five industrialized nations met today and decided to work together toward weakening the overvalued U.S. dollar. This initiative on the part of the Group of Five, or G-5 as it's now being called, represents an entirely new policy for the industrialized nations.' "

I continued to ignore him. I was so angry that if he'd told me the Russians had invaded I wouldn't have listened.

"This is really big news. It says here they've agreed to intervene to devalue the dollar."

"So what?" I said irritably.

"Honey, the dollar's going to react to this news. There's going to be a big move tonight in the Far East."

My wounded ego flared up again in anger. How dare he presume to tell me my own business! I was the head trader, not he!

"Don't be ridiculous," I said haughtily. "You don't know what you are talking about. Nothing's going to happen tonight."

"You'd better check it out," he warned.

"Forget it," I said, dismissing him. "Not only am I not going to read the article, I'm not even going to call the market tonight. I'm going to bed, and I'm going to turn off all the phones."

Larry doesn't argue with me when I'm in this mood.

"Fine," he said, shrugging.

I turned on my heel and went into the bedroom, closing the door behind me. What did he know about anything? I'd show him a thing or two.

I sure did.

I rode up in the elevator to the trading room on Monday morning, well rested for once. I nodded good morning to one of the spot foreign-exchange traders. He returned the greeting.

"Some move, huh?" he said, shaking his head in wonder. "I've been in the business for fifteen years and I've never seen anything like it."

I started to get a queasy feeling.

I hurried into the trading room. A crowd had gathered at the spot foreign-exchange desk. I recognized the president of the bank among them.

Now, the president of the bank does not make regular visits to the trading room. Correction: he never visits the trading room. In fact, I'd never even seen him in person before. Yet there he was, clapping the spot trader on the back, and smiling at the rest of the desk.

The queasy feeling in my stomach increased.

I walked over to my own desk and looked at the glum expressions on Peter's and Phillip's faces. Then I looked at the Reuters screen.

It was the single largest overnight move in the history of the currency markets. As a result of the G-5 initiative, the dollar had lost almost 10 percent of its value in fewer than five hours. And I'd missed it.

I sank into my chair. Peter saw the expression on my face.

"You didn't hedge anything last night?" he asked, horrified.

I shook my head in misery. I'd never seen a move of such magnitude. I hadn't thought such a move was possible. I didn't have any idea of how much we'd lost.

John chose this moment to stop by the desk.

"Isn't it terrific!" he gloated. "The spot desk was short dollars and they made a fortune overnight!"

"Wonderful," I smiled wanly.

It was difficult to hide the tremor in my voice. Even John picked it up.

"Everything's okay over here, isn't it?" he asked.

"Just fine. I mean, wonderful." I corrected myself.

"Good!" he said, relieved. "How much did you make?"

"How much did I make?" I repeated stupidly. "How much—uh—it's hard to tell exactly. You know how complicated options are."

"Are you sure you're all right?" he peered at me.

"Perfectly," I was recovering now. "You know, it was just an exciting night for me."

"Oh! Of course," he said. His attention was drifting back to the spot desk. The president of the bank was making movements as if to leave. "Well, let me know your P and L when you're sure," he shouted over his shoulder as he ran back to hold the door for the president.

As soon as he was out of earshot, I turned to Phillip and Peter.

"Input the new information into the computer and get me some updated reports right now!"

Our computer system was so slow that it took almost two hours to print out new reports. Two hours later I knew where I stood.

We'd lost the half million dollars in profit we'd been accruing for the month of September, and were now showing an additional loss of $250,000.

I decided that John did not need to know the specifics of the situation right away. If I avoided him, perhaps I could even make some of it back before he found out. As it turned out there was no need for covert maneuverings: in his joy over the spot desk's performance, John forgot all about me.

I had ten days to act before my month-end results would be available to senior management.

The first thing I noticed about the G-5 initiative was that it turned much of the trading community from snarling wolves into bleating sheep.

Options provide protection in the event of large currency moves. The more likely people consider the prospect of a significant currency move, the more expensive options become. Potential buyers compete with each other for the privilege of paying, and potential sellers, sensing danger, back away from their offers. The risk to the buyer is that he or she will end up purchasing a very expensive option only to see the market quiet down and the option expire worthless, resulting in the loss of the entire premium. The risk to the seller is that, after the option has been sold, the market will fluctuate even more wildly than before the sale, and the money earned through the sale of the premium will not make up the loss incurred trying to hedge the damn thing. The buyer acts conservatively, the seller acts aggressively, and both risk loss. The mediating factor is the price of the option. At some point the option becomes so expensive that the risk of loss flip-flops away from the seller and over to the buyer. It's like buying a house at the height of a real estate boom: you find to your chagrin that the house was not worth the money you paid for it.

All my rough-and-tumble-big-brave counterparts at the other banks saw the big overnight move and behaved precisely the way you would expect them to. They panicked.

Traders who had sold options before G-5 were desperate in their attempts to buy them all back as quickly as possible. "Mine! Mine!" they shouted into their phones, bidding up the price. Tension heightened as other members of the community took their lead. Soon everybody was buying. The price of options soared. Potential sellers became confused. If everybody was buying, what were they doing selling? Offers of "Yours! Yours!" dwindled, and were replaced by the now-frantic screams of "Mine! Mine!" as the sellers, too, rushed to turn their positions around from short to long.

I watched this process, bemused. Had everyone gone completely crazy? We'd just had the largest overnight move in recent memory, a direct result of a specific action taken on the part of the industrialized nations. The damage was done, in my opinion. Did people really expect the dollar to move like that every night? I mean, when were we all going to sleep?

In addition, every newspaper report I'd read about G-5 had emphasized that one of the key objectives of the initiative was a slow, nondisruptive but steady decline in the value of the dollar. No shocks. No roller-coaster rides. Just the gentle, wafting motion of a feather, as it drops ever so slowly to the floor.

Does that sound to you like a cause for panic?

Maybe, I thought, there's a way out of this mess after all.

▲ ▲ ▲

The very first thing I did was to sell dollars. It's not often that a trader gets the kind of broad hint on currency direction that the G-5 nations dropped that weekend. If the leaders of the industrialized world wanted to devalue the dollar, I certainly wasn't going to argue with them. As the dollar trended down, I knew this position would become profitable. The only thing I had to worry about was where we'd eventually hit bottom, but I figured that we still had a ways to go before that became an emergency.

I then turned my attention to the options market. The prices were unbelievably high! If I acted quickly, I could make back everything I'd lost and more.

I got Bob on the phone.

Bob was now working for a successful brokerage operation. We were on much better terms now that I was a customer. He even remembered my name. It didn't hurt that when he was first getting started I had helped him by giving him all of my business. At the time I had wanted a friend in the industry, and I sensed great potential in Bob. He was so clearly superior in terms of charm and intelligence that I knew he would make enormous inroads into the other brokers' territories. That meant he would get the best and most competitive prices, and I would be one of the first to see them. At least, I hoped I would be one of the first. You could never tell with Bob.

"Nancy, my dear," said Bob as soon as I got him on the phone, "how nice to hear from you. What can I do for you, my love?"

"You can get me a bid, my love," I said.

"Right!" he responded. "Be back in a jiffy."

I waited impatiently.

"The bid is 150," he came back.

Too good to be true.

"For how much?" I asked.

"Five dollars."

That's broker jargon. He meant $5 million.

"Yours for $5!" I said.

"Done."

"Who is it?" I asked.

He named a large commercial bank, a competitor of mine in the market.

"Ask them if they've more to do."

Silence while Bob consulted the other bank.

"They say nothing more at that price," he came back.

"Where's their new bid?" I asked.

"They say they can only bid 145 now," Bob replied after another brief silence.

"For how much?"

"Another $5."

"Yours again!"

"Done."

"More to do?"

"No. They hung up."

"Get me somebody else."

"The next bid is 142."

"Yours! Any more there?"

Pause.

"They say no," said Bob.

"Fine. Get someone else."

"The bid's only 140 now."

"For how much?"

"Ten dollars."

"Yours. Ten dollars done. More?"

I did this every day for a week.

The price dropped steadily. Soon the people who were holding options started to worry. Their options were losing value daily. The market was quieting down, as I had predicted. Other traders started to sell. Suddenly everybody was selling.

I decided to hold the position and milk it for everything it was worth.

"Well!" said John when he saw my September results. "I see that everything is going well for the options desk. How do things look for October?"

"October will be even better," I assured him.

"Great! Keep up the good work!"

G-5 was a turning point for the currency markets, and a turning point for my career. No one at the bank (except for Phillip and Peter, of course) ever knew what had actually happened. I got off scot-free.

In retrospect it would have been better for me if things hadn't gone so well. My impulsive reaction to the fight with Larry should have highlighted some of the more serious problems that were beginning to evolve.

The ease with which I glided through the G-5 fiasco exacerbated my worsening condition for the next few months. The only lesson that I drew from the entire experience was that I was one terrific trader.

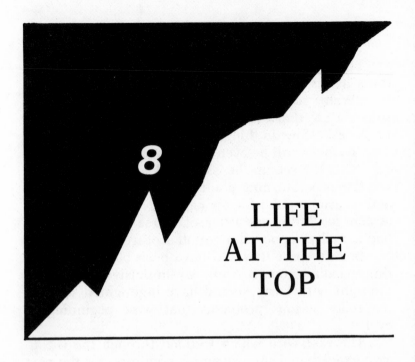

8

LIFE
AT THE
TOP

I was not alone in that opinion.

The money I had earned in the aftermath of G-5 was enough to cement my already strong position within the bank. Pleased with the undeniable success of my operation, John Anderson began to take more notice of me. Not more notice of what I was doing or how I was doing it; more notice of me, personally.

In recognition of my efforts, he showed his appreciation in the only way he knew. He rewarded me with those tributes that lay closest to his own heart.

He signed me up for meetings.

There is a very simple way to tell when you get to be a somebody at a bank. It's not by title, because titles are often misleading. In fact, most titles were invented to mislead people into believing that what they were getting was more power, more authority, more money (oh, yes, people can even be fooled into believing they are getting more money when they're not), when actually all they were getting was more title. I know of one man who was demoted three times in one year and never knew it. But I knew it because at the end of that year he had the longest and most impressive title at the bank.

You're not a somebody only if you have a great income, either. You can earn a healthy income at a bank simply by standing around doing nothing for years and years and years. In fact, this is the position that most people in banks aspire to with the greatest energy.

Importance at a bank isn't determined by seniority. Seniority works pretty much the way income does.

The way to tell if you're a somebody is not by any of these things. It's by the meetings you are invited to attend.

And so, in reward for a job well done, John began to invite me to a variety of meetings. These meetings fell into two basic categories: private meetings between John and myself, and group meetings.

On the private side were our lunch meetings. These were arranged so that John could "bring me up to date" on all of the various and sundry projects associated with his global strategy, and the management of the trading floor in general. ("Now that you are one of my managers," he told me, "I feel that we should see each other on a more regular basis.") These lunches were held upstairs in the bank's executive dining room. The bank had two dining rooms, and management was none too subtle in its distinctions.

Downstairs in the basement was the employee cafeteria, which was available to all employees of the bank but used primarily by those persons who had not yet achieved the rank of vice president. Upstairs on the fifty-first floor was the executive dining room, which was available only to people holding at least a vice presidential title. Downstairs it was dark and rather unpleasant smelling, with plastic tables and chairs crammed together for the staff. Upstairs was light and airy, with a panoramic view of lower Manhattan and carefully arranged tables draped in long white tablecloths. Downstairs you stood in line with a plastic tray, and your food was dished out by a surly individual dressed in a soiled gray uniform; upstairs you were seated by an appropriately obsequious maître d' in black tie, and served by a battery of waiters dressed in clean white uniforms.

Accordingly, one of the principal benefits associated with becoming a vice president was the ability to dine upstairs, away from the common hordes. Remember that it often took as long as ten years to achieve this title. Most people looked forward with great eagerness to the exercise of this particular privilege, having spent many years imagining the culinary delights of those who dined above. It therefore came as a disappointment to the newly promoted to discover that the two cafeterias, so different in appearance, were bound together by a common thread. The same food was served at both. Thus it was possible for a piece of meat labeled "chopped meat with gravy" downstairs to masquerade as "Salisbury Steak Supreme" on the printed menus distributed upstairs.

No one ever let on, however.

My lunches with John were conducted in the following manner. I would meet John at his office at 1:00 P.M. sharp, and we would ride the elevator together to the fifty-first floor. We would make polite conversation during these rides, being careful to discuss nothing of a sensitive nature in front of the other passengers, who might or might not be employees of the bank. This served a dual purpose: to protect the integrity of the trading floor, at the same time increasing our importance in the eyes of the other passengers, who couldn't help but notice from John's conspiratorial manner that our meaningless chatter was merely a smoke screen for more weighty topics.

After being escorted to our regular table by the maître d' ("Oh, yes, Mr. Anderson! Of course your table by the window is ready!"), we would order our lunch and get down to business.

After the obligatory discussion of the "global plan," John would turn to more pressing management issues. Today's subject was the high turnover rate that was currently decimating the trading floor. Many people were leaving the bank to go to work for the competition. The most recent blow was also the most crushing: the man in charge of the interest-rate desk, a ten-year veteran of the bank, had announced his intention to accept a similar position elsewhere.

"Why do you think everyone is leaving?" John asked, as the Consommé Brunoise was served (Vegetable Soup downstairs).

"The bank isn't paying them at a competitive rate," I replied, eyeing my bowl uneasily. You never knew what was floating around in the vegetable soup.

"But we're implementing a new bonus system," John protested.

"But no one's exactly sure how it's going to work," I observed. "You haven't named any figures yet."

"It's still with the board of directors," said John. "It's out of my hands at the moment. I've done what I could. I honestly want to keep good people working here."

"I understand your problem," I said, "but you must

understand mine as well. Options traders, for example, are greatly in demand at the moment. I must pay Peter and Phillip competitively at the end of the year or I'll lose them."

I didn't say anything about myself, but the implication was clear.

"Have they been approached by anyone?" John asked quickly.

I shrugged.

"I don't think so," I replied. "But there are lots of banks looking. Most of them are looking for head traders, but it's only a matter of time before they begin on more junior people."

"I see," he said.

The soup was removed. Golden Glow Aspic (Jell-O with Mixed Fruit) was served.

"Nancy," said John. "I've been meaning to congratulate you. Your unit is doing very well."

"Thank you," I said.

"And it appears not to be a one-shot deal," John continued. "I mean, the income flow is pretty consistent month to month."

"That's true," I said.

"How is it done?" John asked.

"Excuse me?"

"How is it that you produce a fairly constant flow of income on a monthly basis?"

Well! I thought. This is encouraging! John wants to know something about what I do.

I started to give a very simple explanation outlining the nature of options trading in a general way. Knowing that the subject was complicated, I tried only to explain the basics. John listened attentively, occasionally nodding his head. My commentary continued through the arrival of the main course, Glacé Boeuf à la Mode (Pot Roast).

"And that," I said in conclusion, "is pretty much how we do it."

John nodded again and finished swallowing a potato. He wiped his mouth with his napkin.

"That's very interesting," he said. "But I have a slightly different concept of the way it's done."

"You do?" I asked.

"Uh-huh," he said. "I figured it out for myself. Every option has a premium associated with it, correct?"

"That's correct," I said.

"So the way you make money is simply by selling all of these options and pocketing the premium. Isn't that really it?"

"No, not really . . ." I started over. I explained that sometimes we bought more options than we sold, because we expected the price of options to increase. And that even when we sold more options than we bought, we didn't just pocket the premium because we had to manage the risk of the options we'd sold and that cost money.

When I finished speaking he looked at me.

"I still say it's the premium income," he insisted.

I gave up. After all, he was the boss.

"If you say so," I said.

We decided against dessert, which was Blancmange (Tapioca Pudding), and returned to our respective posts: I to the options desk, he to his next meeting.

Then there were the group meetings. Group meetings were regularly scheduled affairs with specific names, like Strategic Planning or Policy Analysis. These meetings were generally attended by the same people and were usually chaired by John.

One of the first meetings that I was invited to was the Risk-Management meeting.

There is nothing more important to a financial institution than the management of risk. On a trading floor, where enormous sums are involved, the stakes are that much higher. In a sophisticated trading environment, the Risk-Management meeting is the place where senior management sets the parameters within which its traders must operate.

Before G-5 I had been left out of this meeting. It was a testament to my new success that I was asked, and I was aware of the honor of being admitted into its select confines.

There was one little problem. Risk-Management meetings were held every Thursday at 10:00 A.M.

In most areas of business, 10:00 A.M. is the ideal time to hold a meeting. It's early enough in the morning for everyone to still be fresh, but not so early that everyone is still asleep.

But on a trading floor, it's different. By 10:00 A.M. you are in the heat of battle. Trading is extremely active. The London, European, and New York markets are all open at that hour.

Important economic information is sometimes released at 10:00 A.M. Senior officials like the chairman of the Federal Reserve Board give speeches to members of Congress at that hour, and their remarks (accompanied by an appropriate storm of bells and whistles) are broadcast over the Reuters and Telerate machines. These remarks are dissected with surgical accuracy, then digested at light-speed by members of the trade, causing the markets to roll and pitch with each successive inference.

Corporate treasurers like to get their funding and foreign-exchange requirements accomplished at 10:00 A.M. because they know the market is liquid at that hour and they are able to get the best prices from their banks. Traders are in the act of establishing large positions at

10:00 A.M.. Literally billions of dollars trade at 10:00 A.M.

Not the best time for a meeting.

Having only just earned the right of attendance, however, I judged it best not to begin by questioning the scheduling. When the time came, I simply left the desk to Peter and Phillip and proceeded down the hall to the conference room.

Risk-Management meetings were held in a small conference room close by John's office but away from the noise and energy of the trading floor.

The conference room was a long, thin, airless room, fitted with a long, thin table, a blackboard, and a grim portrait of the chairman of the board. I was there promptly at 10:00 A.M. A handful of people were there, lounging around in their chairs or staring vacantly out of the only window. I recognized a bank economist and the credit manager responsible for the trading floor. I nodded hello and took a seat in the corner at the foot of the table.

A few more people drifted in slowly. I glanced at my watch. The meeting was already ten minutes late in starting. I couldn't resist the urge to tap my foot with impatience. I wasn't used to being away from the desk during the most active period of the morning. I didn't like leaving the desk in the hands of junior traders.

Finally John arrived, having only just come from an earlier meeting that had run over into this one.

"Everybody here?" John asked. "Good. Let's get started then."

Conspicuous by his absence was the head spot foreign-exchange trader. A fifteen-year veteran of the markets, he handled all of the bank's positions in foreign exchange (except for those I took in options). But whereas I would often try to hedge my positions, the nature of his business was to take large, outright positions. He traded successfully with hundreds of millions of dollars. His knowledge of the markets was unparalleled at the bank. His gains and losses made everyone else look as if they were playing pinochle instead of trading. How any risk-management meeting could be held without him was beyond my comprehension.

Yet clearly he had no intention of showing up. A slight feeling of uneasiness crept over me but I ignored it.

"Today's discussion focuses on the probable direction of the dollar and interest rates in the near term," said John, referring to some handwritten notes for a moment.

He began to speak on the current climate affecting the foreign-exchange market, referring often to his notes. I was impressed to see how well prepared he was. His appraisal was concise and to the point. I relaxed a little. I didn't mind being away from the market if my time was spent usefully.

I listened carefully. After all, this was my field.

He was in the middle of a careful analysis of the significance of some recent actions taken by the Federal Reserve Bank when I realized that I knew what he was going to say before he said it. His comments were based upon a column that had appeared in the previous week's *Wall Street Journal*. In fact, he seemed to have lifted whole paragraphs from the article.

I glanced furtively around the room to see if anyone else recognized the analysis. If others did, they gave no sign.

I settled back into my chair, wondering once again what was happening in the market in my absence.

"Well," said John, finishing up his remarks, "I think

I've set a context for the rest of the discussion. Does anyone else have something to add?"

"I do." It was Hal White, the economist.

John indicated that he had the floor.

"Well," said Hal importantly. "As you know, I've just returned from a high-level policy meeting in Washington. There is a great deal of sympathy for the concept of fixed exchange rates. In my opinion, exchange rates will be fixed by year end."

I sat bolt upright in my chair.

Fixed or stabilized exchange rates would radically affect the price that people would be willing to pay for foreign currency options. In fact, it could wipe out my market altogether. If what he was saying was true, and he seemed quite confident that this was indeed the case, it meant at the very least that I would have to change my current trading strategy radically, and possibly close down the currency options book altogether.

Hal was elaborating on the subject.

"It's almost a fait accompli. . . ," he was saying.

"Excuse me," I interrupted.

Everyone looked at me.

"Yes?"

"Fixing exchange rates is a pretty drastic step," I pointed out. "People have been talking about returning to a fixed exchange rate system for years, but the suggestion has not, to my knowledge, been seriously considered before this. Are you quite sure that the government has definitely decided in favor of this proposal?"

"Jack Kemp has been talking about it for some time," Hal responded.

"That's true," I agreed, "but Jack Kemp is only a congressman, and doesn't have responsibility for the decision. Was the chairman of the Federal Reserve Board at this meeting?"

"No."

"The secretary of the treasury?"

"No."

"How about the German, Japanese, or British finance ministers? Were any of them there?"

"No."

"Well," I said, "who was there?"

"Well, let me see now," said Hal. "There were several economists from the banking community, along with a smattering of academicians from some of the better schools. There were also some congressmen present. And the assistant to the under secretary of commerce dropped by."

I decided not to change my trading strategy on the basis of the assistant to the under secretary of commerce's word, and relapsed into silence.

The meeting continued.

John called on one of the traders responsible for the bank's interest-rate position.

"What is your opinion of the direction that interest rates will take?" he asked.

The interest-rate trader reported that while it was anyone's guess which way interest rates were going, he, the interest-rate trader, assumed that they would stay put if they didn't go up or down.

John then called on the gold trader to discuss possible outlooks for gold in the near term.

Although he had no firm opinion on the direction that gold would take, the gold trader was willing to venture an opinion on interest rates.

"Interest rates are going up," he said.

Here the interest-rate trader felt called upon to speak out—on the subject of gold.

"Gold is going down," he said.

The gold trader acknowledged this bit of advice by pointing out that, with all due respect, the interest-rate trader didn't know the gold market and that gold was a much more difficult instrument to predict than interest rates.

The interest-rate trader responded that, on the contrary, interest rates were much more difficult to call than gold.

The meeting continued on in this vein for the better part of an hour. It was finally ended by the necessity of John's having to attend another meeting.

It was almost noon by the time I got back to my desk. I'd missed the most active part of the day.

At about four o'clock, when trading slowed down and everyone was sitting around waiting for reports of the day's activities to be printed by the operations department, the head spot foreign-exchange trader approached me.

"Did you attend the Risk-Management meeting today?" he asked.

"Yes," I replied.

"What did they have to say?" he wanted to know.

"Not much," I answered.

"Yeah," he sighed. "That's what they always have to say. That's why I never go."

It was the end of October. I'd just had one of my best months ever.

It was late in the day. All of us were engaged in our normal postmarket activity. The gold trader was playing Yahtzee with the Canadian dollar dealer. The Bankers Acceptance dealer was in the middle of a fierce paper-airplane duel with the Fed Funds trader. And my intrepid crew, Peter and Phillip, were testing their athletic mettle at Computer Olympics. This is a computer game in which each player uses the keyboard to participate in a variety of Olympic events. For example, if Peter and Phillip were competing in the 100-yard dash, each would be assigned two keys on the keyboard and they would have to press these keys as fast as they could in order to make each of their little men on the screen (actually, it was more like each of their little dots) run. When the winning man (dot) crossed the finish line, the computer launched into a stirring rendition of the Olympic theme. Peter and Phillip took these contests very seriously.

Consequently, when the phone rang they took no notice.

"Options desk," I answered.

"May I please speak with Nancy?" asked an unfamiliar voice.

"This is she."

"Hello, Nancy. You don't know me but my name is Fred Berkstein and I work for C.W. Associates."

"C.W. Associates?" The name sounded vaguely familiar.

"We are an executive-recruitment firm."

Translation: headhunters.

"What can I do for you, Fred?" I asked.

"Nancy, believe me, it's not what you can do for me. It's what I can do for you," said Fred. "We're not just any executive-recruitment firm. We're the best in our business. And our business is you."

"Right."

"People are our business. We're not in this for ourselves. We're in this for people."

"Right."

"You, Nancy," said Fred, "are our kind of person."

This guy's in the wrong business, I thought. He should be selling used cars.

"Yes?" I prompted.

"Nancy, have I got a job for you!"

"You have?"

"Yes, I have. Do you want me to tell you all about it?"

"No."

"It's a great . . ." Fred continued, then stopped. "No?" he asked incredulously.

"That's right. No."

"But why not?"

"Because I'm quite happy where I am, thank you."

"But this is a wonderful opportunity. . . . Just let me tell you about it. . . . It's at another major commercial bank . . . you'd be running the whole show. . . ."

"I run the show here," I pointed out.

"I know you do, but this is even more visibility, more challenge . . . this bank has had a high turnover in options traders and this time they are really committed to doing the job right . . . ," Fred hurried on.

Of course I knew which bank it was. Everybody in the industry knew which banks were looking for options traders.

"The base salary's going to be $100,000 . . . ," Fred continued.

"That's not enough," I said. "I make that now." (Small lie.)

"It's negotiable, everything's negotiable. The bonus will be up to 100 percent of your salary . . ."

"That's not enough," I said. "I make that now. More than that." (Another small lie.)

"Like I said, everything's negotiable. They may be willing to pay anything you want. Why don't you just let me make you an appointment? . . ."

"I'll tell you what," I said, to get him off the phone, "I'll consider it and let you know."

"All right," said Fred, accepting the compromise, "I'll call you again tomorrow."

"You needn't bother—" I began, but he was already gone.

I hung up to the rousing strains of the Olympic March.

C.W. Associates, I mused. Now where have I heard that name before?

Then I remembered.

While I was still a loan officer, but wanted to move into trading, I'd thought to approach a headhunter to see if there were any jobs available in the field. Larry had done business with a number of these firms and suggested I talk to David Silverman at C.W.

I'd called up and spoken to David. I gave him my credentials, and told him a little bit about what I wanted to do. He suggested that I come in and see him at his office.

I went to C.W. Associates' offices, bringing along a copy of my résumé. David looked it over as I sat beside him in his office.

"Let's see," he said, reading aloud. "Bachelor's and master's degrees from two excellent Ivy League schools. That's good."

He sounded encouraging. I relaxed a little.

"Went into commercial banking immediately upon graduation. Passed the bank's MBA training program. That's good."

I relaxed a little more.

"Assigned to the commodity lending department. That's good!" He looked up and smiled at me.

I smiled back.

"Nancy," said David. "I think we're in business."

"That's great!" I said. "Do you have any positions available right now?"

"I sure do. With your experience, I have some terrific positions available in the lending areas of a number of commercial banks."

"But, David," I said. "You don't understand. I told you on the phone that I don't want to go to the lending area of another commercial bank. Of course I've got experience! I've been in lending for three years! That's why I want to get out!"

"You want to get out of the lending business?" David asked. "But everything on your résumé points to commercial banking."

"Of course it does!" I said. "I've only been working for three years. Commercial banking was just the first thing I did, before I knew better. Now I want to get into something else."

"Like what?" David asked.

"Like trading," I said.

David laughed.

"You must be dreaming," he said.

I looked at him.

"Nancy," said David. "Let me explain the facts to you. You've been in commercial banking for three years now, right?"

"Right," I said, glad to see we'd made headway on that point.

"By staying in commercial banking for three years you have labeled yourself a commercial banker for life. No trading department is going to pick you up."

"Really?" I asked.

"Really. I'll tell you something else. I've been in this business a long time."

By which I assumed he meant three years.

"I know people," David continued. "I can look at you and see that you couldn't do the work of a trader. I wouldn't even send you up for the interview, you understand? Stick with what you got, kid. Why don't you let me place you at another bank for, say, a 15 percent increase? If you don't like it I can place you again in another six months."

"No, thank you," I said. "I don't need you to place me at another job just like the one I have already. I guess I'll just look around on my own."

"Suit yourself," said David, shrugging. "But you can take my advice and save your energy. You'll never be a trader."

▲ ▲ ▲

Fred called me every day for a week.

"Come on," he urged. "I hear you are one of the best traders on the Street. What harm can there be in just going and checking it out?"

I went home and asked Larry what harm there could be in just going and checking it out.

"None that I can see," said Larry.

"But what if someone at the bank finds out?" I asked.

"So much the better, really. The bank is more likely to place a higher value on you if they think you're wanted elsewhere. It might even help you with your upcoming bonus negotiations if they think you've received a competing offer. Also, it never hurts to see what you are worth in the open market."

I arranged for an appointment with the other bank.

The day of the interview arrived.

I was in a very good mood. Everything seemed to be going so well that I went into the cosmetics store across the street from the bank and bought myself $100 worth of the best makeup as a treat for myself. (One hundred dollars' worth of the best makeup buys you one mascara, one lipstick, some face powder and a little eyeshadow. A very little eyeshadow.)

Slightly startled by the meager purchasing power of $100 in what most people would classify as a drugstore, I struck off for the interview, carrying my very expensive cosmetics in a very inexpensive brown paper bag.

Fred had told me to report to the ninth floor. I'd made only one request when we made the arrangements.

"Listen, Fred," I'd said, "since I'm only going to the bank to listen and am not really interested in the position, I don't think it's necessary that I go through the personnel office. Just have me speak with whoever is in charge. There's no need to get Personnel involved until we are close to a deal, and we are certainly not close to a deal at the moment."

I lived in dread of personnel offices. They perform no real function and are notorious for all kinds of bureaucratic nonsense. I wanted to get the interview over quickly and not waste anyone's time (particularly mine) in the process.

"Fine. No problem," said Fred.

I got off the elevator at the ninth floor.

It was the personnel office.

I tried to make the best of the situation. I went up to the receptionist and gave her my name.

"Yes, you are expected," said the receptionist. "Please fill out this form."

I looked at the form. It filled two sides, single-spaced, of a sheet of legal-size paper. It asked for all kinds of interesting information, including the color of my eyes, which I was not aware was a component of the job description. It also asked for my last five places of employment, including summer jobs held during high school, and for the names, addresses, and telephone numbers of my immediate superiors at each of those positions.

Aside from the fact that it was not common practice for me to carry around the addresses and telephone numbers of my previous employers, I objected to filling out the form. As I didn't really want the job, and didn't expect to take the job, and was only there to discuss the position because I'd been talked into it by a headhunter, I didn't expect that the bank would ever need a record of the color of my eyes.

Accordingly, I handed the form back to the receptionist, politely responding that I had no intention whatsoever of filling out the form.

Apparently, no one had ever refused to fill out the

form before. I could see that I was shaking the receptionist's belief in the system as a whole.

"But you must fill out the form," she said. "It's procedure!"

"I don't care what it is," I responded. "I'm not filling out the form."

The receptionist decided that it was time to call in the big guns, in the form of her boss, an overweight man in his mid-thirties.

"What's the problem?" he asked abruptly.

The receptionist explained that I had refused to fill out the form.

"Oh!" said her boss. Evidently deciding that the misunderstanding must be due to physical infirmity on my part, he turned to me and spoke very slowly, enunciating clearly.

"You-have-to-fill-out-this-form," he said.

I looked at him.

"I'm-not-going-to-fill-out-that-form," I said.

"You- have- to- fill- out- the- form- to- get- the- job," he said.

"If-I-take-the-job-then-I'll-fill-out-the-form," I said.

This threw him so much that he forgot to enunciate.

"But that's not standard procedure!" he said.

"I don't care," I said.

He glowered at me.

"I have to check it out with the person in charge," he said.

"Do so," I said.

He got on the telephone. When he got off, he turned to me.

"Okay, you can go to the interview without filling out the form first," he said. "The interview is upstairs on the thirtieth floor."

"Thank you," I said.

I turned toward the elevators.

"Don't forget!" he cried as I stepped into the elevator. "If-you-get-the-job-you-have-to-fill-out-the—"

The elevator closed on his last words.

I got off the elevator on the thirtieth floor. A woman in a dark suit and bow tie was waiting for me.

"Nancy?" she asked.

"Yes?"

"My name is Jane. Please follow me."

I followed her. Along the way I stopped her to ask a question.

"Jane?"

"Yes?"

"The headhunter . . . er . . . executive recruiter neglected to mention the name of the person I'm to be meeting. What is his name, please?"

"Her name is Kathy Arnold."

This took me aback.

"And what is Kathy Arnold's position?" I asked.

"She is administrative head of the trading department," Jane replied.

John Anderson's position!

Just as there are very few women who run their own trading desks, so are there equally few women administrators in the field. In fact, Kathy was the first one I'd ever heard of.

I began to look forward to the meeting.

Jane ushered me into a small office at the far end of the bank's trading floor. A brunette woman wearing a dark suit and white shirt (but no bow tie) held out her hand to me.

"Nancy? I'm pleased to meet you. I'm Kathy Arnold."

Her grip was as strong as any man's.

I took a quick glance at Kathy. She was a woman

of medium weight, which is to say that although she didn't strike me as heavy, she didn't strike me as thin either. What she did strike me as was the kind of girl who played field hockey in school. She was reasonably attractive, with regular features.

"I'm very glad to meet you," I said.

"Sit down," said Kathy, "and we'll begin."

I took a seat across from her. Jane sat down in a chair by the door, pen and notebook in hand.

"Tell me about yourself, Nancy," said Kathy.

"What do you want to know?"

"Why don't you begin with how long you've been trading and what made you go into trading in the first place?" she suggested.

I gave her the short version of my rags-to-riches tale. Periodically she would nod in Jane's direction and Jane would take notes of whatever it was I was saying.

"Very interesting," she said when I'd finished. "And how do you trade now?"

I explained a little about the way I traded.

"*Volatility* trading, is it?" she said, picking up on one of the words I'd used. "Yes, all you volatility traders are in vogue right now." She said it as though I were the result of someone's fashion sense.

"Now for the important questions," she said, leaning forward in her chair.

"Yes?" I replied, leaning forward in mine.

"Do you have any brothers or sisters?" she asked.

I was unprepared for the question. It took me a moment to remember that I did, in fact, have a brother, and I said so.

"Aha!" she said. "An older brother or a younger brother?"

"A younger brother," I said, slightly puzzled.

"No sisters?"

"No sisters."

"That makes you the oldest child," she said.

Upon reflection I agreed that that did seem to sum up the case pretty well.

Kathy nodded approvingly. Jane wrote.

"Very good!" said Kathy. "And where are your parents?"

"In Chicago," I said.

"Are they both alive?"

"They are," I said.

"And you left them in Chicago?" asked Kathy.

"Uh, yes," I replied, slightly confused by this line of questioning.

"Very good again!" said Kathy, smiling at me. "Eldest child, a woman, leaves home, strikes out independently! Exactly the pattern I was looking for!"

I took this to mean that she was satisfied with my credentials.

"Now," said Kathy. "Before we go any further, do you have any questions?"

Well, yes, I had a few. Could she describe the job?

"Oh, yes," said Kathy. "Well, as you probably know, we've had a number of options traders here in the past, and they've all left for one reason or another. We want our bank to become a force in the options market and we're willing to devote the resources necessary to do the job."

Really? Such as?

"Well, we were thinking of hiring someone like you, and a junior trader of your choice."

What about the back office?

"Well," said Kathy, hesitating for the first time, "the back office does need a little work. We'd expect you to take care of that."

How is your back office currently accounting for the bank's options portfolio?

141

"Well," said Kathy, looking more and more uncomfortable, "they're . . . not."

Should I take that to mean that I would have to install a fully functioning accounting system?

"Well," said Kathy slowly. "You don't have to, but I'd imagine it would be difficult to work without one."

Translation: Yes.

What about credit lines? Would I be able to trade size with all the other banks if I wanted to?

"Well," said Kathy, "credit lines have always been a problem at this bank. If you wanted to trade options with another bank, you would have to get approval from the credit department."

And how long does that take?

"Approximately six months," said Kathy. "Per bank."

Since the bank is committed to becoming a force in the market, couldn't the process be speeded up a little?

"Unfortunately not," said Kathy. "It's against bank procedure."

So I would be walking into a position where there is no back office and no credit lines available to trade under.

"That's right," said Kathy, nodding.

Jane wrote.

"But do let me point out the advantages of the position," said Kathy.

Please do.

"It's a position of high visibility within the bank," said Kathy. "Very prestigious. You'll get to go to all sorts of high-level meetings!

"Nancy," said Kathy, "I'm going to be honest with you. I like you. I like your background. I think you're perfect for the job."

"Thank you," I said.

"Let's talk about salary and bonus," said Kathy.

I knew I was in trouble.

To walk into another bank with no back office and no credit lines meant that I would have to spend a minimum of six months working just to establish the unit, with no real trading income to speak of. As bonus is usually related to trading income, that meant I would have only six months of trading income to show for my first year at the job. To say nothing of the fact that I would be leaving a fully functioning options unit in order to work under conditions that were at least as bad as (if not worse than) those I had started out with originally.

In other words, I didn't want the job. I prayed she wouldn't offer me so much money that I would be tempted to take it.

"What are you offering?" I asked.

"We are offering $120,000 plus bonus," said Kathy. "Bonus would be up to 100 percent of your salary, depending on performance."

I breathed a sigh of relief.

"That's not enough," I said, gathering up my makeup and my coat.

Kathy stopped me.

"What would be enough?" she asked.

"What?" I asked.

"I said, what would be enough?" she repeated. "I'd really like to have you. What kind of money were you looking for?"

"What I want doesn't matter," I said, "It's what you are offering that counts. Are you improving your offer?"

"Just tell me what you want," she pressed.

I made some rapid calculations. I really didn't want the job. Also, I'm a trader. I wanted to make sure I wasn't going to ask for anything less than what she was willing to pay. I came to a figure. But what if I named an amount and she agreed? What was I going to do then?

I made my decision.

"I wouldn't do it for less than a quarter of a million dollars," I said. Then, seeing her face, I added "plus bonus," just for safety's sake.

"I see," said Kathy, nodding her head.

Jane wrote.

"Well, Nancy—" said Kathy, standing up and holding out her hand.

I held my breath.

"—while the bank is committed to becoming a force in the options market, it is not committed to that extent. It was nice to meet you."

"My pleasure," I said, shaking her hand and escaping out the door.

Who would ever have imagined that I'd be so relieved at not being offered a job that paid somewhere between $120,000 plus bonus and $250,000 plus bonus? I thought. Oh, well, that's life at the top, I guess.

How would I ever explain this to my father?

9

THE HEIGHT OF POWER

John Anderson stopped by the desk.

"I have something important to discuss with you," he said. "Can you come by my office around four o'clock today?"

"Certainly," I replied.

"Good. See you then," he said, abruptly turning his back and walking away.

I stared after him. He was visibly upset. This was highly unusual. He rarely lost his equilibrium. What could it be?

Had he heard about my interview at the other bank? Impossible. Besides, I'd turned that job down. Was somebody else leaving the trading floor? The only person left of any importance was Andy, the head spot trader. I looked over at Andy. He was standing at his desk, screaming into two telephones at once, happy as a clam.

No, that wasn't it.

Perhaps the board of directors had turned down the bonus requests? This was likely, but it wasn't the kind of thing that would upset John in this way. After all, it wasn't John's compensation that was affected by the bonus negotiations; it was just his staff's.

No, I decided, no way to guess. Have to wait for four o'clock to find out.

John's office door was closed when I arrived promptly at four. I knocked.

"Come in," came John's voice from inside.

I opened the door and went in. My eyes widened with surprise.

John was sitting at his desk, waist-deep in papers. The normally neat and uncluttered office was littered with documents and files.

"Have a seat," said John, flinging an arm in the direction where the table and chairs had once been.

I followed his signal to an unusually high stack of papers and notebooks and started digging. Sure enough, the initial search revealed the presence of a chair somewhere beneath the piles. I redoubled my efforts and eventually cleared off enough space to be able to sit precariously on the end of the seat.

"Sorry about that," John said glumly.

I looked over at John. There was clearly something wrong. For one thing, his hair was slightly disheveled. Not the "casually tousled" style he usually sported. No, this was definite muss, as though he'd actually run his fingers through it before he'd remembered not to. Another surprise: he wasn't wearing his jacket. In fact, I couldn't even find his jacket. Also, he had actually loosened his tie. He was the very picture of the careworn executive.

Totally out of character. Something was terribly amiss. I almost felt sorry for him.

"What is it you wanted to see me about?" I asked.

He turned to me.

"It's London," he said, his voice trembling with rage.

"London?"

"London," he confirmed. He could barely speak.

I was having trouble understanding him. Surely he wasn't upset with the city as a whole.

"Can you be more specific?" I asked.

John started to explain.

Our bank was owned by a large foreign bank that had offices all over the world. It was so large it actually had three offices of its own in London. As our bank also had an office in London, that meant that there were four representatives of the same organization in that city.

This would have been all right if each of those offices had had its own specialized function. For example, one office could have lent funds for the development of real estate, another could have financed the import-export business, a third could have handled trading, and so on. In this way, each branch would have its particular expertise and all the offices would have flourished.

But our parent bank, it appeared, believed in a decentralized environment. So each of the offices operated as a separate little bank, trying to handle every type of banking function. The result was that no office was able to establish an expertise in any one area. They were much too busy competing with each other for the same business.

Our parent bank had no real expertise anywhere in trading. Up until now, our bank had been the recognized source of all market knowledge and initiatives. It was very much a feather in John's cap, for instance, that I ran the only options unit in the whole organization.

But now it appeared that one of our parent bank's London offices wanted to compete with us by trading options.

"They want to trade options?" I asked, surprised. Options are very complicated financial instruments. They aren't usually the first choice for a beginner.

John nodded.

"Well," I said. "Why don't they send somebody over here for six months or so and I'll train them to trade options and then they can handle all the options business for us out of London?"

"They don't want to do that," said John.

"Well," I said, "what do they want to do?"

"They want to give all the business to an outside trading organization."

"Why would they want to do that?" I asked. "They are just giving away income that would go to the organization as a whole."

"They don't want to give us the business," said John. "That would make us more important than them."

"Of all the ridiculous . . ." I didn't know what to say.

"I know," said John, shaking his head in misery. "And the worst part is—do you know what this does to my 'global plan'?"

"You're sure they won't cooperate with us?" I asked.

"I'm positive," said John. "They already paid the outside trading organization something like $250,000 for an options accounting system."

"You're kidding," I said. "But they could have had mine for free! All they had to do was ask me! And mine is just the kind of system they need to start an operation!"

I eyed John with new respect. And I thought senior

management at our bank was bad! The parent bank's management was beginning to make our management look like the three wise men.

"What are we going to do?" John asked.

I was angry, too. I didn't like the London office's approach. Incompetence on that level bothers me. Also, I didn't like having my turf invaded like that.

"When are they scheduled to begin trading?" I asked John.

"Sometime after the first of the year," he replied.

I made my decision.

"If it's competition they want, it's competition they'll get," I said grimly.

"What do you mean?" John asked.

"I mean we're going to open up an options trading desk in London, too."

John perked up.

"Nancy, I like your thinking," he said. "Can it be done?"

Can it be done? Hadn't I learned to manage a billion-dollar options portfolio while on the job? Hadn't I put together a terrific team in New York? Hadn't I traded brilliantly through G-5?

"Of course it can be done," I assured him.

He stood up and shook my hand.

"I'm glad you're on my team," he said.

"Thank you," I said.

I turned to go.

"By the way," he asked. "How quickly can you get it set up?"

"What choice do we have?" I asked. "I'll have it open by the first of the year."

It was November 15.

On the way back to my desk I thought about it. The thing about a London desk was that, clearly, somebody had to go there and run it. Later on, additional traders could be hired, but to begin with someone would have to go.

Who was that someone going to be?

Well, there were only three of us to choose from. It shouldn't be that difficult to decide.

I ruled out Phillip immediately. I wasn't sure Phillip could find London.

That narrowed the choice to Peter or me.

Whoever went might have to go for an indefinite period of time, perhaps as long as six months or a year. I was married, Peter was single. (I could just imagine Larry's reaction to my going abroad for six months without him. I could take him with me, of course, but then there was the problem of finding him something to do. I wasn't up to that kind of challenge.) Besides, as I pictured it, the London office would take most of its instructions from New York. The head trader had to be in New York. That narrowed the choice to just Peter. Peter it was.

Good, I thought. That's decided. Of course, sending Peter might be a little inconvenient. That would leave me alone with Phillip, and Peter alone in London. It's difficult to trade with just two people and impossible to trade alone.

Well, I thought, there's a very simple solution to all of this. I will simply hire a new trader in New York, train him or her before Peter leaves, and instruct Peter to hire someone immediately upon arriving in London.

No problem.

I held a short staff meeting when I got back to the desk. I told Peter and Phillip about the parent bank's London office. They were both indignant. I informed them of my decision to open an options desk in London. They applauded. I asked Peter if he would be willing to go to London for a few months to start up the operation. He was enthusiastic.

(Actually, Peter had an English girlfriend whose visa was up and who was going to have to return to London shortly anyway. So it wasn't an entirely altruistic decision on his part.)

I told them we'd have to have the whole thing up and running by the first of the year in order to beat the competition.

No problem, they said.

I went home that night and told Larry. He listened carefully until I'd finished explaining. Then he spoke.

"Are you crazy?" he asked.

"How difficult can it be? I just scoot Peter over there, get our name established in the London market, hire a few new traders, and presto! a London office."

"Why don't you open up in Timbuktu as long as you're at it?" Larry commented.

"Maybe I will," I returned.

"How do you intend to control your London operation?"

"Control?" I asked.

"Yes. How do you intend to keep from overtrading? How will you manage two positions? How will you get information back and forth between the two offices?"

"The operations department will have to come up with something, I suppose," I answered. "They must have the capability to communicate between the two offices by some sort of on-line computer system."

"I'd check that out if I were you," said Larry.

"Don't worry about it," I said. "That won't be a problem."

"Well, assuming that that is no problem, how do you intend to trade?"

151

"What do you mean?"

"I mean, how do you intend to staff your unit?"

"I told you," I said. "I'm going to hire someone in New York right away and train him before Peter leaves."

"Someone with experience, I hope," Larry said.

I thought about everyone I knew with experience. Most of them weren't worth hiring. The ones that were made more money than I did.

"No," I decided. "I'm going to hire someone with little or no experience. That's the best way."

"And train him in less than a month?"

"Of course," I said. "Why, anyone can trade options."

"Of course!" said Larry. "I forgot that!"

I ignored the sarcasm.

"I'm not kidding. Nancy! Have you thought about the kind of commitment involved in expanding along these lines? You'll have to trade for two operations; you know you'll be helping Peter trade while London is open. You'll have to train new people. You'll have to supervise the installation of communications equipment."

He paused for breath.

"By my calculations, it will take at least three of you to do the job."

Larry's words notwithstanding, I continued with my plans for expansion. The first thing to do was to hire someone in New York.

This was not as easy to do as I had first imagined.

As soon as word got out that the Options Unit was expanding into London and that there were positions in New York opening up as a result, I suddenly became everybody's best friend.

Thoughtful people from all over the bank took time out of their busy schedules to stop by my desk and congratulate me on how well I was doing and to impart to me the interesting information that they'd wanted to be an options trader since the fifth grade. Women would stop me in front of the mirror in the ladies' room to compliment me on my choice of lipstick, and before I knew it these tête-à-têtes would turn into hard-sell job applications. It got so that I couldn't walk into an elevator without being flattered or fawned over by some devoted acquaintance, and then pitched to with the practiced adroitness of a theatrical agent.

Unfortunately, none of my newfound admirers met any of the qualifications of the job. I was forced to look outside the bank for a suitable applicant (to the intense displeasure of all my new friends who promptly reverted to their old attitude of haughty disdain).

Two people were immediately recommended.

The head spot trader referred me to an intelligent young woman who was currently working for a computer company. I interviewed her twice and was sorely tempted to hire her. She was obviously diligent and industrious. Unfortunately, she hadn't the vaguest idea what an option was, or what trading was all about. There was no telling how quickly she'd catch on, or if trading was even the right place for her. Although I was convinced that I could "teach anyone" to trade options, the prospect of training someone who lacked even a rudimentary knowledge of the marketplace daunted even me.

I turned down her application.

At John Anderson's insistence I interviewed a man in his late thirties who held a Ph.D. in something or other. Market knowledge was not a problem here. This man had plenty of experience with options, having just lost a significant sum of money trading them for his own account. Actually, losing money is not, in itself, a reason for turning down someone's application. Every trader loses money at one point or another. But this man had picked up a lot of bad habits in his trading that would be hard to break him of. He thought he was a great trader and blamed everything on the market. It was easy to see why he'd lost money. I wanted someone with rather more experience than the head spot trader's choice and rather less experience (or at least a better quality of experience) than this man. Besides his questionable attitudes, there would be the additional problem of having the junior trader on the desk (him) being a good ten years older than the senior trader on the desk (me).

I turned down his application.

Having interviewed all of two people, my patience was wearing thin. There was also the pressure of time running out. Thanksgiving was just around the corner. I was ready to hire the next person who walked through the door.

The next person to walk through the door was a handsome blond man in his early twenties who had just graduated from the University of California at Berkeley. His name was Randy Miller.

On the surface Randy's credentials were excellent. He'd graduated the spring before and had gone to work for a small California investment bank for the summer. This meant that he was familiar with the way the markets worked. And, wonder of wonders, he'd written his senior thesis on options! Perfect. Now he was looking for a job in New York. This was where it was at, he drawled.

I arranged for a series of interviews.

Randy arrived at 5:00 P.M., after the market had closed. I sent him off with Peter and Phillip for the next round of interviews. When they had finished, I sat down with him myself.

I asked Randy a number of questions about options. He had all the right answers. Although his knowledge was limited, he appeared to be on the right track. I was encouraged.

He was enthusiastic about the position, yet I felt a certain spark was missing from his manner. Nonsense! I chided myself. That's just the way they talk on the West Coast. You'd better watch yourself. You're turning into an Eastern snob.

I sent Randy on to interview with John Anderson. While he was gone I talked to Peter and Phillip about him.

We all agreed that he seemed like a nice guy, and had a basic knowledge of the business. They, too, found him lacking in energy, but were willing to discount the feeling.

"Well," I said, finally. "What do you think? Should we hire him?"

"He seems all right," said Phillip.

"It's so hard to tell after just one interview," said Peter.

"Look, guys," I said. "I've got to make a decision. Peter's leaving in one month. This guy seems okay. Unless one of you has an objection to him, I think we should take him."

The truth was that I was bored with the whole interview process. Besides, I was sure that I could fix whatever was wrong with him. More evidence of trader head. I was deep in the throes of the disease. Perhaps it was all the attention. Perhaps it was all the meetings.

John came out of his office after Randy had left.

"What did you think of him?" I asked.

"On a scale of one to ten," said John, "I'd say he's about a five. He didn't impress me very much. He actually seemed kind of slow."

I explained about the California mentality.

"I don't know," said John.

What does John know? I thought. He'd sent me a university professor with a midlife crisis.

"Look," I said. "I'm not looking for a rocket scientist. I'm looking for a junior trader. This guy knows enough about the business already that he should be able to pick it up pretty easily. We have to get somebody quickly, you know. The first of the year will be here before you know it."

"Well," said John, "it's your decision."

I hired Randy on the condition that he start work right after Thanksgiving. He accepted.

We were on our way to London.

November turned out to be significantly less profitable than any of the preceding months. We made less than $100,000. I blamed the reduced income on a slow market and on all the time I'd had to spend interviewing people and planning for the London office.

John stopped by the desk a few days after I had hired Randy. He motioned me away from the others.

"Great news," he said. "The board of directors has approved the bonus plan."

"That's terrific!" I said.

"Why don't you stop by my office later this week and we'll discuss some of the specifics," said John.

"Fine," I said, returning to my work.

Larry and I had talked of little else but my bonus for weeks.

"How much do you think you'll get?" Larry asked every other night.

"I don't know," I replied, never tired of discussing the subject.

"You must have some idea," said Larry.

"It's so hard to say," I said. "The bank has never really paid bonuses before."

"That's why they're losing everybody," said Larry. "They have to begin to pay competitively."

"Yes," I said. "I know that, and you know that, but the question is, Do *they* know that?

"I think you should prepare for your bonus negotiations," Larry said.

"Prepare? What do you mean?"

"Well, what are you going to say to John? Suppose they only give you a bonus of $10,000. Will you stay working for the bank for that?"

"They wouldn't!" I said, shocked. "All the work I've put in! All the money I've made for them!"

"I didn't say they were going to. But what if? It is a possibility, you know."

"What would I do?" I said hotly. "I'd quite on the spot, that's what I'd do. Let John or the board of directors run the portfolio if they think it's so easy."

"Calm down," said Larry. "I'm just asking. You see my point? You should go into any negotiation knowing your price in advance. Not only does it save a lot of time, but it will help you to bargain more effectively."

But I was still mumbling to myself.

"Ten thousand dollars, indeed! Let them do it if they think it's so easy!"

"Nancy," Larry said, "Stop dwelling on the $10,000. I just used it as an example. Much more likely would be, say, $30,000. How would you feel about $30,000?"

I thought about it.

Thirty thousand dollars was more money in one lump sum than I'd ever been paid before in my life. Nine months ago, $30,000 would have been a sheer impossibility. I would have laughed if anyone would have suggested it to me.

But I'd just turned down a job at another bank for a salary of $120,000 and a bonus of up to 100 percent of that amount. Thirty thousand dollars didn't seem like such a big deal in the light of that offer. And there were plenty of other banks still looking for head options traders.

"For $30,000," I said, "I'd leave. I wouldn't quit on the spot, but I'd leave. I'd start interviewing immediately."

"Okay," said Larry. "You'd quit on the spot if it's $10,000, and you'd leave at your leisure if it's $30,000. What amount would you be satisfied with? What amount would you stay for?"

I thought again.

I didn't really want to go to another bank. I loved working with Peter and Phillip. They were my friends. We had a good time together. If I left, there was no telling who I would have to work with.

"I'd be satisfied with $50,000," I said, finally. "I think I deserve more, but I'd stay for $50,000."

"That's what I was thinking," said my spouse.

"I deserve more," I pointed out. "They should pay me more."

"I agree," said Larry, "but what you deserve has nothing to do with it. This bank has not paid substantial bonuses in the past. This is entirely new for them. If you get $50,000 you'll be fine."

I was forced to agree with him.

"Now," said Larry. "Let's talk about attitude."

"Attitude?"

"Yes," he said firmly. "Before every big game the coach always lectures about attitude."

"Big game?"

"In the first place," said Larry, ignoring my questions, "no matter what number he gives you, you will not quit on the spot."

"But, Larry . . ."

"You will not quit on the spot, do you hear me? It doesn't do you any good. The object is not to ride off into the sunset like Clark Gable."

"Gary Cooper."

"Whoever. The object is to get the money. You have

to set the tone of the negotiations," he continued. "If he gives you an unreasonably small number, you might want to tell him that the number is so much below what you consider to be fair that you are unprepared to discuss it at the present time, and ask to reschedule the meeting."

"Why would I want to reschedule? I'd rather get it over with in one sitting."

"Because the second you leave, he'll assume that you intend to look for another job, and he knows you'll get it."

"So you think he'll increase the offer at the second meeting?"

"If he can, he will."

"Why doesn't he just give me a fair number to start with?"

"Because he has to try to get away with anything he can. He's trying to keep *his* P and L for the bank showing a profit too, you know."

"That's true."

"On the other hand, if he gives you $50,000 to start with, you probably shouldn't act too pleased."

"Why not?"

"Because if he thinks you're unhappy with that number he might make some other concessions. I don't think he'll give you more money, but he might give you some other form of recognition."

"I don't know," I said. "There are only so many meetings one can attend in a day."

"You know what I mean. All I'm trying to say is, play to win. You're in an excellent negotiating position. You've done a fantastic job."

"Yeah!" I said.

"They don't want to lose you. You are more likely to walk away from the table than they are."

"Right!" I said.

"People spend their lives dreaming about holding the kind of cards you're holding."

"Yeah!" I said.

"So go out there and win, win, win!"

I went to John's office to discuss the details of the bonus plan. His door was closed when I got there. I took several deep breaths before knocking. This was it!

"Come in," John said in response to my rap.

I went into the office.

Both John and his office had returned to their normal state. The office was neat and uncluttered. So was John. He seemed perfectly in control.

"Have a seat," he said, gesturing to the now-visible table and chairs.

I sat down. He came and sat next to me. He had a folder in his hands. Inside the folder were some papers with numbers on them.

"Nancy," said John, "I can't tell you how pleased I am that this bonus package went through. I knew we were going to have to start paying people competitively, and I pushed for it."

I thanked him for his efforts.

"Now," said John, opening the folder, "let me explain how the bonus package works."

I drew closer to him.

"It's based on a percentage of what you earn," he said. "Your section gets about 15 percent of your bottom line."

I made a rapid calculation in my head. My section had earned $1.8 million before expenses in the last six months. Of course, this did not include the half-million-dollar loss left by my predecessors. My direct expenses, except for brokerage, were about $150,000. Brokerage was another $250,000. That left me with $1.4 million. Fifteen percent of $1.4 million was $210,000!

I couldn't help smiling.

"Now," John was continuing, "for your section, we have the income you earned for the year. That's $1.3 million less expenses."

So he was going to subtract the initial loss. I did another quick calculation: $1.3 million less about $400,000 in expenses was $900,000; 15 percent of $900,000 was still $135,000.

"Your direct expenses for the year came to about $400,000," said John.

"That's correct," I said.

"Now, your indirect expenses came to—"

"My indirect expenses?" I asked.

"Of course. Your bottom-line percentage comes after indirect expenses. That's what bottom line means."

I still wasn't worried. I mean, how much indirect expense could a three-person section have incurred?

"How do you calculate indirect expense?" I asked.

"It's done as a percentage of the indirect expense allocated to the whole floor."

"And how much is that?" I asked.

"Twelve million dollars," he said.

"Twelve million dollars?" I repeated. "Twelve million dollars? Why, that's absurd! How could the trading floor have spent $12 million in indirect expense?"

"Easy," said John, smiling at my naïveté. "This floor makes a lot of money. We have to help pay for everything at the bank from the library to the president's limousine."

I wasn't sure, but I didn't think it was right that the president's car should get a part of my bonus. I didn't remember the automobile having contributed much to the formation of key trading decisions.

"And how much of the $12 million will be allocated to my section?" I asked.

"About $750,000," he said.

▲ ▲ ▲

"Three quarters of a million dollars in indirect expenses?" exclaimed Larry later that evening when I had finished explaining about the bonus plan. "Three quarters of a million dollars for a three-person unit? What did you guys have for lunch every day? Caviar?"

I explained about the president's limousine.

"Nancy," said Larry, "$900,000 less $750,000 leaves $150,000. Fifteen percent of $150,000 is $22,500. Are you telling me that you are expected to pay your entire unit out of that stock? Why, you have to pay Phillip and Peter at least $10,000 apiece just to keep them."

"More," I said miserably.

"Well, you can't pay them more unless you want to go without entirely. As it is, you'd be paying each of them $10,000 and you'd be left with $2,500."

"I know," I said. "It's even worse than I expected. What should I do?"

"Don't spend it all in one place," Larry suggested.

"How can you joke about it?" I asked.

"Because it's just too ridiculous for words. You have only one choice."

"What's that?"

"Throw away the formula completely and go in there and tell him what you want."

I knocked on John's door again.

"Come in," he said.

"I'd like to discuss the bonus plan again," I said.

"Something wrong?" asked John.

"Nothing's wrong exactly," I said uneasily. I was nervous. "It's just that I'd like to say something."

"Yes?"

"About the indirect expenses . . . they seem rather high . . ."

"Well," said John. "I'll tell you what. Why don't

162

we sit down and go over your bonus recommendations for your people?"

"That would be fine," I said, relieved.

"What do you suggest we give to Peter and Phillip?" John asked, pencil in hand.

"Well, you know, John," I said, "Peter and Phillip have worked very hard this year."

"I know that."

"And they've done very well. They are intelligent, diligent individuals. They are assets to the organization."

"That's right," said John.

"I really think we should try to keep them. I've told you that options traders are greatly in demand."

"And I've told you that I intend to keep them," said John. "So what is your recommendation?"

I made my recommendation. He wrote down the number. He didn't even blink.

"Do you agree?" I asked, cautiously.

"I expected something like this," he said.

"What about the indirect expenses?" I asked.

"Well, we'll have to be flexible with the indirect expenses," he said, winking. "This has been a good year for all of us. I want next year to be just as good. That means I have to keep people around."

I was completely floored. He was being so reasonable.

"Now, for your bonus," he said. "I've been thinking about it."

"Yes?"

"Would you be satisfied with $80,000?"

"What happened to the indirect expenses?" asked Larry when I told him what happened.

"I guess," I said slowly, "that they were indirectly applied—somewhere else."

10

GROWING
PAINS

Larry and I went out to dinner to celebrate my bonus.
Larry selected a beautiful restaurant on the river, and
made sure we were given a table by the window. We
got all dressed up for the occasion. Heads turned as we
made our way to the table. Larry knows how to make
an entrance.

We sat down and ordered champagne. It was poured
into delicate crystal flutes.

Larry raised his glass.

"To you," he said. "I want you to know how proud
I am of you. This is your night."

We touched glasses and drank. The crystal rang
pleasantly.

"That's nice," said Larry. "Let's do it again." He

raised his glass. "You're beautiful and I love you. I wouldn't want to be married to anyone else."

"Me either," I said.

This time we kissed.

"Isn't it wonderful!" I said, looking out over the water and toward the lights of the city across the river.

"Yes," Larry agreed, holding my hand.

"No," I said, realizing he thought I meant the view. "I meant about the job and all. How well everything has turned out. And it's certainly nice to have the money."

"Nancy," said Larry, "it's not the money. It's never the money. It's that you tried. That's what you should be proud of."

"Sure, sure," I said, a little impatiently. "And I bet I can make three or four times as much next year. Look at Adam. He makes twice that."

The waiter came to take our order.

"Which way do you think the dollar's going?" I asked, as soon as we were alone again. "There seems to be sentiment on both sides—"

"Nancy." Larry stopped me. "No market talk tonight, okay?"

"Oh, right. I'm sorry. What would you like to talk about?"

"How about your eyes?" Larry suggested. He paused. "Hey, why don't we go away next weekend?"

"Where?" I asked.

"I don't know. Let's go out to Montauk. There's no one there this time of year."

"Sure," I answered without much conviction. "We'll see."

I smiled at him. We drank some more champagne. The first course arrived.

"Randy starts this week," I confided over the lobster salad. "I'll have to whip him into shape quickly."

"Nancy," said Larry. "Go slowly here. You don't realize what you're getting yourself into. It takes a long time to train someone properly. And opening a new office, especially overseas, is more work than you expect. A lot more. You don't have the resources. Frankly, I don't know how you're going to do it."

"What are you talking about?" I asked. "It's not that big a deal."

"We've had this discussion before," said Larry, shaking his head. "Let's just drop it and try to enjoy dinner."

"You just don't think I can do it," I accused. "You think I've just been lucky this whole time."

"I'm not saying *you* can't do it," said Larry. "I'm saying it would be difficult for *anyone* to do it. And you have been lucky. There's a lot of luck involved in trading. You know that as well as I do."

The main course arrived. We ate in silence.

"How did we get off the subject of your eyes?" Larry asked finally.

"You started it."

Like all junior traders, Randy was caught between his position and his ignorance. He knew he had to ask questions in order to learn. I recognized this necessity as well. But that didn't make it easier for either party.

For example, suppose you are the head trader. You have just made a decision to buy the dollar, expecting it to go up. As soon as you buy it, the dollar drops in value. You are losing money.

"Why did you do that?" asks the junior trader.

A perfectly reasonable question. A perfectly innocent question. Not, however, the question that you most feel like answering at that moment.

Possible responses include:

1. "I did that because I'm pretty sure the dollar is

going up, but I could be wrong, so I have to concentrate a little bit on the market right now."

2. "I did that for a very good reason but I don't have the time to discuss it with you right now."

3. "Shut up and watch the screen."

Although I was confident that I could teach Randy to trade in no time flat, I'd never considered how annoying it could be to have someone new on the desk. From the very beginning, Peter and Phillip and I had worked in complete harmony. Trading demands total concentration. We knew when to avoid idle conversation and unnecessary questions. Each of us had different strengths and weaknesses, which we understood and to which we deferred. Each of us did what we had to do. We were comfortable with one another. There were strong, unspoken bonds between us.

Into this environment, I had suddenly thrust a complete stranger. Under the best of circumstances, it was a difficult situation. And Randy did nothing to help. In fact, from the very first day, I could find nothing in his manner reminiscent of the person I'd interviewed. Gone was the quiet, respectful, junior trader, eager to learn. In his place was a chattering, boisterous know-it-all.

Randy's biggest problem was that he was insensitive to his surroundings. I had assumed that, coming from a trading environment, Randy would already understand the cardinal rules of trading etiquette. The most important was, it is all right to ask questions, but it is definitely not all right to say whatever comes into your head no matter what the circumstances.

I watched Randy and Phillip together. As I have already mentioned, Phillip is one of the nicest individuals on the planet, with the patience of a saint.

Phillip bought some dollars.

"Why did you do that?" asked Randy.

Phillip explained that he thought the dollar would be having a correction soon (it had been going in one direction—down—for about nine months). He took out his charts and carefully unfolded them for Randy's benefit. He started to teach him, in a painstakingly thorough way, how to read the charts. While he was explaining, the dollar started to fall again. Phillip began to lose a little money on his position.

Still he ignored the market in an effort to teach Randy about the charts.

"Oh!" said Randy, looking from the charts to the screen. "Well, I wouldn't have bought the dollar where you did. I would have sold the dollar. Maybe I would have bought it back here," he added.

Now, there is nothing so irritating to a trader as a person who announces what he or she would have done after the fact. Hindsight does a lot for someone's trading ability.

Phillip showed considerable restraint and said nothing. But I saw that he set his mouth a little firmer, and he put his charts away.

A little while later, after the dollar had fallen substantially more, and Phillip had been forced to take out his position at a loss, Randy approached him once again.

"I would have bought my dollars back here," he said, continuing with the conversation as if nothing had happened.

"I thought you said you would have bought them back fifty points ago," Phillip reminded him.

"I didn't say I would have, I said maybe I would have," Randy began.

"You have the right to your opinion, of course," said Phillip, cutting him off.

It was the sharpest I'd ever heard him get.

It was also a part of Randy's style to pretend to

know everything—even questions to which it was clear he couldn't possibly know the answers. His was a very chipper ignorance. It never occurred to him that he made a bigger fool of himself by pretending to know the answer to something than by simply admitting he didn't. Thus, no matter how many times he was caught in a blunder, he continued cheerfully to bluff his way through his training. This made it very difficult to isolate what he did know from what he didn't.

"Did you figure out the delta position of that trade?" I asked him.

"I don't have to—I know the delta position," came the response.

"Really? What is it, then?"

"It's—it's—let me see, the delta position would be . . ." Randy would start to mumble and stare at the trade.

"Do you know how to figure out the delta position?" I asked.

"Of course I know how to do it!"

"Well, then, if you know how to do it, tell me what it is."

Of course he didn't know how to do it, and I had to show him.

Randy's omniscience went far beyond simple trading matters. He was, it appeared, an expert on everything. One day Peter and I were having a discussion of the application of one of the rules of the exchange.

"I know that rule," said Randy, butting in to our conversation. "I know how it applies."

Peter and I looked at each other. It was a pretty obscure ruling. We only knew about it because we were having a problem with the exchange. It was odd that Randy would know the rule as well.

"Really?" said Peter. "What is the rule, exactly, Randy?"

Randy made up a rule on the spot for our benefit. He showed great imagination, but little factual knowledge.

"Right," said Peter, smiling his funny little smile, and turning back to me.

I began to wish that I was going away to London instead of Peter.

In addition to training Randy, I was spending a large part of my day helping Peter set up the London office. This, too, was taking more time than I'd imagined.

We were in daily contact with the man who was the administrative head of the bank's trading room in London, a very pleasant gentleman who had never heard of options. That was all right; we didn't expect him to trade. We simply wanted him to arrange for the delivery of the necessary equipment.

Before we could determine what equipment was needed, however, we had to find out what was already there.

"We've found a lovely spot for you in the corner of the room," said the London manager, when I'd gotten him on the phone. "It's right by the tea table."

"That's terrific," I said. "Thank you very much."

"Don't mention it," he said. He was always very polite.

"Does the space you've so kindly provided for us—" I began.

"Don't mention it," he said.

"—have any equipment associated with it?" I asked.

"Oh, yes!" he said. "There is some equipment here."

"Good," I said. "What kind of equipment is it?"

"Well," he said, doubtfully. "I don't really know the proper names for some of these machines. . . ."

"Can you describe them for me?"

"Well, yes, I suppose so. Let's see," he said, "there are two little screens built nicely into the desk."

"What information is transmitted by those screens?" I asked.

"Well," he said, hesitating again, "I don't really know. . . ."

"Try turning them on," I suggested.

"Oh, yes, of course!" he said, vastly relieved. "Yes, I see now that they relay information concerning the spot foreign-exchange market."

So I had two machines that performed the function of a Reuters screen. A good start.

"Thank you," I said. "That's very helpful."

"Don't mention it," he said.

"Now," I said. "Are there any PCs on the desk?"

"PCs?" he asked, puzzled.

"Personal computers. We're going to need two personal computers. IBM personal computers. Do you think that you can get them for us?"

"Oh, certainly," he said. "But I'm afraid I'll have to call you back tomorrow about that."

"All right," I said. "And thank you very much for all of your help."

"Don't mention it," he said.

Three days later he called back.

"I found you some personal computers," he said.

"Wonderful!" I said.

"Yes," he continued. "Just imagine! The bank has twelve computers available that nobody is using."

"Twelve!" I said. "That's terrific, but I only need two. What kind are they, AT or XT?"

"Well, let me see," he said, "I have one right here. It says 'Wang' on it—"

I stopped him. "Wang computers?"

"Yes. The bank discovered that Wang computers

were cheaper than IBM computers so they bought a dozen of them."

"But I can't use Wang computers," I said. "I need IBM."

"We don't have any IBMs," he said. "But you can have all twelve Wangs, if you like."

"But I don't need twelve Wangs," I persisted. "I need two IBMs."

Silence.

"I'll tell you what," I said. "This is much too difficult to organize over the phone. Why don't I just come to London for a few days and handle all of these administrative problems?"

"I'd appreciate that," said the London manager.

"Don't mention it," I sighed.

I decided to go to London the week before Christmas. The market appeared to be quieting down for the holiday season.

Peter was going with me, to find a place to stay and to help sort out some of the organizational problems. He would return to New York for the holidays and then move to London on a more permanent basis.

I tried not to think about what it was going to be like without Peter on the desk. Oh, well, I thought. It's only for about six months.

Concerned about possible operational problems resulting from the expansion, I decided that I needed someone with operations experience along on the London trip. The obvious choice was Sam Antonio from the back office. Sam knew his job cold. So far, in my experience with the operations department, this type of expertise was rare, almost unheard of.

The back office was responsible for the smooth functioning of my department. It was their job to make sure that payments went out to the right place and on time, and that all payments received were properly accounted for. Margin requirements at the exchanges had to be proved and met lest the exchange close out our position for lack of funds. Every day, Sam's department had to enter the day's trades into its computers and print out the reports that were so necessary to the managing of the position.

Operations people at the bank were generally underpaid, and there was always the risk of their being lured away by the competition. Sam had done such a terrific job over the past eight months that I wanted to reward him in some way. The trip to London was the perfect vehicle.

I asked Sam if he would like to go to London for a few days right before Christmas. He was thrilled.

"But I'll have to ask the Field Marshall," he said.

"The Field Marshall?" I asked.

"My boss. William Hambrecht."

"Oh!" I said. "I don't know him."

"I know you don't," said Sam, grinning. "If you knew him you wouldn't have to ask."

Sam's group didn't report to me, even though they provided my section with technical support. The bank kept the supervision of the operations department separate from that of the Trading Sector in order to reduce the risk of theft or fraud.

"Okay," I said, smiling back at Sam. "You ask the Field Marshall for permission."

Two days later, Sam came up to me at the desk. He looked unhappy.

"What's the matter?" I asked.

"The Field Marshall says I can't go to London," he said.

"Why not?"

"He says it's too expensive and, besides, I'm too junior to go."

173

"Too junior to go?" I repeated. "Why, that's ridiculous! Who would I take besides you? Nobody else knows how everything works."

"I guess," said Sam slowly, "that the Field Marshall thinks that if anyone should go, it should be him."

"But he doesn't know anything about our requirements," I said. "What does he expect to do in London?"

"I don't know," said Sam. "I hear it's a good place for shopping."

"Well," I said, "in that case why don't you just go back to your Field Marshall and tell him that I'll pay for your trip and that you are plenty senior enough for me."

"You mean it?" asked Sam.

"I mean it."

The Field Marshall was hard pressed to find a reason for forbidding Sam to go to London once it became clear that I was willing to absorb the expense. He couldn't very well claim that Sam was needed in New York when I said he was needed in London. Sam was allowed to go.

It was my first encounter with the Field Marshall.

I paid very little attention to the market in December. The dollar started to fall again, but I barely noticed. Between training Randy and organizing the expansion and getting ready to go to London, I was only vaguely aware that the market, contrary to my expectations, hadn't really quieted down at all.

What did I care? My bonus was set. I was one of the highest paid officers of the bank. I'm not sure, but I think I was the highest paid woman.

I gave myself until the first of the year to get the unit organized. I was in too good a humor to bother about the market. I was successful! It was the holidays! And I was going to London for the very first time!

11

WE
WISH YOU
A MERRY
CHRISTMAS . . .

"I'm going to London on business," I announced to Larry.

"When?" he asked, barely looking up from his newspaper.

"The week before Christmas."

We had just finished dinner, a delicious repast of leftover Chinese take-out.

"How long will you be gone for?"

"Three or four days." I hesitated. "You won't even notice I'm gone."

"I don't notice when you're here."

He rose and started to clean up the empty cardboard chow mein boxes.

"Let me do that," I said, jumping up.

"That's all right, I can do it," he said. "It's not like there are any dirty dishes."

I followed him into the kitchen.

"I'll tell you what," I said. "If I leave on the red-eye I can go right to the office and if I plan things right I can finish everything in two days. How's that?"

"Suit yourself. It doesn't seem to matter to you what I say anyway."

"Of course it matters."

"What do you mean, of course? I've been trying to talk to you for months now—" he stopped himself.

"Larry. It's only a two-day trip."

"Why bother to take a plane at all? Why don't you just slip into your red cape and fly to London yourself?"

"What's the matter with you?"

"I don't know why the hell you got married. It doesn't seem to be what you want. I think you'd be much happier at this stage of your life living alone."

"How can you say that?" I was stunned.

"How can I say that?" Larry shook his head in disbelief. "How can I say that?" He threw up his arms and walked into the bedroom.

I stared after him. Go to hell! I thought. Who needs this?

I stuffed the rest of the garbage into a bag, stalked out to the incinerator, and threw out the remains of the dinner with a vengeance. Who does he think he is, I fumed. I probably would be happier living alone!

No, I wouldn't.

I had a brainstorm. The perfect solution.

I went back into the apartment and stood at the bedroom door. Larry was lying on the bed reading a book.

"Why don't you come to London with me?" I said.

He looked up.

"It'll be great." I hurried along. "I'll schedule all my meetings in the morning so we can have the afternoons together. And we can stay for the weekend. It will be romantic."

"It's a nice thought, but I don't see how it's possible to organize a new operation in three mornings. It's far more likely you will not only spend the entire day at the bank, but you'll end up having dinner with them, too."

"No, I won't. I promise."

"Look, Nancy, I've been to London. I don't want to end up spending three days wandering around by myself. If you don't think you can do it, be honest. I'd rather you went alone."

"No, no. I can do it. I want to be with you. I want things to be the way they were." I sat down next to him on the bed.

"In that case, we'll have a great time. I know all kinds of wonderful little places. I'd love to show you around."

I began to get excited.

"We could go to the theater," I said. "And out to lunch."

"Shopping," said Larry. "You'd like that."

"And tea!" I said. "I've always wanted to have a real English tea, with scones and clotted cream and raspberry jam!"

"I know just where to go," said Larry.

We started kissing. The phone rang.

"Don't answer it," he whispered.

Two rings. Three rings.

"You know I have to." I pushed him away.

"Ah, yes. This is Singapore calling," said the voice on the other end of the wire. "Is Nancy there?"

"This is Nancy."

"Ah, yes! Good evening, Nancy! The market is remaining relatively calm. . . ."

We landed at Heathrow Airport on a Tuesday evening in December and checked into the hotel. The next morning I left Larry still sleeping soundly in the big double bed and went downstairs to look for Sam and Peter. The desk clerk told me that they'd already left. I hurried off to the London office, located somewhere in the financial section of town, known simply as the City.

I didn't have a map or a guide; I didn't need one. I simply found the subway and followed all of the men wearing bowler hats and Burberry raincoats. They led me directly to the London office.

The London manager was waiting for me when I got to the office that first morning. He was a thoroughly nice man, very reserved, who wanted only to do his job.

And do his job he did. He was as much a fixture of the London office as the electric light bulbs. He'd started with the bank when he was nineteen years old, beginning as a clerk in the back office. He worked hard, going from job to job, promotion to promotion, slowly inching along the path to success.

A full twenty years after walking into the bank as a young man, he finally reached his ultimate destination: manager of the entire office. Since the office of London manager carried with it the title of vice president, he and I were of equal rank.

He hurried up to greet me. He was very tall. Even with my heels on, he towered over me.

"You must be Nancy," he said. "I'm Alec Carter. How do you do?"

"How do you do?" I asked, shaking his hand.

"Won't you come into my office?" he asked, leading the way.

I'd walked into, out of, and through trading rooms in New York for nearly nine months. I knew what to expect, and it didn't even bother me anymore. It shouldn't come as a surprise to anyone that the atmosphere inside most trading rooms is overwhelmingly male. Walking into a trading room is the closest I'll ever come to visiting the inside of a men's locker room immediately following the big game.

I had learned to live with the jokes. Traders love tasteless, off-color jokes. Thanks to my experience in trading, I was now the master of an almost unlimited number of these knee-slappers (an accomplishment that unfortunately does not carry over well into other areas of social discourse).

I could stand the jabs. Whenever a piece of equipment broke down on my desk, there was always someone there to ask if I was sure I'd plugged it in. Or, "It figures a woman wouldn't be able to fix a printer," a male colleague would announce to the room at large, neglecting to mention that he couldn't fix it either. I was used to veiled looks, double entendres, half-concealed smirks. I thought I was ready for anything they could dish out.

I was not ready for the London office.

For all its talk, the New York trading community is much more receptive to the concept of women's rights than it cares to admit. There is an underlying acceptance that times have changed and women have to earn a living just like everyone else. Remember that the trading community comprises mostly men under the age of thirty. These men went to school with women. They've been beaten, first at spelling, and later at math, by women. They've had to compete for the same jobs as women, and they've had to take that competition seriously. Consequently, they have lost some of that air of male superiority held by their fathers and grandfathers. It can take some of the wind out of your sails to discover that the woman standing next to you on the subway platform earns four times as much as you do.

But in London it's different. The all-male networks are much stronger there. The core group resists the persuasions of the intruder. When I walked into the London trading room that first morning, I felt the shock ripple through the room.

What's the matter with these guys? I thought. You'd think they'd never seen a woman trader before.

They hadn't.

I followed Alec into an office just off the trading floor. We sat down facing each other. He stared at me.

"How . . . uh . . . how long have you been with the bank?" he asked me, to break the silence.

I explained that I'd been with the bank about three years.

"Three years," he repeated blankly. Then: "And how long have you been trading options?"

I told him I was in my ninth month.

"Had you had much experience in trading before this?"

"None whatsoever," I replied.

He struggled manfully to suppress his horror.

"Well," he said finally. "We're very pleased to see that you are opening shop here. I'll do everything in my power to help you."

"Thank you," I said, touched. He really was a nice man.

"Don't mention it," he said. "Shall we have a look at your space?"

We walked through the room toward the back. On the way I saw something that made me start. *Playboy* centerfolds had been tacked to the wall. Alec walked right by them. He gave no sign of having noticed.

Alec ushered me to a desk in the corner of the room. It was exactly as he had described it.

"What do you think?" Alec asked anxiously. "Will this do?"

"Oh, yes," I hastened to reassure him. "This will do nicely."

"As for the two computers you need, I thought that we might put one right here, and the other one back there," he flung his arm in the direction of the wall, some twelve feet away.

"No, both will have to go right here," I said, slapping the top of the desk with my hand.

"Where?" started the London manager. "Oh no! It can't go on top of the desk!"

"Why not? We need both PCs right on the desk so we can price options while we are on the phone."

"You couldn't run back and forth I suppose?" he asked hopefully.

"I'm afraid not."

"But it can't go on the desk!"

"Why not?"

"It will ruin the decor," he said dramatically.

I looked around. Sure enough, all the other traders' screens were built into their desks.

That stopped me. I have to confess that interior design was an issue I hadn't considered before. (Although now that he mentioned it, I certainly wouldn't want to do anything to ruin the effect of the centerfolds.)

"I'm afraid we have no choice in the matter. One of the PCs must go on the desk."

"Yes . . . well . . ." Alec struggled between his loyalty to aesthetics and his innate politeness. Politeness won. "Yes, of course, whatever you want," he murmured unhappily.

While we were talking one of the junior spot traders approached Alec and whispered something in his ear. Alec turned to me.

"There's a phone call for you," he said. "Why don't you take it in my office?"

On the way back to Alec's office I glanced at one of the spot traders' screens. The market wasn't particularly active. Still, it could only be Phillip calling from New York with some problem. I braced myself for trouble.

"Hello?" I said into the phone.

"Hello, sweetie. How's it going?"

My husband.

"Larry," I said. "Is something wrong?"

"Nope. Just calling to see how you're doing over there."

"I'm just fine, honey," I said. "But I'm busy."

"Well, I won't keep you," he said. "I just called to see where you wanted to meet for lunch."

"Lunch?"

"I thought afterward we could do a little sightseeing. . . ."

"Honey," I said sweetly, praying that no one was listening in (you never can tell on a trading floor; the phone lines are communal and most of them are taped as well). "I'm afraid I'm running a little behind schedule. I can't take the whole afternoon off as we'd planned."

"Well, when can you get off?"

"I think it's safer to skip lunch today. Why don't we meet for tea?"

"Fine. See you then."

I caught Sam as he was coming out of the back office. He was laughing.

"What's so funny?" I wanted to know.

"They can't get our accounting program up. They're using the wrong kind of computer," he said.

I groaned. "Not the Wangs again," I said.

"Yep. They want to use Wangs," he said, shaking his head. "I can't for the life of me figure out why. I told 'em Wangs won't do the job."

"It appears," I said, "that the bank is having a fire sale on Wangs and we are supposed to be the happy recipients."

"Yeah," he said. "That's another thing. They want to give us twelve of the things. What would we possibly do with twelve?"

"Never mind," I said. "What are we going to do about it?"

"Well," said Sam, "just to show me, they've got someone coming over from Wang today to give us a demonstration. He is supposed to know how to get our accounting program up on his computer."

"Any chance of it working?" I asked hopefully.

"None," Sam grinned. "But it ought to be fun watching him try."

I saw Sam again later that afternoon.

"Did it work?" I asked.

"Nope."

"Tell them to order some IBMs," I said.

"I already have," said Sam.

Peter, who had been meeting with some of the other traders, met me in Alec's office to discuss where he'd be living during his stay in London.

"Nothing to worry about," said Alec. "We've arranged a place for you."

Peter and I exchanged looks.

"You have?" I asked.

"Yes. A terrific little efficiency apartment not far from here," he continued.

"Well," I said. "I must say it's very nice of you to have gone out of your way like that to find Peter an apartment."

"I'm afraid I can't take the credit for it," said the London manager. "The bank keeps an apartment all year round for visiting executives. You can have it rent-free."

That stopped me. Having had some experience by this time with the London office's free equipment, I thought it behooved me to find out a little more about the free apartment before accepting it.

"What kind of neighborhood is it in?" I asked.

"One of the best in London," Alec replied.

"What kind of condition is it in?"

"I've had assurances that it is in excellent condition."

"How large is it?"

"There's a bedroom, living room, dining room, and a small kitchen attached," he answered. "I'm sure it's quite suitable for Peter. You know, all the bank's executives, including the president himself, stay there whenever they are in town."

I had to admit it sounded perfect. I threw out one more question, just to make sure.

"How are all of those executives going to feel about having to stay at a hotel whenever they come to London?" I asked.

"Stay at a hotel?" The London manager repeated. "Now, why would they stay at hotels?"

"I mean, because Peter will be staying in the apartment," I explained.

"They won't be staying at hotels," said Alec. "Peter will be."

"You mean Peter's supposed to move out of his apartment every time some official of the bank comes into town?" I asked.

"Why, yes, of course," Alec said.

"And just how often do you anticipate that to be?" I asked.

"Oh, no more than two or three times a month," he replied.

We decided to turn down the free apartment.

A spot trader poked his head in the door.

"Telephone call for Nancy," he said.

Alec and Peter looked at me.

"I'll take it in the other room," I offered. "I won't be but a minute."

"Hi!" said a familiar voice when I answered the phone. "Me again."

"Hello, Larry," I said.

"How's everything going?"

"Just fine. But I can't talk now."

"Just confirming. The Connaught, three o'clock."

"Better make it four."

I returned to Alec's office.

"Everything all right in New York?" Alec asked.

"As far as I know," I answered honestly.

"Now," said Alec, "I understand that you need my help in one last area."

I swallowed nervously. I'd already had just about all of the help I could stand for one visit.

"I have been informed," he continued, "that you intend to hire a trader here in London to supplement your group."

"Actually," I said, "we are looking for two people. A senior trader and a junior trader. Peter's job is to find them, train them, set up the desk, and get back to New York as quickly as possible."

He didn't seem to hear me.

"I have just the person for you," he said. "I'll have him assigned to your group."

Free computers, a free apartment, and now a free person. I was instantly on my guard.

"Do you mind if I ask a few questions?"

"Not at all," he replied.

"Who is he?"

"He's a very nice young chap who is currently working in our back office. His name is Robert Wilkins, but everyone around here calls him Bobby."

"How old is he?"

"Nineteen."

I blanched. It's a young business, but not that young. Even the junior trader would have major responsibilities. I shuddered to think how I would have behaved if someone had hired me to trade options at nineteen. I'm quite sure Wall Street would never have lived through the experience.

"How did you happen to choose him—I mean, Bobby—for this position?" I asked casually. "Does he show a special aptitude for options?"

"Oh, dear, no," Alec laughed. "I daresay he's never heard of options."

"Has he a quantitative background then?" I asked.

"Pardon?"

"Does he know math?"

"Oh, yes. I've never had any trouble with his addition or subtraction. He's splendid in the back office. Rarely an error."

"What about his calculus?" I asked.

"Calculus? Don't tell me you need to understand calculus to trade options?"

"I'm afraid it helps," I said. "You know, options trading is a little bit more complex than straight-out foreign-exchange or eurodollar trading."

"No," said Alec. "I didn't know that."

"Well," I said. "How did you pick him for the job?"

"The same way we always do," he replied. "He's the next in line. I promised him the very next job to open up on the trading floor. That's yours."

"I see," I said.

Having only just hired Randy, and having lived for an entire month with the results of my handiwork, I wasn't quite so cavalier about adding personnel as I'd been in November. I was just beginning to see what the addition of a grating personality could do to the overall atmosphere of a trading desk. The wrong disposition was as much of a distraction to the orderly functioning of the unit as hiring someone to bang on a drum during working hours. I had no intention of making the same mistake twice.

"Well," I said. "I don't suppose you'd mind if Peter and I talked to Bobby before you assigned him to our group?"

"No," Alec said slowly. "I don't see why that couldn't be arranged. In fact, I know he's looking forward to meeting you."

"He knows we're here, does he?"

"Oh, yes! I've already told him that he'll be working with you."

Peter and I exchanged looks.

Bobby sat nervously on the end of the couch in an office adjacent to Alec's, where Peter and I had arranged for a short interview. He was tall and skinny. His jacket was too small. His pants were too large. His skin showed traces of a liberal application of Clearasil.

"Hello, Bobby," I said. "I'm Nancy, and this is Peter. We're glad to meet you."

"Same here," he murmured.

"Bobby," I said. "I understand that you want to be an options trader. Is that true?"

"Yes."

"Why do you want to be an options trader, Bobby?"

He mumbled something about its being fun to trade.

I felt very bad about all of this. It wasn't his fault that he was so young, and so terribly unsuited to the position. Who knows but that in four or five years he wouldn't be one of the most successful traders in London? It's just that I didn't have four or five years to spare.

187

"Wouldn't you rather trade foreign exchange or eurodollars?" I suggested hopefully.

The reply was indistinct, but I did catch the words "doesn't make much difference."

"Oh, but there is a difference," I said, seeing a way out of the situation. "Options are very difficult to trade."

"They are?"

Peter caught my meaning instantly.

"You'll have to work very hard," he cautioned. "You'll have to begin right away. You've a lot to learn."

"That's right," I nodded. "Don't worry. I've a number of books I can lend you on the subject. And don't be put off by how long and difficult they are. They're quite useful."

"I'm going on holiday," said Bobby. "It's Christmas."

"So much the better!" I said. "You'll have plenty of time for reading then."

"Now, as to your hours," said Peter.

"I work nine to five," said Bobby. "Sometimes they let me out at half past four, though."

"Well," said Peter. "I'll be getting into the office at seven-thirty sharp every morning, and of course I expect you to do the same. We'll have to stay later than the others because we need our reports from New York and we'll have to discuss the position with Nancy."

"Oh!" said Bobby, not very enthusiastically.

"And then, of course," I said, "because we're new in town, there'll be a great deal of socializing after work."

"At the pub?" Bob perked up.

I realized I'd overdone it. Besides, I had no idea what the legal drinking age was in London.

"We can't drink too much," said Peter, coming to my rescue. "We have to always be on top of our game. We often have to trade in the evenings as well."

"In the evenings?" asked Bobby, amazed. "You mean, after work?"

"We all have to be available on a twenty-four-hour basis," I said. "We might need to consult with you at any time."

"We're not asking you to do anything that we don't do ourselves," Peter reminded him.

"Oh!" said Bobby looking from me to Peter and then back again.

I popped back into Alec's office. "May I speak to you for a moment?" I asked.

"Certainly," he said.

"Peter and I have just had a little chat with Bobby," I said.

"How did you like him?"

"He's lovely," I said honestly. "But I'm afraid he doesn't want to trade options."

"What?" asked Alec, amazed.

"Haven't you a spot for him on your eurodollar desk?" I asked quickly. "That's where he really wants to be."

"Well," said the London manager. "If that's what he wants. . . . You're sure you don't mind?"

"Not at all," I said, graciously.

"Well, thank you, then," said Alec.

"Don't mention it."

The spot trader knocked on the door again. "Pardon me, but there's a phone call. . . ."

"I'll be right there," I sighed.

I never did meet Larry for tea. We had dinner that night with people from the bank. The next two days were more of the same.

I met with Sam and Peter on Friday afternoon.

"Let's sum up the situation," I said. "We'll begin with the equipment. Sam?"

"I've two IBMs on order," said Sam.

"When are they expected?" I asked.

"Not for three weeks," he replied.

"Oh!" I winced. "We can't hurry them at all?"

"No," Sam shook his head. "It's Christmas. Everyone's on vacation. If they'd only been ordered earlier . . ."

"Right," I sighed. "What about the other equipment?"

"Well," said Sam. "It seems the phone company takes awhile around here as well. I've ordered you some additional phone lines. I assume they'll get here about the same time as the computers."

I looked at Peter. "That pushes your starting date back to the third week of January," I said.

"It's just as well," he said. "I'll need some time to round up my things. I can get here a little early and start looking around for people to hire. Start making friends with the rest of the community, that kind of thing."

"Right," I said. "Did you find housing?"

"Yes, I did. It's available immediately."

"So you'll leave on schedule," I said. "Will you be all right on your own for a while?"

"Yes, Mom."

"I'm not being motherly. I'm being professional," I snapped. "Nobody trades well on his own. There are too many mistakes made that way."

"I'll be careful."

"You'll call me if there's anything going on?"

"You'll be the first to know," he assured me.

I went to say good-bye to Alec.

"Thank you for all your help," I said.

"Don't mention it," he returned. "How did you find your first trip to London?"

"Hectic," I said, laughing. "I had no idea it was so much work organizing a desk."

190

"What do you mean?" he asked.

"You know," I said. "Ordering all the equipment, getting the people, and the space, and the phone lines. I'm glad I don't have to do this again!"

"Why—" Alec stopped. "Don't you know?"

"Know what?" I asked.

"Why, the bank has decided to move the entire London trading floor to a new building in six months. We'll have to rearrange everything at that time. I'm surprised you weren't informed."

I got back to the hotel Friday evening to find Larry waiting for me.

"Get everything done?" he asked coldly.

"Larry, honey, I'm sorry," I said. "I had no idea how much work was involved."

"That's always the problem, isn't it?" he said.

I was silent. We stared at each other.

"We have a choice here," I said finally. "We can spend these last two days fighting, or we can make up and try to enjoy ourselves."

"I would certainly rather we had a good time," said Larry.

"So would I."

And we did. We had breakfast in bed. We took long, hot bubble baths in the room's gigantic tub. We walked all over London and I finally had a chance to see some of the world's most breathtaking architecture. We shopped, we had tea at the Savoy Hotel. We went dancing. We were lovers again.

We were walking down South Moulton Street, one of the most fashionable shopping areas in London. Larry stopped in front of a lingerie shop, which sported a life-size picture of a beautiful woman clad only in a silk chemise and sheer stockings with rhinestones up the back.

"Stop drooling," I said.

"I'm not drooling," he protested, wiping his mouth.

He continued to stare.

"You'd look great in those stockings," he said. "I want to buy them for you."

I hugged his arm.

"That's not necessary," I said.

"I know it's not necessary," he said. "I want to. You'd look better in them than she does," indicating the model.

"I don't know," I said, hesitating. "This place looks expensive."

"Who cares? You're worth it."

"I don't know," I said again. I'd had some experience with lingerie shops.

He was in the shop before I could stop him.

"This place is great!" he said when I'd followed him inside. "Just look at all of these terrific stockings!"

The stockings were sensational.

"I like this one and this one and this one," he said. "What do you think?"

"They're great," I said. "But one's enough. They must be expensive."

"How much can panty hose be?" demanded my husband.

Before I could tell him, he walked over to a saleswoman who had been watching the proceedings.

"We'll take these," he said, giving her three pairs.

"Are you sure you want all three?" she asked slowly.

"Of course," said my husband, with a grandiose gesture.

The saleswoman hurried to wrap up the purchase in lilac-colored, perfumed tissue paper.

"What do I owe you?" asked Larry, while she was busy folding.

"Ninety-six pounds," she replied.

There was a moment of silence while Larry tried to compute the exchange rate in his head.

"Ninety-six pounds," Larry repeated. "That's $140."

He seemed to think he had either heard wrong or calculated wrong.

"That's right," the saleswoman nodded to him.

"For three pairs of stockings?" asked Larry, struggling to maintain his composure.

"That's right," the saleswoman repeated.

He turned to me.

"Let me put them back," I said.

Larry recovered gallantly. "Do you like them?" he asked.

"Of course I like them."

Larry turned back to the saleswoman. "We'll take them," he said.

The saleswoman smiled sympathetically and gave him a piece of chocolate at no extra charge.

12

...AND
A HAPPY
NEW YEAR

I had a plan.

After the weekend in London, Larry and I spent the holidays with some friends in a big, old house in the Pennsylvania countryside. It snowed Christmas morning, right on command. In this peaceful environment, I realized something important: romance and passion must be worked at in a marriage, just like everything else.

If anyone had asked me what was more important to me, my marriage or the direction of the dollar, I would have instantly answered "my marriage" and would have vehemently denied that my behavior implied otherwise. But, in fact, I had been siphoning all of my energy away from my husband and into the bank.

I decided to put a stop to it. I was determined to make the marriage work.

In this I was being completely selfish. It's no great secret that the most satisfying experiences in life are those you share with someone close to you.

Don't misunderstand me. I had no intention of giving up my job. I recognized that my marriage could be truly successful only if both parties involved led full, satisfying lives outside the bounds of the union. For me, this meant continuing along my chosen career path. But it was necessary to begin to balance the requirements of a very demanding vocation with the responsibilities of being a wife.

Hence my plan.

I needed to spend time with Larry, I needed to spend time at the office, right? The solution seemed to me to be a very simple one. I would trade brilliantly in January, so brilliantly that I would earn the whole year's income for the bank in that one month. Management would be more than satisfied with the results, and I could relax and pay attention to my husband for the other eleven months of the year.

This is not as crazy as it sounds. The nature of the market is such that most traders make the bulk of their profits in two or three months of the year. The difference is, they don't pick the month in advance.

The alarm went off at 5:30 A.M. on January 2, 1986. As usual, I groaned as I came to.

Getting out of bed was the hardest part of the day for me. I love to sleep. Given a choice, I would probably spend ten hours out of every twenty-four unconscious.

I pulled myself together in the morning long enough to get dressed, and lured myself out of the apartment by picturing the freshly baked, piping hot, homemade cherry turnover I'd buy when I got to the croissant shop directly across from my office. At 6:15 A.M. I plunged into the cold darkness of pre–rush-hour Manhattan, and hurried down the block to the bowels of the universe, otherwise known as the New York City subway system. I picked my way carefully down the subway stairs, avoiding the large puddle of evil-smelling liquid on the last step, misting suspiciously, like some terrible lake. I put my token in the slot and hurried to the subway platform.

No train. Silence, relieved only by the steady drip, drip, drip of moisture leaking from a crack in the ceiling and the mumbling of a bag woman stretched out on one of the platform's four benches. It was in this congenial atmosphere that I put the finishing touches on my master plan.

Clearly, I reasoned, the only way to earn an entire year's income in one month was to take an enormous position as soon as possible. But what position to take? That was the question. That was always the question.

I started my analysis with a quick review of the market's past performance. The dollar had been falling pretty steadily since March 1985. There had been a short period in August when the dollar rallied, but the charge was short-lived. Fresh troops, in the form of the industrialized world's finance ministers at G-5 in September had taken deadly aim and killed the dollar for all intents and purposes. What most of us were engaging in at the moment was merely a mopping-up exercise. The dollar had lost a full 15 percent of its value since September, 25 percent if you took March as your starting point, when the dollar was at the height of its power.

That was past history. But what would the future hold?

The arrival of the train (heralded by a shriek that has always conjured up for me the vision of ten thousand souls being whipped simultaneously by ten thousand fiends) interrupted my thought pattern. I followed my fellow travelers into the car and found a seat. One good thing about getting into work so early in the morning is that at least you get a seat on the train. The doors closed. The engines roared. The conductor screamed piercingly but unintelligibly over the microphone. We were off!

I returned to my analysis. Because the dollar had been steadily falling for such a long time already, market perception was that 1986 would be a much quieter year than 1985. Volatility, the market's measure of how rapidly the value of the dollar would fluctuate in the upcoming months, was low. I knew that some people (including the bank's gold trader, who, as usual, had an opinion on everything except gold) were loudly predicting that the dollar wouldn't move very much at all; that all of the major moves had already taken place, and that volatility would collapse even further.

Fifty-ninth Street. Time to change for the express. No express yet. I wait patiently on the platform, surrounded on all sides by the human condition. It's rather early in the morning to appreciate fully the human condition. Consequently, I do my best to ignore it. I escaped back to the market.

I didn't believe what the other traders were saying. I didn't think that the market would stay calm. It's not human nature to stay calm, and the market is, after all, made up of human beings. Everything in life works in cycles, and the dollar is no exception. Besides, nobody makes any money when the market's quiet. How would all the foreign-exchange traders on Wall Street justify their existence (not to mention their salaries and bonuses) if the dollar spent a whole year trading in a narrow range?

The express train arrived. Because all of the trains

were running late, a crowd had formed. I was unable to secure a seat this time. I returned to my analysis.

The problem was, I had no clear feeling which way the dollar was going to go—up or down. It had already fallen so far so fast that I was afraid we were in for a correction. A *correction* is the technical term for everybody's deciding to take their profit all at once. Since the only people with profit were the people who were short the dollar (which was just about everybody in the market by this time), taking that profit meant buying back all those dollars they'd sold. The force of all that buying could propel the dollar up.

But, on the other hand, the Reagan administration did not seem to want the dollar to go back up. They wanted to improve the trade deficit. There are two possible ways to improve the trade deficit. The first is to force American producers of goods and services to make their products more competitive by cutting costs or by producing a better product that everyone (even other Americans) will want to buy. To choose this way is to invite a possible confrontation with American labor. The second way is willy-nilly to make all foreign goods and services more expensive than American goods so that, even if the foreign goods are better, Americans will buy American goods because they are so much cheaper. To choose the second way is to face a possible confrontation with America's trading partners: the Germans, the Japanese, the French, the British.

The choice for American politicians was simple. Foreigners don't vote.

Decisions, decisions. What to do? And then, suddenly, somewhere between Forty-second and Fourteenth streets, it hit me: the perfect position.

Don't bet on direction at all. Bet on volatility. Options were cheap now. Buy every option in sight and then sit back and wait for a breakout in the dollar. Make sure that you have options on both sides. Whichever way the dollar goes, the options on that side will more than pay for the cost of the others.

Well satisfied with my plan (after all, hadn't I devoted nearly an hour to it while trying to get downtown?), I got off at the World Trade Center and made my way to the little croissant shop directly across from my office. I was painfully disappointed to discover that the store had changed management during the Christmas holidays, and that the new proprietor thought it a good idea to substitute the previous day's stale cherry turnovers for freshly baked ones, a ruse that was detected with the first bite.

Could it have been an omen?

I walked into the office and immediately got to work buying options. I bought and bought and bought. I spent three days buying everything I could find. I didn't distinguish between long-term and short-term options. I didn't care about the price. I bet heavily on a big move.

Usually when somebody comes in buying big, the price goes up. But when I bought, the price went down. That meant there were plenty of people in the marketplace who held a view directly opposite to mine, who were more than willing to sell to me. Did that discourage me? Not a bit. I bought more. By the time I was finished buying, I had the largest position I had ever accumulated.

Nobody at the bank noticed. Nobody at the bank asked. Nobody at the bank seemed to care. And the market remained ominously quiet.

Peter was gone. In his place was a squawk box that was supposed to link us to him in London. As the box disconnected on the average of once every twenty minutes, transcontinental communication was spotty. This was actually a lucky break. I found out later how much it costs to leave a telephone line open all day to London.

So, Phillip and I continued to man the desk. Of course, there was also Randy.

Sam came by at the end of the day with our reports.

"I think there's something wrong here," he said.

I looked at the reports. They showed a gain of $9 million in one day. While I am a good trader, I'm not that good.

"There's obviously an error here," I said.

A thorough examination of the reports revealed that one trade had earned us over $9 million.

"Here's the error," I said, pointing out the trade to Sam. "The information on that trade must have been entered incorrectly into the computer."

"Let me get the ticket," suggested Sam.

Everyday we wrote up the tickets detailing the day's trades, which were later used to process the reports vital to understanding and trading the position. Recently I had given this job to Randy.

Sam returned with the ticket.

"Here's the problem," he said. "The handwriting is so sloppy we misread the information and entered the wrong date into the computer."

I turned to Randy. "Please try to be more careful in the future," I said. "Now Sam will have to reprint all of our reports." I turned to Sam. "How long will it take to fix the error and reprint?" I asked.

"About an hour and a half," he replied.

I sighed. It was already 5:30 P.M.

"Do it, please," I said wearily.

The very next day Sam again arrived with the reports.

"You're not going to believe this," he said, handing me the thick sheaf of papers.

I looked. This time, we were down $11 million. Once again, it was easy to find the error. Once again, inspection of the ticket revealed that Randy had been careless. Once again, I had to wait until 7:00 P.M. to get the new reports.

The next day I taught my secretary how to write the tickets. She learned how to do it in fifteen minutes. Careless errors on tickets became a thing of the past.

Randy's carelessness extended beyond routine chores. He tried to do everything so quickly to prove that he was on top of the situation that he made senseless errors. I understood that the mistakes were a result of his nervousness at wanting to do a good job, but good intentions are not enough on a trading desk. He often miscalculated the number of contracts that were necessary to cover a trade, and would end up buying too few or too many. Since I didn't check his multiplication and division every step of the way, I wouldn't find out about the problem until it was too late and we'd already lost money.

But it was his continuing insensitivity to his surroundings that bothered me the most. He chattered constantly. He said anything that popped into his head. Even ordering lunch became a big production.

"I'm hungry," I announced around one o'clock. "I'm going to order in some food. Does anyone want something?"

"No, thank you," Phillip declined politely. "I have some lunch here." He indicated the ever-present cold beef and mashed potatoes. "May I offer you some?"

"No, thanks, Phillip," I smiled at him. "I'll just order my own. What about you, Randy?"

"Sure, I'd like some lunch," Randy replied.

I picked up the phone to dial for a delivery.

"What do you want?"

"Let's see," said Randy. "Do I want a hamburger? No. Do I want ham and cheese? No, I don't really feel

201

like ham and cheese. It's not a ham-and-cheese kind of day. Do I want tuna fish?"

I put down the telephone. Experience had taught that this process could take up to a quarter of an hour.

"Just let me know when you've decided," I sighed.

"Do I want egg salad? Uh-uh. Do I want bologna? I hate bologna. Do I want . . ."

I have to admit that I wasn't in the best spirits to begin with. It had been two weeks already and so far the market had stubbornly refused to live up to my subway revelation. Meanwhile, Peter was in London, attempting to trade without benefit of instruments or reports.

"We have a problem, Sam," I said one afternoon.

"What's the matter?" Sam was instantly on the alert.

"It's the reports. Peter's not getting copies of our reports for the opening of London. He can't trade without those reports. He doesn't know what the position is."

"Well," said Sam. "It's a sticky problem. After the reports are printed out in the evening, I've been having one of my people Rapifax the pages to Peter in London."

"I know," I said. "But the Rapifax doesn't work that well. All the pages come out blurry and Peter can't read them."

"I also send him copies by courier," Sam pointed out.

"I know," I said again. "But the courier doesn't get to London until noon. That means he has to trade for four or five hours without crucial information."

"I don't know what else we can do," said Sam, shaking his head. "Rapifax is the only way to get it there in time. We'll just have to keep trying."

Eventually what happened was that Peter would call me at home when he got into the office at 8:00 A.M. London time (3:00 A.M. my time) and I would read the position to him over the phone. I can't tell you how thrilled Larry was with that arrangement.

It's only temporary, I kept saying to myself. The market will heat up and the position will come in and I'll look back over these last few weeks and laugh.

As I got less and less sleep, Randy's behavior seemed to get worse. The time I spent with him decreased as I tried to focus on the market. Instead of using his spare time to study options or to go over his position, he would play video games on the computer. After a while you couldn't tell the difference between the desk and a penny arcade.

I started to hate him.

Something happened to me in those last three weeks of January. The strain of expansion, with the resulting overflow of operational and management problems, combined with insufficient sleep, were beginning to take their toll. Gone was the confident, optimistic, bright-eyed trader of the previous year. In her place was a frothing maniac: unsure, overworked, exhausted.

I put every ounce of faith that I had in that position. It was, I thought, the one thing that could rescue me from the unhealthy atmosphere that was beginning to surround me at work like some toxic cloud. It was to be my salvation. The deeper I sank into the morass of operational quagmire, the more I clung to that position.

Suddenly, I had completely lost my perspective. And perspective is the one quality a trader needs most.

It was the end of January. Phillip was poring endlessly over his charts. Randy was playing Yahtzee on the computer with the gold trader. Sam delivered the day's reports.

I was exhausted. I had been up in the middle of the night every day for a week giving Peter the position. As it was late Friday afternoon, I picked up the reports without looking at them and decided to go home.

I read the reports on the subway. I walked into the apartment. Larry was out shopping for dinner. I took off my coat and hung it up in the closet. I went into the bedroom. I carefully removed the spread from the bed. I took off my shoes. I took off my earrings. Then I threw myself on the bed and cried.

I cried long and hard. I cried at the top of my lungs. I cried uncontrollably, inconsolably. Instead of going up as I had predicted, volatility had crashed. The market was as quiet as I'd ever seen it. My beautiful position had lost approximately $350,000 in just three weeks.

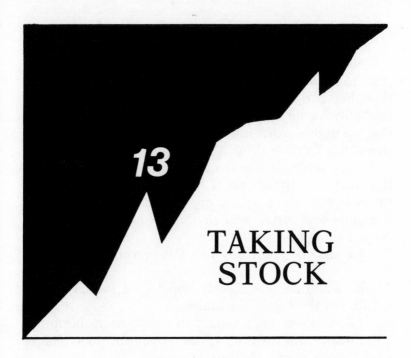

13

TAKING
STOCK

Wait a minute. Hold everything. A $350,000 loss? Why, that's nothing. That's peanuts. I'd lost more than that in one night during G-5. And made it all back and more. So why the hysteria? The uncontrollable sobbing?

Because during G-5 I was still new. Even by my own inflated standards, success was measured in those first few months by the barest survival. Now, however, I was a seasoned professional. I was paid to be right. Everyone else—Adam, Thomas, Chuck—all of them must know my position. I had bought from all of them. Surely they were all laughing at me now, raking in their profits at my expense. No doubt, I agonized, I had replaced Qaddafi as their favorite source of trading-room humor.

Never mind that it was impossible for my competitors to know my position or my P and L. Never mind that they had their own problems. Some of them were probably losing a good deal more than I, and were sitting up nights worrying that everyone was laughing at them. But I didn't think about any of that.

Over the past months I had enjoyed the spotlight that comes with success. I had just received an enormous bonus. My parents, my friends, my associates—everyone was proud and envious. Now all of that was gone, I thought—lost forever.

I guess you could say I took it personally.

As the situation was clearly hopeless, I just lay there wailing at the top of my lungs.

Larry chose this moment to return from shopping.

I heard him turn the key and open the door. Thank God Larry's home! He'll understand.

Larry came running into the bedroom.

"Nancy!" He was pale. "My God! What is it? Are you hurt? Did something happen to you?"

"No, no," I reassured him, between gulps. "I'm not hurt. I'm perfectly all right. Nothing happened to me. I'm fine."

He sat down on the bed and tried to put his arms around me.

"Nancy, sweetheart," he said tenderly. "I've never heard you cry like this before. What's the matter?"

I cried louder.

"Please, honey, tell me what it is," he said, stroking my hair.

"Oh, Larry," I sobbed. "I . . . I . . . ."

"Yes? You what?"

"I . . . I . . . I'm losing money!" I wailed.

There was a moment of silence.

"You're what?" he asked.

"I'm losing money! Oh! I've lost $350,000 in just three weeks!" The statement brought on fresh sobs of self-pity.

Larry stopped hugging me. He stood up.

"Let me get this straight," he said. "You are crying over an options position?"

I cried harder.

"You are crying over a $350,000 loss?"

Heartrending sobs punctuated by hiccups. Another moment of silence. I could feel him glaring at me. Finally, he spoke.

"Are you nuts or something?"

Not the reaction I was expecting.

"Stop it," he said. "That's enough. I mean it."

Surprised, I raised my head from the pillow to look at him.

"You are not going to cry like this over an options position," he said. "That's the stupidest thing I've ever heard of."

"What do you know about it?" I sniffled.

"What do I know about it! Do you think you're the only person who ever lost a little money?"

I stopped crying.

"But don't you see?" I demanded. "Everybody will know I've lost. They'll laugh at me!"

"Who cares if they laugh at you? Who are they? Every trader loses! Did you think you were an exception? Did you think you'd be right every time? You're in the wrong business. You want to be right every time? Sell Hondas.

"This has been coming on for months," Larry continued. "You've been running around like a maniac, begging for disaster."

"What are you talking about? I've never worked this hard in my life!"

"Just working hard isn't enough. You have to work

effectively. You know what it takes to be a good trader? I'll tell you. Discipline, management, and attention to detail. You, my dear, are lacking some of these traits."

"Which ones?" I demanded.

"All of them."

"That's not true," I said.

"Oh, yes, it's true. You've sown your own seeds. Your management style is worse than bad. It's non-existent. Look at how bad Randy has turned out. Let me tell you something. That's your fault. Not his. And why take on the burden of a London office at this time? I told you to make sure you had support systems in place before you went ahead with it."

That I knew was true.

"But what can I do?" I asked.

"The first rule of trading is knowing when to take a loss. If the London office was a mistake, close it. Bring Peter back to New York and wait until the thing can be organized properly."

"No! No way!" I was adamant.

"Why not?"

"Because that would be admitting I was wrong and I'm not going to do that. The whole world knows we opened a London office. We can't back down now. That would mean the whole bank would lose face. I won't do that. I'll work harder, I'll try to rectify my mistakes. But I can't close a desk I just opened."

"All right," said Larry. "Leave it open then. But get your act together or get out."

He went to put the groceries away.

How could I argue with him? He was right. I'd brought all these problems on myself. Well, I thought grimly, if I got myself into this, I can surely get myself out. It's simply a matter of putting my mind to it.

I got up and washed my face. It's hard to take yourself seriously with streaks of mascara running down your cheeks.

▲ ▲ ▲

I spent the weekend strategizing. Looking at the matter from a cool, dispassionate point of view I came to the conclusion that what was needed in this situation was a three-pronged approach.

Lack of adequate operational support was the most significant obstacle in my path. The absence of a satisfactory communications network between New York and London was causing unnecessary foul-ups. In addition, the sheer volume of my trading had increased to the point where I was having trouble controlling the position. At present, the operations department was incapable of generating the kind of reports that were necessary to the smooth functioning of my unit.

Rather than using a computer system to give me accurate, up-to-the-minute information (as all of my competitors did), I was calculating the position by hand. Calculating the position by hand when you're dealing with millions of dollars and hundreds of trades is ludicrous. Punching the wrong number on your calculator can cause an error. Skipping a trade by accident can cause an error. Adding the thirty-third number wrong out of a string of fifty can cause an error. And, of course, by the time you've finished (it takes about two hours to do the job properly), the market has already changed, so your labored calculations are no longer relevant. But they are the best you have, so you use them anyway. It was like living in the Stone Age.

I'd seen other banks' trading operations so I knew it was easy to purchase or develop a system that was capable of calculating in two seconds what currently took me two hours. Not only that, but an on-line computer system could constantly update as the market changed and could show what would happen to the position for a number of different scenarios. Having a good support system does not guarantee good trading, but it certainly helps.

I'd let my section fall behind in installing the necessary support systems. Luckily, I thought, this was a problem easily rectified.

But operational support wasn't the only problem I had to tackle. There was a management problem as well. Larry was right. I wasn't a manager at all.

Trading is a very straightforward business. A trader deals only with numbers. Managing people is a different business altogether. People tend to complicate otherwise rational issues with irrational tendencies to have hopes, dreams, desires, ambitions, and so forth. A good manager has to take all of this into account for each of her subordinates and plot the one course that will maximize that person's potential—a very difficult task, requiring much hard work and patience. A task significantly more difficult than trading.

My most obvious problem was Randy. Instead of ignoring him, I was going to have to sit down and talk to him and tell him all the things that were bothering me and find out what was bothering him. An uncomfortable interview, but necessary if Randy was ever to become a productive member of the group.

The last area of self-improvement was in my actual trading style. I was simply going to have to be more disciplined. I was going to have to take my loss this time and work harder to make it back. I was going to have to think up new trades and watch the markets more closely.

Here once again I came back to the computer system. I knew that there were ways to trade options more conservatively than I'd done in the past. But to analyze the market and find the appropriate strategy required precise data; hand calculations were out of the question.

For the first time I realized the full importance of upgrading my system.

▲ ▲ ▲

The first thing Monday morning I put my plan into action. I began by speaking to Sam.

"I want to talk to you about our computer system," I told him.

"Yes?" said Sam.

"It's not working out," I said flatly. "We need a better system. We need more sophisticated reports and we need them instantaneously. We can't wait two hours every time we have to update the position. And we desperately need to link London to New York."

Sam broke into a smile.

"What's so funny?" I demanded.

"Nothing," he said. "It's just that I couldn't agree with you more."

"I want you to investigate possible ways to improve the situation," I said.

"I'm way ahead of you," said Sam. "I've already started to look into it."

I was impressed. "Fantastic," I said. "Make it a top priority. I need to know my alternatives as soon as possible."

"Got you," said Sam.

"And I want to know everything," I emphasized. "Cost, time to installation, possible problems. Everything."

"Got you," said Sam.

I went back to my desk and looked at the screen. The currency prices had barely moved. I sighed. Time for part two.

"Randy," I said. "I'd like to talk to you."

"Sure," he replied, surprised.

"Not here," I said. "Let's go find someplace quiet."

Randy and I sat facing each other in an empty office off the trading floor.

"So what's the deal?" Randy asked.

I opened my mouth to speak and then closed it.

Now that the time had come for a heart-to-heart, I didn't know what to do. I've always shied away from unpleasantness.

"Are you happy here?" I said finally.

"Happy?" Randy repeated. "Sure. I mean, yeah, I'm happy here."

"Well," I said, getting up my nerve and plunging in, "I'm not."

"Not happy here?"

"No. Not happy with you."

"Oh."

"I don't know quite what to do about it. I'd like to talk about it."

"Go ahead," Randy said coldly.

"You know," I said slowly, trying to choose my words carefully, "it's very important that the atmosphere on a trading desk be congenial to all the participants."

"So?"

"So, I'm afraid that you are detracting from the overall productivity of the desk," I said, hating myself. "I'm sure you don't mean to do it, and that's why I thought if I pointed it out to you we could rectify the situation."

"What do you mean?"

"I mean that sometimes—often, actually—you show a lack of sensitivity to your surroundings. I'm afraid that you tend to chatter during the course of the day and this disturbs the people working around you."

"What do you mean, chatter?"

"Well, Peter and Phillip and I are all pretty quiet people and we need time to concentrate. I don't think you are paying enough attention to that."

"But—" Randy began.

"Let me finish." As long as I had begun, I figured I might as well get it all out before I lost my nerve. "It

212

seems to me that your inclination to talk is also taking your attention away from your own work. You've made any number of careless errors since you've been here. I think if you said less and concentrated more, you'd get farther."

"Fine," Randy replied, his mouth set in a straight line.

"Also, I have to say that I am dissatisfied with the rate at which you've picked up trading. I don't want to see you playing computer games in your spare time in the future. I think you should be working to improve your understanding of options."

"Peter and Phillip play computer games."

"Peter and Phillip," I emphasized, "have been here a lot longer than you have, and they have already demonstrated their abilities to produce. You haven't. You should be using that time to learn."

"Fine," Randy said, shrugging.

He wasn't taking it very well. This made me angry. Couldn't he see that it was just as hard for me as it was for him? If he didn't listen to me, how were we to get anywhere? I felt I'd gone out of my way to be reasonable.

"The last thing," I said, trying to ignore his attitude, "is that I'm going to change your training around a bit. You've been responsible for overseeing the Swiss franc book up until now. That doesn't appear to be working out. I'll take over that book again. What I'm going to do is to give you a specific amount of money to trade with. You can trade it however you please. Phillip, Peter, and I are all available to help you. You can ask us what we think whenever you wish. But you will be responsible for making the ultimate decision. It's yours to win or lose with as you see fit."

"I see," said Randy.

"I hope that by giving you this responsibility you

will learn how difficult it is actually to make decisions in trading. Also, since you often second-guess some of our decisions, this will allow you to put your money where your mouth is."

Randy was silent.

"Well, what do you think?" I asked.

"What difference does it make what I think?" Randy muttered. "You've already made up your mind."

Oh, dear.

I went back to the desk. The market was still quiet. What to do? What to do?

I decided to inform John Anderson of the situation.

"It's important," I warned his secretary.

John's secretary disappeared into his office.

"He can see you now," she said when she re-emerged.

I went into the office. John had just come back from a ten-day ski vacation in northern Italy. He looked terrific: tan, relaxed, fit. The contrast between his appearance and mine is one that I will remember for a long time.

"Well, Nancy," said John smiling. "How are you? Have a seat."

I sat. He was so chipper it was positively disgusting.

"Now, what can I do for you?" he asked, leaning back in his chair expansively.

"Well, I'll tell you, John," I said, leaning forward in mine. "The position is out of control. We need a new, updated computer system. Communications between New York and London are not sufficient to meet our needs. I'm having to get up in the middle of the night and it's affecting my ability to trade. The new trainee I hired in November is not working out. In addition to all of that, I took a large position and we're losing on it. I don't know what to do."

There was a moment of silence. Then John spoke.

"Well," he said, "you do look tired. If you ever want to go on vacation, I can recommend some perfectly charming villas in Italy."

I went back to the desk. There seemed to be no alternative. I took a deep breath, and closed my eyes. Then I picked up the phone and started taking out the position. I sold every option I had bought at a loss.

Three days later the market started to heat up. If I had held that position, I would have indeed made my entire year's projected earnings in one month.

14

OUT
OF THE
FRYING
PAN . . .

Thus I entered into a joyless period during which my mood alternated between frustration, discouragement, and outright gloom. By attempting to pull my section together I was unintentionally committing an unforgivable breach of etiquette. I was trying to get something done.

The bank responded to the threat by calling an all-points bulletin and labeling me Public Enemy Number One. My efforts to acquire an updated computer system were viewed as subversive, suspect, and possibly Communist-inspired.

If I had to do it all over again, there is no question that I would have bypassed the existing bureaucratic structure and settled the matter by walking over to the nearest Radio Shack and purchasing the appropriate computer equipment with my bank-issued MasterCard. That simple act of defiance would have saved the bank so much time and money that they could have bought their own Radio Shack outlet with the proceeds, and so gotten themselves into a real business. But I didn't do that. I tried to get my system by working through the bank's normal channels.

Oh, well. Nobody's perfect.

Sam reported his findings about a week later. "It's like this," he said. "You have two basic alternatives."

"Okay," I replied eagerly, pen and paper in hand. "Shoot."

"Alternative one: you can update your present system by purchasing a minicomputer."

"A minicomputer," I repeated, writing it down. "What is a minicomputer?"

"A minicomputer is bigger and more advanced than a personal computer, but not so big as a regular mainframe computer."

"Will it satisfy all of our needs?" I asked. "Will it have enough memory to solve the problem?"

"It will."

"Will it be able to update the position on a moment's notice?"

"It will."

"Will it be able to put together all kinds of sophisticated reports?"

"It will."

"Will it be able to link New York to London?"

"That," said Sam, "is something I can't answer at the moment."

"Okay," I said, writing. "You check that out. Now, you mentioned a second alternative. What is it?"

217

"Alternative two: link into the bank's mainframe computer."

"Will they let us do that?"

"Well," said Sam slowly, "they should be able to. Basically, what we've got to do is to ask them."

"That doesn't sound too hard."

Out of the mouths of babes.

"Before we ask them, though," I continued. "Will linking into the mainframe satisfy our requirements?"

An expression of pity settled on Sam's features. It's the same look that the TV repairman gives me when I ask if everything's fixed now.

"Nancy," he said, "the mainframe will knock your socks off."

"That's nice," I said. "But will it link New York to London?"

"It will," he said.

Sam went back to further investigate costs and installation. I went back to the desk.

"Anybody want some lunch?" I asked brightly.

"No, thank you," Philip was quick to respond. "But may I offer you some—"

"No, thanks," I said. "Randy?"

Silence.

"Randy?" I repeated, more pointedly. "Would you care for some lunch?"

"No, thanks," he muttered.

There had been quite a change in Randy's attitude since our little chat. And it was all for the worse.

Sam came back after a few days.

"We have to talk," he said.

"Did you find out anything more?" I asked.

"Well," said Sam. "I found out that a minicomputer will be able to link New York to London."

"Terrific," I said.

"And I found out how much it will cost." He named a figure.

"All right," I said, writing it down. "And how long will it take to install?"

"Well," said Sam, "if I order one right now, it will probably be up and running in a month. Two weeks to deliver, two weeks to run tests."

It was then the beginning of February. That would mean I would have an updated system by March.

"Okay," I said, writing. "Now, what about the mainframe?"

"About the mainframe . . ." Sam hesitated.

"Yes?" I said.

"To be honest with you," said Sam, "I'd rather go with the mainframe. It seems silly to buy a brand-new minicomputer when the bank already has a mainframe that will serve the purpose. I mean, we've got the capability right here. It's a waste of money to duplicate effort."

That sounded reasonable.

"Well," I said. "How long would it take to link up?"

"The actual linkup time," said Sam, "is nothing. Two weeks. Just the time it takes to run the tests, same as on the minicomputer."

"That sounds good," I said. "So what's the problem?"

"The problem is getting the approval," said Sam. "That can take serious time."

"Well, before we go to the trouble of getting approval," I said, "will the cost of the mainframe alternative be competitive with that of the minicomputer?"

Sam hesitated.

"It should be," he said finally. "In fact, it should be much cheaper. But . . ."

"But what?" I asked.

"Well," said Sam uncomfortably, "I wasn't able to

get an exact number from the people in charge of mainframe time. It seems they can't do anything unless I fill out a number of forms."

"So fill out the forms," I said.

"I already started to," said Sam.

"So what's the problem?"

"Well," said Sam, "they say it can take up to two months to get an answer after the completed forms are received."

"To get an approval?" I asked.

"No. To get an estimate of cost. The approval process can't start until the cost is estimated."

"Oh!" I said. "Not very speedy of them, is it?"

"No," said Sam.

"I assume the problem is not one of literacy?"

"Sorry?" Sam asked.

"They can read, can't they?"

"As far as I know," Sam grinned.

"In that case," I said, "we should be able to speed up the whole process by going right to the top."

"What are you going to do?" asked Sam.

"I'm going to enlist the aid of John Anderson," I announced.

"Oh!" said Sam, not very enthusiastically.

"He is administrative head of the trading floor," I reminded him. "This is his job. It's right up his alley."

"Uh-huh." Sam looked at me.

"It's at least worth a try," I argued.

I made an appointment to see John.

"What can I do for you?" John asked when I got in to see him.

I explained about the new system and the two alternatives. I outlined the problems I was having getting information from the people responsible for the mainframe. As this was a matter of priority, I was wondering if he couldn't be of assistance.

"Glad to help out," said John. "I know just what to do."

"What's that?" I asked.

"We'll set up a meeting and . . ."

The need for the new system was becoming more and more pressing.

As quiet as the market had been in January, when I needed it to be active, that's how active it was in February and March when I needed it to be quiet. The economic forecast for the year was getting worse. Even the Reagan administration was forced to revise downward its estimates of the gross national product.

Recognizing the need for action, Secretary of the Treasury Baker began a concerted policy of talking down the dollar. This apparently fell into the category of: when in doubt, do what's easiest. Even though the dollar had already depreciated by about 25 percent since its high in March 1985 to no appreciable effect, it was certainly simpler to continue this policy than to try to reduce the budget deficit (which many argued was the real culprit), a more formidable task.

But the dollar's slide was a subject for concern by one of the most intelligent and respected members of the financial community: Federal Reserve Chairman Paul Volcker. Volcker, one of the unsung heroes of the last decade (he single-handedly broke the spiral of inflationary expectations that had hurled the country into a recession), understood that too rapid a decline in the value of the dollar would cause more problems than it would prevent. He also seemed to be more familiar with market psychology than the other members of the Reagan administration, and knew that government intervention was likely to provoke extreme price movements that hadn't been intended. Accordingly, he tried to temper Secretary Baker's announcements by ad-

221

dressing himself to all of the problems inherent in a too-rapidly-falling dollar.

The trading community interpreted these actions as a power struggle between Baker and Volcker. They sold the dollar when Baker spoke and bought it back when Volcker replied. Since these verbal tugs of war often came without a moment's notice, and increased in frequency as the participants became more intense, the markets became extremely volatile. The dollar swung like a yo-yo.

Under these circumstances, it was almost impossible for me to calculate my position by hand. As trading was extremely active, my portfolio was growing. I was having to trade off of the barest estimates of what I actually had. As I continued to speak to London at three o'clock every morning before coming into work, I became more and more exhausted. My fatigue was evident in my attire, my face, the very way I walked. I started taking a nap at my desk at about four o'clock every afternoon, in order to prepare myself for the evening's trading.

I couldn't just stop trading, either. I had to protect my existing portfolio, sometimes by putting on new trades. And other bank traders were calling me often to make them prices. Since I needed them to make prices for me, I had to reciprocate. Otherwise when I needed them, they wouldn't be there. It should come as no surprise that I was continuing to lose money.

Although Randy's attitude was unbearable, I waited a week before speaking to him again. When I couldn't stand it anymore, I called him into the empty office again. This time there was no pretense of pleasantry. I simply told him that he was on probation, and that if his attitude didn't change I'd have to let him go.

"Probation?" he squeaked.

"I can't see why you're surprised," I said flatly. "You can't tell me you've tried since our last talk. You've been impossible on the desk. Can't you see that I have enough to worry about without you? Do you really think there's another trader on the Street who would have put up with what I've put up with? How can you sit there and add to my problems? Have you so little conception of what is happening right under your nose?"

There was a moment of silence.

"You're right," he admitted suddenly. "I was angry and I suppose I acted badly. I'm sorry. You have every right to be angry."

"Do you want this job or don't you?" I asked.

"I do. I do." He assured me. "You'll see. I'll change."

In fact, he did try to change. I could see that he was trying, now that he was under the gun.

But did I really want someone who worked hard only when threatened with dismissal? Did I want someone so unsuited to the work and to the rest of the section? Was I being fair to Randy, to myself, to the unit by keeping him on?

The first meeting to discuss my new computer system was called for 3:00 P.M. When I arrived I was surprised to see how many people had already assembled. Besides Sam and myself I recognized Kashir Rameshwar, two assistant administrators, the head of credit for the trading floor, and a couple of unfamiliar faces, including that of an older man, with close-cropped silver hair, who sat ramrod-straight in a hard chair. He was in incredibly good physical condition. His expression was severe. This could only be William Hambrecht, head of the operations department, the infamous Field Marshall.

What's going on here? I thought. Surely all of these people aren't involved in the decision! I started to have

223

a very bad feeling about all of this. By now a veteran meeting-goer, I knew that the larger the crowd, the more difficult it was to get anything accomplished.

John entered and called the room to order. "Let's get started," he said briskly. "We are here to discuss—" he consulted some notes "—Nancy's request for a new computer system."

Murmurs of surprise up and down the table. The two administrative assistants began taking notes.

"I'm going to turn the floor over to Nancy," said John. "Let's all try to get together on this one!"

Everyone looked at me.

"The expansion into London and the corresponding increase in the volume of our options trading business," I began, "has pointed out the inadequacies of our current computer system. We must upgrade. Sam has already done some research on this subject." I explained about the two alternatives and the problems we were having getting answers from the bank's mainframe department.

"I'd like to make this a top priority," I concluded. "That means that someone who is in charge here" (I looked meaningfully at John) "will have to speak to someone in charge there. That's all that's necessary. I'm sorry that most of you had to waste your time attending this meeting. I'm afraid there's very little most of you can do."

For a moment nobody spoke. Then: "Can you explain again why you need the new system?" asked one of the administrative assistants.

"Can you explain again the system you are currently using?" asked the head of the credit department.

"Vot are de choices again?" asked Kashir.

"What is an option?" asked one of the people I couldn't identify.

An hour and a half later, after I had repeated my story at least five times, I tried to make the point again that what was necessary was a high-level conference and a willingness to make my request a top priority.

"I don't see that that's a problem," said John, finally. "I suppose I can speak to someone in charge. What do you think, William?" he asked, turning to look at the Field Marshall.

We all turned to look at the Field Marshall. Obviously relishing the moment for dramatic effect, the Field Marshall frowned at his pencil. Finally, he spoke.

"Let's start over again from the beginning," he said.

The decision to fire Randy was the most agonizing one of my entire career. The night before I fired him, I was miserable. Yet there was no alternative. Randy's employment was a glaring error that needed to be corrected. It was a lesson that I would never have to learn twice.

The conversation with Randy the next morning was brief. I couldn't even look at him. I simply told him that it wasn't working out and that he would have to go. Randy packed up his few belongings and left without saying good-bye to anyone. I went into the ladies' room and cried.

In the midst of all of this, I got a call from Thomas, the investment banker.

"Hi, Nancy. How's it going?"

"Oh, hi, Thomas. Everything's fine. The usual," I lied. My heart sank. Thomas dealt only in large numbers. If he asked me for a price I might end up trading $50 million worth of options that I didn't really want. It would be the icing on today's cake. But I couldn't say no to him. That would be a sign of weakness.

"Glad to hear it."

"What can I do for you, Thomas?" I asked, taking the plunge. Might as well get it over with quickly. "Would you like me to make you a price?"

"Actually, no."

"No?" What luck!

"I'm calling because I'd like to ask you to dinner," said Thomas.

"Dinner?" I repeated stupidly.

"Yes. It's important. I have something I want to talk to you about."

"Sure. Fine," I said. What could Thomas have to say to me?

I met Thomas at a restaurant frequented by members of the trading community. He didn't waste any time. He got right down to business.

"Nancy, I suppose you've guessed what I wanted to talk to you about," he said.

"Actually not," I replied.

"Well, then, let me tell you. I have an opening on my desk for a trader. I want you to apply."

With everything that had been happening to me, this was the last thing I'd expected. I stared at him with my mouth open. He waited for me to say something, and when I didn't, he continued.

"You'd be working for me. It's an extremely prestigious position. I went to a lot of trouble just to get management to agree to see you."

"Why?" I asked.

"Don't you know why?"

"No."

"You're a woman," he said.

I started to laugh. "You're kidding, right? This is the 1980s."

"I'm not kidding at all. The position I'm offering you is one that involves trading the firm's own capital. They've never had a woman doing that before. It took me two months just to get them to agree to meet you."

Well. Here it was. The kind of job offer that every trader dreams of. A way to get away from the bank and leave the frustration and turmoil of the past two months behind me. Thomas was the best. Whenever I'd spoken with him, I'd always learned something new. His firm had enormous clout in the market.

"No," I said.

"No?" he repeated, astonished. "Wait a minute, before you give me your answer, let me finish. You haven't heard me out. Maybe you don't understand what I'm offering you. You get all the responsibility you can take. You'll trade for larger sums than almost anyone else in the market. I don't have to tell you what kind of power my firm commands."

"I know."

"I haven't even talked about money yet. Don't you want to know what I'm offering? These aren't firm figures, you understand—everything's subject to negotiation—but the compensation is excellent. Your salary is minimal, of course—something over $100,000, just to cover living expenses—but the bonus is substantial. If you perform well and the desk has a good year, we could hand you a check for half a million dollars at the end of the year."

So investment banks did pay that kind of money.

"Take some time to think about it," he urged.

I looked at him.

"I appreciate the offer," I said. "I really do. But I don't need time to think about it. The answer is no."

Larry was waiting up for me when I got home that night. He knew I was having dinner with Thomas.

"What happened?" he asked.

"He offered me a job."

Larry looked at me. "What did you say?"

"I refused."

A look of relief passed over his face. "Why?" he asked.

"I don't know. I just knew it was the right thing to do."

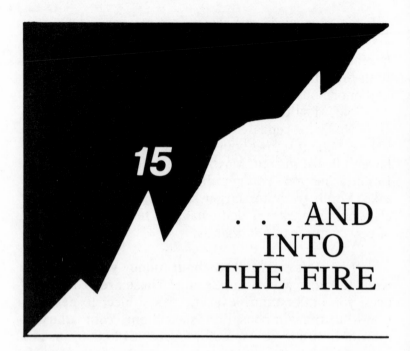

15

. . . AND INTO THE FIRE

Why didn't I take that job?

On the surface, it seemed the culmination of everything I'd worked for since graduate school. It represented achievement with a capital *A*. Here was power and money on a scale that most people only dream about. I didn't know another trader on the Street who would have turned it down.

But something inside of me said no. It was a purely instinctive reaction. I guess I was beginning to understand at just what price such power is bought. It would be bought at the price of my marriage. It would be bought at the price of all my time and energy. The pressure would have been enormous. Even more than what I was currently experiencing. I would have had

to be single-minded in my determination to accumu-
late wealth. Nothing could interfere with that commitment.

A very expensive trade.

My instinct for self-preservation, however, did not yet
extend to my present circumstances. I was at my desk
a few days later when Sam approached me.

"I have to talk to you," he said.

"Sure," I said, surprised.

"Not here," he said, looking around.

We went and found an empty office.

"Did we get those cost figures yet?" I asked him.

"Just got them."

"Terrific! Is the mainframe cheaper or more expensive than the minicomputer?"

"Significantly cheaper than the minicomputer. Also,
once you go on the mainframe you never have to worry
about it again. If you expand to other cities you won't
have a problem. With a minicomputer you might have
to go through this again as you continue to grow. I
strongly suggest that you go with the mainframe alternative. There's absolutely no reason why that couldn't
be up and running soon."

"Well," I said, "I'll do what you suggest. You're
about the only person around here who knows what
he's talking about."

"Thanks," said Sam, looking uncomfortable.

"You're also one of the few people who really works
hard and has tried to help. I want to thank you for
everything you've done, and let you know how much I
appreciate you. I don't know what I'd do without you.
Now, what was it you wanted to tell me?"

"I'm resigning."

"You're what?" I could hardly believe my ears.

"I'm resigning. I got a better offer from another

bank. It's for $10,000 more a year. I'm sorry, but I can't turn down an increase like that. It's too much money."

I tried to think. If it was only a matter of money, perhaps I could stop him.

"What are you earning here?" I asked.

"Twenty-five thousand a year," he replied. After a short pause he added: "You can see why $10,000 more a year makes such a big difference. You know, I'm married, and my wife and I have always wanted to buy a house. . . ."

"Yes, yes, I can't say I blame you," I assured him. "You're underpaid at $25,000 a year."

"You're telling me." He grinned.

"Listen," I said urgently, "what if I got the bank to match your increase? Would you stay then?"

"Save your breath," Sam said flatly. "William will never approve the increase. He'll be happy to see me go. He's never liked me."

"But if I did," I persisted. "Would you reconsider?"

"Nancy," said Sam, "I've always liked working with you. I've had my problems working here, but you've never been part of them. In fact, I hope that I have the chance to work with you again sometime. But just accept it. There's no way you're going to keep me here. You'll just be wasting your time."

"Please answer me, Sam. If I get you the extra $10,000, will you reconsider?"

There was a pause. Then Sam smiled at me.

"If the bank matches the offer, I'll reconsider."

The thought of life at the bank without Sam was frightening. I made yet another appointment with John Anderson to see if I could get Sam the $10,000 increase, a small raise, even by the bank's standards. It was getting to be a regular visitation.

"But, Nancy," said John, after I'd explained the

problem, "Sam's not my responsibility. He's in William Hambrecht's department."

"I know," I said, "but you are one of the highest-ranking officers in the whole bank! You are senior to Hambrecht. I know you have no direct authority over operations, but I'm sure that if you talked to him, he'd listen. He'd have to."

"I can try, I suppose," John admitted.

"Please," I urged him. "It's really important. I wouldn't come to you if it wasn't. It's only $10,000. If William's upset about the money, tell him I'll pay it out of my section. We just can't risk losing Sam right now. Even if he only stays until he trains someone else to take his place! Please."

"I'll see what I can do," said John.

After another series of meetings (almost three months since I had initiated the request), a philosophic decision was reached to pursue a link into the bank's mainframe computer. William promised to obtain the necessary approval to perform the actual task as soon as was humanly possible.

In the meantime, the days passed bleakly. Nothing had really changed. Phillip and I were struggling to keep our heads above water in a churning market. This was nothing, however, compared to the quality of my home life.

"Look at you!" Larry exploded in one of our never-ending battles. "You look awful! You're losing weight! The phone rings at three in the morning every night! How can you expect to trade under these conditions? You're not doing your job or your marriage any good. Don't you see how hard it is for me to stand by and watch you destroy yourself?"

"Please try to understand," I moaned.

"What is there to understand? I'm worried about you! You promised me you'd change. Well, you have. You've gotten worse!"

"Have some chow mein," I urged. "You'll feel better after you've eaten."

"I don't want to feel better! I want something done! If you can't handle it, quit!" He paused. His expression changed. "Nancy, is this really the way you want to spend your life?"

"What do you mean?"

"It's just that you don't seem very happy."

"Please," I said. "We'll get that system soon. You'll see. Then things will get better. Just hang on a little longer."

"Oh, Nancy," Larry sighed. "It's not just the system. You're kidding yourself."

"Nancy," said John Anderson, "I'm afraid I have some bad news."

"What is it?" I asked, bracing myself.

"William Hambrecht absolutely refuses to raise Sam's salary by the necessary $10,000. He says your back office can survive perfectly well without him."

"How would he know?" I asked sharply. "He's never even been in my back office."

"He says that no one is irreplaceable. I'm afraid I have to agree with him."

"But, John," I began again, despairingly, "you don't understand all the risks—"

"I do understand," said John. "I understand that you are a highly emotional young lady. I believe you are upset over losing Sam. I'm sorry, but there's nothing I can do."

Highly emotional?

"Look," said John with a grin, "if it makes you feel any better, William has absolutely guaranteed the smooth functioning of your back office. He promised me that you wouldn't even notice that Sam was gone."

Sam left a week later.

"Good luck," I said, kissing him good-bye on the cheek.

"No hard feelings, I hope?" he asked.

"Of course not," I said. "I would have done the same in your place."

"Well, good luck to you, too," he said. Then he paused.

"I guess you'll need it."

For the first week that Sam was gone we did not get one single report produced on time. No reports got to London. The reports that we did get were wrong. I don't remember the exact amount of money that we lost that week. I do remember that it was significantly in excess of the $10,000 it would have cost to keep Sam.

On the Friday afternoon of that memorable week, I went to the back office to check on my reports. I paused at the door and surveyed the scene. The room looked as if it had been hit by a hurricane. There were heaps of paper everywhere. On the desks, on the shelves, on the floor, in and out of the wastepaper baskets, on the window ledge, on top of the computers, on top of the printers. Only the ceiling remained uncluttered.

Buried beneath the mountains of paper were two people, working frantically. There was no sign of William Hambrecht. I wanted to ask when my reports would be ready, but one look inside that room changed my mind. I returned to my desk.

"Phillip," I said.

"Huh?" Phillip looked up from his charts.

"We have to help them back there. They're so disorganized. It's no wonder they're having problems."

"Yes, I know." Phillip looked grave.

"We have an even bigger problem, though," I continued. "Over the weekend the leaders of the industrialized nations are meeting again to plan economic policy."

"I know," said Phillip.

"This could be a big weekend," I remarked. "The dollar could really move depending on what's decided there."

"I know," said Phillip.

"It could be another G-5," I said.

"I know," said Phillip.

"What do you think our chances are of having an up-to-date report on our position by the end of the day?"

"Uh," said Phillip, "I guess not very good."

"I agree," I said. "I'll tell you what. Why don't you go back there and see if you can be of any assistance while I stay here and try to run up the position by hand?"

"Okay."

At 6:00 P.M. I had my reports. They were obviously wrong. Phillip and I found the errors. Phillip went to correct and reprint the reports. I went to see John Anderson.

"Hello, Nancy," said John.

"I just thought I'd let you know that there's a G-5 meeting this weekend," I said coldly.

"I know," said John.

"As of right now," I said, "I want you to know that I don't have a report of my position. If it weren't for hours of manual calculations, I wouldn't even know if I was long or short the dollar. The back office is a shambles. I'm going home now. I'll come in on Sunday. If there are no reports on my desk, I will not take responsibility for what happens Monday morning."

I turned and left. Highly emotional, huh? Let him worry for a change.

▲ ▲ ▲

234

I got my reports on Sunday. I spent all day in the office preparing for every possible scenario. An on-line computer system could have done everything in five minutes.

The G-5 meeting turned out to be a nonevent. All that work for nothing.

Somehow we got through the next few weeks. Faced with mounting losses, I developed a gambler's mentality. It was impossible to trade conservatively without accurate data. It seemed that my updated computer system was no closer to installation than it had been in January. There was always some new delay.

Hoping against hope for a windfall, I took larger and larger positions on the dollar. I wanted to make it all back quickly and start afresh. This resulted in some truly horrendous trading decisions as my exhausted brain strained to wrestle with a volatile climate. I threw caution to the wind as I threw money at the market.

I was completely, totally, abjectly miserable. I believed that it was all my fault. The losses, the disorganization, the disintegration of my unit, everything. I had invested every particle of my being into this job and I was coming up negative.

Ensnared within the bounds of my own paranoia, I felt my failure in the glances of my associates and superiors. I felt they blamed me for what was happening, and that they looked down on me. That they all knew me for the loser I was. And I believed them. I developed into a person I didn't recognize. I snapped at people for no apparent reason, but actually as a preemptive strike, anticipating their rejection. The marketing desk lived in fear of me. I hated myself. I retreated behind the fortresslike safety of my wall of screens.

I found myself sitting in the conference room again, victim of yet another meeting on the subject of my phantom computer system. I'd lost count of the number of times we'd met to discuss the issue. The same faces, the same questions, the same excuses. I was experiencing an eerie feeling of déjà vu.

The Field Marshall was explaining why the system wouldn't be ready for at least another month. The administrative assistant was wondering aloud whether we shouldn't go back and reconsider the minicomputer alternative. The credit official was asking if the new system would have an impact on credit lines. If so, he was against it.

They were wearing me down. This must be what it feels like to be a political prisoner, I thought; having to repeat the same story over and over again to stony-faced interrogators. The only thing missing was the bright lights shining in my eyes. On the other hand, I had William Hambrecht.

I wearily opened my mouth to reiterate how important this system was to my operation, how I couldn't trade without it, how it couldn't be put off another day, another hour, another minute. I looked from one blank face to the other. Slowly, I closed my mouth.

I'm the kind of person who feels first and thinks second. Suddenly, I had a feeling.

I don't belong here.

This truth freed my thought process. It was so instantaneously obvious that I wondered how I had ever felt different. In that moment, for the first time in months, I was able to look at the situation with some semblance of objectivity. Look at them! I thought. They don't care what's happening. They all know what a problem it is by this time. They all know that it's costing the bank money. I'm the only one who cares. Each of them is caught up in his own little fiefdom. They are actually enjoying watching me suffer. They view passive obstruction as a means of increasing power and influence. It's more important to them that they reaffirm their individual superiority than that they do their jobs in the general interest of the bank.

I don't, I mused, have anything in common with any of them, do I? It's as if I'm from another planet. I actually believe that they resent me for bringing this problem to their attention and making such a fuss about it. They think I'm just making waves.

Look at them! I thought again. Why, they think—they think—

I stopped.

They think *I'm* the problem!

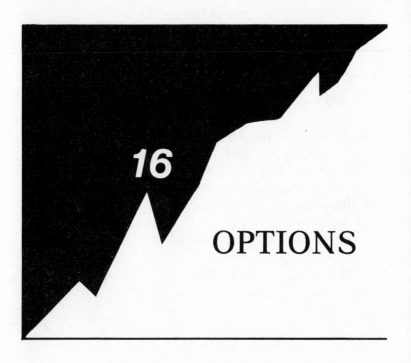

16

OPTIONS

To have worked so hard at something and then to be made a mockery of for the very efforts you've made necessarily provokes some self-examination.

The same conditions that had allowed me to become a head trader in just three months were now preventing me from acquiring the support necessary to do the job properly. I had never, I decided, understood the rules of the commercial banking game. If I was having problems with John, William, and all the rest of them, who was really at fault? If the system was protected, nourished, and promoted by those who functioned within its confines, who was to blame, the outsider or the system? Hadn't I really brought all this on myself by ignoring the obvious and trying to change a system that had no reason for changing?

Put another way, if nobody else cared, wasn't I the bigger fool for trying?

"Larry," I announced calmly at dinner that evening, "I'm going to leave the bank."

"Well!" he said, setting down his chopsticks in surprise. "Other than turning down Thomas, that's the first sensible thing you've said in six months." He paused. "Are you sure you're feeling all right?"

"I don't belong there," I continued, ignoring him. "I learned that today."

"Let me feel your forehead," he said, leaning over. "You're going to stop trading? Maybe I should take you to the hospital."

"Cut it out," I snapped. "It's not funny. Besides, I didn't say I was going to quit trading altogether. I said I was going to leave the bank. I'm going to try to get a job at another organization, someplace where I won't feel like a fool for trying to do a good job."

"Oh!" he sighed, starting to eat again.

"So, where do you think I should go?"

"How should I know?" Larry countered. "Trading is the same everywhere. It's all the same breed."

"That can't be true!" I exclaimed, thinking of John, William, and Kashir.

"Oh, I'm not saying you'll find the same level of incompetence at other institutions," said Larry.

"Of course not!" I said, reassured.

"It will probably be worse," he continued.

"Oh."

"But in some places it will be better. Investment banking, for example, is more professional than commercial banking."

"I'm not going to an investment bank," I said. "I've already made that decision."

"Why don't you face facts? It's basically the same everywhere."

"You just want me to stop trading!" I said accusingly.

"I'm not saying that. But I wonder if you really want to keep trading."

"Larry, you're wrong." I was adamant. "I love trading. I don't want to give it up. I just want to move to a place where there are other people like me."

"There is no such place."

"Larry, think of all the money!"

"Forget the money. Money is a false issue. We're not going to starve. Tell me something. You didn't dream about becoming a trader when you were younger, did you?"

"Of course not," I said. "I didn't know what trading was when I was younger."

"Well, what did you want to be when you were growing up?" Larry asked.

"Secretary of state. But I don't think the position's available at the moment."

"Oh, come on. What did you really want to be?"

"Oh, Larry," I sighed. "This isn't getting us anywhere."

"C'mon, this is the first real conversation we've had in months. Indulge me."

"We've had lots of conversations."

"I don't call speculating on the possible outcome of a G-5 meeting a conversation. Let's talk about something interesting for a change."

I thought for a moment. "When I was growing up I wanted to be a writer," I said finally.

"There you go!"

"But, Larry, that was a dream. A dream!"

"What's wrong with dreams?" Larry demanded.

"They're not real, for one thing!"

"You have to make them real."

"Will you stop being so silly?" I sighed.

"What's so silly about it? I think trying to be a writer is an excellent idea. Why did you want to be a writer when you were younger?"

"Why . . . because it's creative, I suppose. And worthwhile. I have a lot of respect for writers."

"Has any of that changed?" Larry asked.

"No."

"Exactly. And do you feel that way about trading? That it's creative and worthwhile?"

"Well . . . not exactly . . . I mean, some parts of it are creative, I suppose, although not on the same level—"

"What about its being worthwhile?" Larry pressed. "Do you think that trading is a worthwhile profession?"

"It certainly pays better."

"That's not an answer."

"Writing's not practical!"

"I'm glad all writers don't feel that way."

"Larry, I am not going to quit trading to write," I said. "It's not an alternative."

"Suit yourself," Larry shrugged.

"Sometime later, perhaps. But not now."

"Just don't wait too long," he said softly.

Leave trading for a career in writing—what was Larry thinking of? I sighed. Did he really think that people were capable of such abrupt turnabouts, and at my age? (I conveniently forgot that I was only twenty-eight.) Why didn't I take up tap dancing as well, while I was at it? Or lion taming? Or nuclear physics?

Sure, I had wanted to write. Everybody has his dreams. But, honestly, I thought, how many people actually pursue them? And of those that try, how many succeed? That was what was important, wasn't it?

Success? I thought so. Hadn't I found that success brings along with it all those lovely intangibles like power, admiration, respect? To say nothing of more tangible rewards—like money? What was the point of trying something if you didn't have a better-than-even chance for success? I mean, what kind of trade was that?

Larry is so forceful, I thought, he makes almost any argument persuasive. It's odd that someone who is normally so intelligent can sprout such idealistic drivel from time to time. He can't actually believe it.

I know! I thought. It must be all those ideas from the sixties. Every now and then he reverts. I'll bet he's been listening to his old Bob Dylan albums again when I'm not around.

I was still determined to quit the bank. I recognized that I'd make a mistake and I needed to correct it. I planned to interview at small, private trading firms until I found one that suited. Options traders were always in demand. I didn't anticipate having any problem finding a new employer.

I started to check around. A little investigation revealed the names of two or three companies that looked promising. One in particular stood out from the rest.

It was a company that had been started by a man named Brad Rubens, who began trading in the early 1970s and was now enormously successful. His firm had started with a couple of million dollars and was now managing hundreds of millions. Brad Rubens was recognized throughout the industry for his achievement. He'd been written up in the newspapers for his brilliant career. He was wealthy beyond my wildest expectations. He owned a number of vacation homes in addition to a fabulous estate, expensive sports cars, a stable of thoroughbred horses, plus several yachts and private planes. The picture of a man who had wrestled with life and won a unanimous decision.

That sounds good, I thought. I'll go there.

The treasurer of the company agreed to meet me right away. He even sounded enthusiastic. We agreed to meet at four o'clock in the bar at the Waldorf-Astoria. The treasurer told me that he would be bringing along Brad Rubens.

I'm going to meet Brad Rubens! I thought. What an honor! Even if he doesn't need an options trader or want to finance an options trading program, at least I'll have a chance to speak with him and maybe I'll learn something. He would be perhaps the most successful man I would ever meet.

I was really worried about that interview. Not so much about getting the job, but about holding my own. This man held a Ph.D. in applied mathematics from a top university. What if I said something stupid? Stop it, I told myself. Anyone with half a brain listens to someone else the first time, and Brad Rubens will be no exception. If he thinks you have nothing to contribute, he simply won't see you again.

The big day arrived. I excused myself from the office at about three-thirty that sunny May afternoon and made my way over to the Waldorf-Astoria.

The bar the treasurer had chosen was very much a man's province: dark, clubby, with massive leather chairs and an enormous, perfectly polished wooden bar. The waiters wore bow ties, black pants, and immaculate white shirts. The atmosphere conjured up visions of a high-class pool hall.

As it was still relatively early in the afternoon, there weren't too many people drinking yet. What patrons there were were portly male figures dressed in dark suits, clutching heavy glasses of scotch and soda or bourbon.

I saw the bartender and one of the waiters exchange an amused glance as I tripped through the artificial gloom in my light spring dress and high heels. I sat down at a table for four.

At least they won't have any trouble spotting me in this crowd, I thought.

A waiter appeared.

"May I get you something to drink, madam?" he asked, addressing the question to the air over my head.

"Ginger ale, please," I replied.

"Ginger . . . ale?"

One good thing about trading. It teaches you how to scare waiters into action.

"Ginger ale," I said, in the voice I used to deal $20 million.

While he didn't seem to recognize the beverage, he was apparently used to the tone of voice.

"Right away, madam."

The ginger ale arrived promptly.

I crossed my legs, sipped my drink, and waited.

I tried to sit up very straight in my chair. This was a problem as the glossy material of my skirt kept slipping against the shiny leather. It would be just my luck to slip right off the chair and under the table during a crucial moment of the interview. I was preoccupied with this unexpected dilemma when two men entered the bar, glanced around, and started in my direction.

That's them, I thought. I stood up when they got to the table.

"I'm Nancy Goldstone," I said, extending my hand.

The taller of the two men shook hands. "I'm Richard Lewis," he said.

This was the treasurer. "Pleased to meet you," I replied.

"And this," continued Richard, "is Brad Rubens."

I held out my hand. Brad shook it limply and grunted something unintelligible at me. We all sat down. "Let's get a waiter over here," Brad growled.

The waiter appeared, and while they ordered their drinks I had a chance to study the two men.

Richard had a pleasant, open face, but was obviously nervous. He faced me with a frozen smile. Brad was extremely short and given to chunkiness. When we shook hands, I'd towered over him. His expensive clothes couldn't hide the fact that he was uncomfortable with his own body. He sat with his back to me, preferring to fling his comments over his shoulder, out of the side of his mouth. It must have been an extremely uncomfortable position. My clearest view was of the back of his head. This was an interesting study as Brad was going bald and combed what hair he had left up and around, rather like a turban.

There was an uncomfortable silence.

"I'm very pleased to meet you," I said finally. "I'm glad you could make it."

Richard smiled nervously at me. "Have you been waiting long?" he asked.

"Not very—" I started to answer.

Brad cut me off. "Let's get down to business, shall we?" he demanded curtly, turning his head so I got a quick glimpse of his profile. "I don't have all afternoon." He consulted his watch. "I have a train to catch. Let's make this quick."

I was shocked by his rudeness. Richard, glancing down uncomfortably at his Coke, picked up the slack. Both men had yet to look me straight in the eye, although I think Richard wanted to. "You mentioned that you traded options," he said to encourage me.

"Yes," I said, trying to overlook Brad's strange behavior. "I run the options desk for the bank. I've decided I no longer want to work for a commercial bank. The system is too heavily bureaucratic to be conducive to effective trading. I am going to take my trading program to a smaller, more efficient organization. I thought you might be interested. You said you were."

Brad made a noise rather like a snort. "What's your trading program?" he sneered in my general direction. He made it obvious that he considered it unlikely that I could add, let alone trade.

I started to get angry, but I tried to keep my poise. "Well, it's rather complicated," I hedged.

No trader gives away his program until he's sure that the person he's speaking to isn't simply going to steal it. This was an industry rule, and Mr. Rubens knew it as well as I did. He'd done nothing to inspire the necessary level of confidence.

"What are we doing here then?" he snapped triumphantly. "I expected to see a written proposal of your trading program. Where is it?"

The man suggests a bar for the first meeting, and then expects me to hand over a detailed proposal for his casual perusal?

"I don't have a proposal with me," I said.

"Well, we don't have much to talk about then, do we?" he jeered. "If you want to send over a written proposal, I'll look at it." He got up from the table. "Right now I'm afraid we have to catch a train. Will you excuse us?"

For the first time Richard looked right at me. He was openly embarrassed about his boss's behavior and was trying to offer me an unspoken apology. I think he was as surprised at Brad's reaction to me as I was.

They left me at the table. It took me a moment to realize that a man who was worth in excess of $50 million had just left me with the check.

I walked all the way home from the Waldorf-Astoria to my apartment on the upper West Side. It was a beautiful spring afternoon, but I didn't notice. It was rush hour and the streets were packed with people hurrying home from work. I didn't notice them either. Some of them probably noticed me, however. I was the person having a loud conversation with herself.

The nerve of that man! I fumed. Of all the low-down miserable, slimy little twerps! How rude! How boorish! What a totally vile little worm of a man! Oh, why didn't I throw my ginger ale in his face? I seethed.

But wasn't Brad's behavior just an exaggeration of symptoms I'd already spotted among my peers? Could it be that, instead of growing out of their insecurities as they became more successful, they instead grew more firmly fixed in them.? That trading so catered to an individual's uncertainty that, instead of facing it down and overcoming the problem, the person hid from the truth and let the feeling grow until it was overwhelming? That trading built upon your fears of worthlessness, so that you took refuge in numbers and money, money, money? Look what money had done for Brad Rubens.

Was this the kind of person I wanted to be? Did I belong in trading at all?

It certainly was a very good question. What, I asked myself, did I really like about trading? About the business? In the end, I could find only one thing that I unequivocally liked about trading. I liked telling people that I was a trader. Although most people had no idea what a trader was, they were usually very impressed with the statement and tended to treat me with a mixture of fear and respect. I liked being treated with a mixture of fear and respect.

But it wasn't really me they respected, was it? It was the act of trading, and the money it represented. After all, the people I met at parties didn't know me at all. They couldn't respect me because I was a nice person or a good person or a creative person; they only respected me because they thought I did something difficult and flashy for a living. Most people never looked beyond the reputation of the job.

And that was what was so nice about trading, wasn't it? I never had to show any other side of myself; I could hide behind the business. That's what most people did. That was what Brad Rubens had done.

Over the past year or so, I'd really become a trader in that sense of the word, hadn't I? All other aspects of my life and my personality had become subordinated to the business. Creativity, warmth, energy, even my marriage—all sacrificed to the trader in me.

What if I couldn't tell people, upon being introduced, that I was a trader? What if I took away that category, with all the confidence it implied? What kind of person would be left? Would people still like me or respect me if I wasn't a trader? Would I like and respect myself? What would I have left? Why, at the rate I was going, I'd have nothing left.

On that note, I limped into the apartment. "How'd it go?" asked Larry.

"Terrible. Horrible."

"As bad as all that?" asked Larry.

"Worse," I said gloomily, and went on to describe my meeting with Brad Rubens.

"So where does this guy live?" Larry asked innocently when I had finished.

"I don't know," I said. "Why do you ask?"

"Because I'm going to go beat the living—— out of him," said my husband.

For the first time in ages, I laughed. "Me first," I said.

"I guess this means you're not going to work for Brad Rubens."

"I guess not."

"So what are you going to do?" Larry asked.

"I don't know."

I spent the next two weeks following my old routine, but I couldn't miss the fact that it was getting on toward summer. Summer! Stifling subways and stuffy offices. I dreaded it. It was a time when most people are looking forward to a little relaxation; the sun and the beach. I did not look forward to the inevitable arguments with my spouse over why I was devoting so much time to my work when there was a beautiful summer to enjoy.

Summer! Bah, humbug!

Back at the office one afternoon I was staring fixedly at my Reuters screen, apparently engrossed in the market, but actually wondering idly if the rays from the machine had already permanently damaged my chromosome structure, and those of my children and my children's children. When I was younger my mother had always maintained that the beams from our color television were bad for us, and had insisted that my brother and I sit at least three feet away from the set. All that careful protection—for what? Now I sat not six inches away from the combined rays of six color television sets day after day. I'll probably have little green numbers for children, I thought glumly.

All my life I had been forging ahead like a mechanical stuffed animal that, once wound up, paddles along until it runs into a wall, whereupon it simply changes direction and, in single-minded pursuit of some unquestioned goal, merrily advances until it meets the next obstacle. Thus could my life be depicted, with the possible exception that my batteries never seemed to run out.

If trading, the cream of my chosen career path, was not the answer, what did that say about my choices? Could I have made such a serious mistake? And if I had been wrong, and was finally recognizing my mistake, was there anything I could do about it now, after all this time?

Larry and I spent the Memorial Day weekend at a summer house we'd rented in Connecticut. On the morning of Memorial Day I woke up to the sound of birds chirping. It took me a second to place the sound.

I lay in bed awhile until Larry woke up. Then I rolled over on my side and looked at him.

"I'm going to quit the bank tomorrow," I announced.

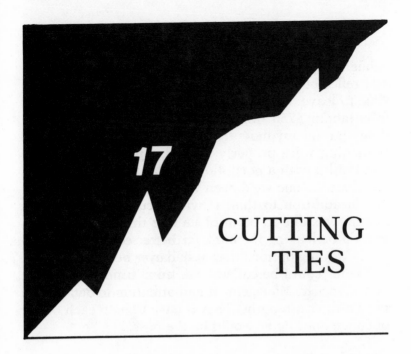

17
CUTTING TIES

Despite everything that had led up to this moment, my actual decision to quit was strictly spur-of-the-moment. I didn't think about losing the prestige. I didn't think about losing the money. At that moment, I only thought how nice it would be if I didn't have to go into work tomorrow. Who knows how many great decisions are made this way?

"Really?" Larry asked.

"Really."

"Just like that?"

"Just like that."

Larry put his arms around me.

"I think you're making the right decision," he said.

I basked in the glory of this sentiment just long

enough to go into the office and actually quit. In fact, as I reflected on my decision, I had chosen the perfect time to leave. Fully one half of the options in my port-folio (about $750 million worth) expired in June. If I didn't put on any more trades, and made sure that those remaining were properly hedged, I would leave Peter and Phillip with a portfolio that was far easier to man-age than the one we'd been working with to date.

In addition to that, it was now June 1. The new system was due to be in place first thing in the morn-ing. I'd be leaving the bank far better equipped for the job of trading options than it had ever been in the past.

Peter could be called back from London to be the new manager. Management and attention to detail were not Phillip's strengths. They'd have to help each other, of course, but Peter would be the boss.

When I walked into the bank on June 1, I did not go directly to the trading desk. I went instead into an empty office and phoned Peter to tell him of my decision. "What?" he gasped, through the three thousand miles of long-distance interference.

"I'm resigning today," I repeated. "I've had it. It's your show."

"You can't do that!" In his panic Peter dropped his customary farm-bred composure. "It's too soon!"

"No, it's not," I said, calmer now than I'd been in months. I was prepared for Peter's reaction. "You can do it. Don't worry. I'll stay until the June options ex-pire. You won't need me after that."

"Please don't do this to me," Peter begged. "Can't you wait a little?"

"Peter, listen to me. You can do this. You can al-ways call me if you need me. I'm not dying. I'm just resigning. You just need to get used to the idea."

"But . . . ," Peter started to argue.

"What's the matter?" I asked. "Don't you want the job?"

"Of course I do," he muttered.

"Then do it," I said.

I hung up with Peter and walked into the trading room. Phillip was already at the desk. I looked around. Nothing had changed. "No system, huh?" I asked Phillip.

"No system," he said, shaking his head.

William Hambrecht happened to be walking through the trading room at that moment. I called him over.

"Weren't we supposed to have a new system today?" I asked innocently.

This simple question unleashed the Field Marshall's wrath.

"I never said that!" he shouted.

"William," I said reasonably, "didn't we sit in a meeting not two weeks ago where you announced that the system would be up and running by June 1?"

"That's a lie!" He was very red in the face. "I never said that! That system won't be ready for another three weeks or so!"

"Okay," I said, shrugging and turning away.

"I never said that!" William continued in a fury. "I don't know how you could possibly think that your system would be in by June 1!"

"I said okay," I returned calmly.

He wasn't prepared for my indifference. He couldn't understand it. He found it maddening that I wouldn't be provoked. "You pull these dates out of thin air!"

"If you say so," I replied. "I'm not going to discuss it further."

"That system won't be ready for three more weeks. At least three more weeks!"

"I said that this conversation is over," I said, in a

voice that left him no choice. And then I turned my back once and for all on the Field Marshall.

He stared at me perplexed for a few moments, then stormed out of the trading room.

Well, it was time to quit. But I had a problem. John was out of the office. He was attending a meeting in Washington. I'd have to quit to somebody else. I resigned to Andy, the head spot trader. He was very upset by my decision, and called John in Washington to tell him he'd better fly back to New York that afternoon. John got back in time for lunch.

Once again, we rode the elevator to the executive dining room. Once again, the fawning maître d' led us to a gleaming table for two by the huge, plate-glass windows. It was a beautiful summer day. The sky was a fresh, clear blue. The view was spectacular. This is the last time I'll eat here, I thought with a sudden pang. Have I made the wrong decision? Shall I miss it terribly, after all?

At that moment the food arrived. On second thought, I won't, I decided, looking at the Pâté du Chef (Chopped Liver).

John cleared his voice to speak. Nothing came out.

"I'm sorry you had to miss your meeting," I said, to break the awkward silence.

"That's all right," he replied. "You won't change your mind?"

I shook my head.

"Why are you leaving?" John asked.

A difficult question to answer. "Well . . . all the problems we've been having," I began. "The delay over the computer system. Even today!"

"I know, I know," said John. "I promise you'll get that system as soon as possible. It's almost here. Why don't you wait and give it a chance?"

"Too much water under the bridge," I replied. "I'm sure you'll get your system. But I won't be here when you finally get it. I've had enough."

John sighed.

"Where are you going?" he asked.

Andy had asked me the same question. "I'd rather not say," I hedged.

How explain to this man that I didn't know what I was going to do? That I'd resigned without any clear plan? He'd think I was crazy. I wasn't sure that I wasn't crazy. It was better to let him think I was taking a job elsewhere.

"I wish you'd tell me," he said unhappily.

"I can't."

"I mean," said John, "if you're going to an investment bank I know there's nothing I can do. I know we can't compete with what they pay. But if it's a job at another commercial bank I think we should at least be given a chance to meet the offer."

I was surprised. I thought he'd be glad to be rid of me, but apparently that wasn't the case. He thought he was losing a trader to the competition.

"No," I shook my head. "I'm not going to work here anymore."

"Are we as bad as all that?" he asked. "Should I shut down the unit?"

The question took me by surprise. Nobody had thought to shut down the unit when it was handed over to me after a mere six weeks' experience. Peter and Phillip had over a year's experience apiece. "Heavens, no!" I exclaimed. "Peter can do it."

Word spread quickly throughout the trading floor that I was leaving. People speculated that I was headed for a big job elsewhere. They envied me the money they thought I would be making. Nobody even considered that I might just be leaving. They knew as well as I did that I could get a job elsewhere on the Street for more money than I was currently earning at the bank. Who walks away from that kind of income?

Who indeed?

Most traders who voluntarily resign their posts are asked to leave immediately. Everybody knows that a trader can do a great deal of damage in a very short period of time, so most institutions will not take the risk that the trader no longer has the bank's best interests at heart. I suppose that I should take it as a compliment that when I offered to stay on for two weeks and help smooth the transition, John took me up on it.

They were an uncomfortable two weeks. I was there but I wasn't. I was involved but I wasn't. I performed the same duties that I'd performed for the past fifteen months, but without the responsibility. The two weeks gave me a chance to reflect on what I'd done. I started to panic.

What had I done? Why, I'd given up the best job I would ever have. I'd given up power and prestige. I'd given up my very identity! I wasn't a writer, I was a trader! My God, what had I done? I looked at the people in the trading room. Would any of them have done what I'd done? Of course not! They're not crazy! Just look at their reaction to me; they think I've traded up to a better job!

Is this what they call having second thoughts?

"Larry," I said nervously that night at dinner. "I've been thinking."

"Yes?"

"I think that you and I should trade together. I know you've been trading on your own for some time, but I think we would make a good team."

"Nancy," said Larry, "I thought you were quitting because you wanted something else out of life. I thought you wanted to do something more creative, like write."

"I do, I do," I agreed. "But, well, it seems silly to give up trading. I mean, I've been a trader all this time and . . . well, I'm not sure that I made the right decision."

"What makes you think you made the wrong decision?"

"Well . . . the people at work wouldn't understand just quitting. They'd think I was crazy or something."

"So? Whose opinion is more important to you, theirs or your own?"

"Well, mine, of course, but—"

"But you're embarrassed? You think people will think worse of you when they find out? That they'll tell themselves you just couldn't handle it?"

I nodded.

"Some of them probably will," said Larry. "Do you think you couldn't handle it and that you're a quitter?"

I nodded again.

"That's too bad," Larry said. "I, for one, am quite proud of you. What you did took a lot of guts. Besides, you did a terrific job while you were there. You gave that bank an effective unit, and one that will survive your resignation. Nancy! Think of how much money the bank could have lost when you first started out! They left a junior trader with six weeks' experience to handle a billion-dollar portfolio! And without systems, support, or guidance. By rights they should have had their heads handed to them on a platter! It was only your dedication and commitment that saw them through a very difficult time. You should be extremely proud of what you did."

"Well, maybe . . . but I lost a lot of money, too."

"They came out ahead on the money. That's more than they deserved. Stop trying to win everyone else's approval! Win your own approval for a change. That's the toughest game in town. Trading plays a poor second to that one."

I knew Larry was right. I didn't regret my decision to leave the bank. The bank was like a shallow lover who had overstayed his welcome. That relationship had lost its allure, leaving me to wonder that I had ever found any magic in it at all. But the decision to give up trading in the pursuit of some crazy dream—that was a different story.

My last day at work was the day that half the portfolio expired. I was in the office at 6:00 A.M., making sure that everything went smoothly. That the money that had to be paid got paid. That the options that had to be exercised got exercised. That the three-hundred-plus tickets got written. (I know they got written, because I wrote them.) It took me until 6:30 P.M.

John had dropped by the desk during the day to say good-bye. He had also written me a lovely note, thanking me for what I had done and wishing me well.

At 6:30, being one of the few people still at work, I said good-bye to my staff and walked out into—

Into what?

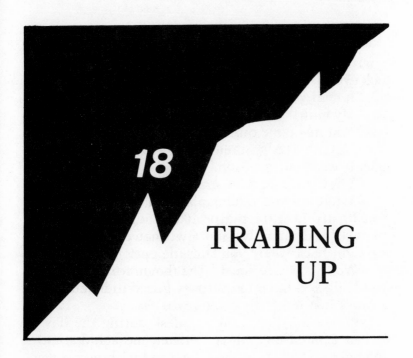

18

TRADING
UP

I wish I could tell you that I rode off into the sunset
without ever looking back. That I faced my new des-
tiny with all the courage and faith of a character out
of *Star Wars* who knows that "the Force" is with him.
That I walked in the brilliant light of my own self-
awareness from the moment I escaped the gloomy,
dungeonlike confines of the bank. However, this was
not the case.

Two weeks after leaving the bank, I was a confused
muddle of conflicting emotions. I felt a complete failure. I felt I had no identity. I didn't trust my own judg-
ments. Ironically, I felt myself to be somehow less of a
person after the experience of high-powered trading than
I had before it.

I reacted to the whole thing in the usual way. I took everything out on Larry.

"It's all your fault!" I screamed at him.

"My fault!" Larry exclaimed. "How is it my fault?"

"You made me quit!"

"Nancy!" Larry breathed. "You know that's not true. It was your decision."

"I never would have made it if it wasn't for you."

"What are you talking about? You hated that job! You finally identify the problem, admit you made a mistake, and after two short weeks away from it you are right back where you started again!"

"*No!*" I was furious. "That's not what happened! You badgered me into quitting! I used to look forward to work just to get away from you!"

At last came a day when neither of us could stand it anymore.

It was a beautiful summer day. We were at the house in Connecticut, sitting out in the yard. What a waste of what could be a lovely time together, I thought. Why can't I enjoy myself anymore? What's happened to me?

"Why don't you try and write something today?" Larry suggested.

I started to cry. "I can't write. I've never written anything. It was all just a pipe dream."

"How do you know if you don't try?" Larry asked. "Why are you so averse to trying?"

"Because—because—" I struggled to answer. "Because I'm afraid to try!"

The words came out of nowhere. They were a complete surprise. But the second I said them, I knew they were true.

"Well!" said Larry. "That was a long time in coming."

"That's true, isn't it?" I said. "That's what this is all about, isn't it?"

"Apparently. But why are you afraid to try?"

"Because," I whispered, "I'm afraid to fail."

And that was the truth. I'd always been afraid to try. I set my standards so high that it was impossible to succeed.

But I hadn't been afraid to try to manage a billion-dollar options portfolio after only six weeks. It was so clearly impossible for me to succeed, that if I'd failed, who could fault me? At the same time, once I failed, I could prove to myself once and for all that I wasn't capable. If a person wants badly enough to prove that to herself, she'll eventually succeed.

But I'd surprised even myself. In the face of incredible adversity, I'd succeeded. But had I proved anything to myself by succeeding? Not I. All I concluded from the experience was that the situation hadn't been that difficult to begin with. After all, even I had managed to come out on top.

So how did I react? I raised the stakes. I expanded without systems, without personnel, without guidance. That was a real no-win situation. I'd arranged everything perfectly for my own failure. After all, who but I could have known my own weaknesses so perfectly? And I'd failed, right on schedule.

All to prove that I was no good to begin with.

There is a calm that comes with truth.

"What should I do?"

"Write."

"But won't the same thing happen all over again?" I asked.

"Not if you've really learned something."

"But I'm still afraid to try."

"Listen," said Larry. "Why don't you take it easy

on yourself for a change? Instead of trying to rewrite *War and Peace*, why don't you tell yourself that the first thing you write will probably be terrible? Let yourself off the hook. Don't try for a masterpiece your first time around."

"Well . . ."

"Maybe you'll surprise yourself," he grinned.

Could it really be that simple—that trying for something you believe in is a worthwhile effort in itself? That that is what success is really all about; that it isn't money, or power, or other people's admiration? That believing in yourself is enough?

I took out a pad of paper and a pen.

I stared down at the empty page.

And then I started to write.